I0646226

The Transplant Web

by

S.R. Maxeiner, Jr.

© 2016 S.R.Maxeiner, Jr.

All rights reserved. Except for fair use educational purposes and short excerpts for editorial reviews in journals, magazines, or web sites, no part of this book shall be reproduced, stored in a retrieval system, or transmitted by any means without the written permission of the publisher.

International Standard Book Number 13: 978-1-60452-110-8
International Standard Book Number 10: 1-60452-110-4
Library of Congress Control Number: 2016935424

BluewaterPress LLC
52 Tuscan Way Ste 202-309
Saint Augustine FL 32092
http://bluewaterpress.com

This book may be purchased online at -

http://www.bluewaterpress.com/web

Please note that address information is subject to change. At the time of printing, the address was correct, but may have changed since. Please check our website for the latest address information for BluewaterPress LLC.

FOREWORD

The complex, intense and deeply emotional world of transplantation is beautifully captured in The Transplant Web. As a female cardiothoracic surgeon trained in the 1990s, the burdens and triumphs of protagonist chief surgical resident, Dana, resonated with me. The story is told in a pragmatic manner that reflects his own surgical background; yet Dr. Maxeiner captures the delicacy of relationships during a time of tragedy and triumph so often present with the transplant experience. Permitting the transplantation of vital organs from the beloved donor to a desperate recipient is an act of grace on the part of donor families. To be among the first surgeons to perform such operations and create miracles must have been humbling yet thrilling.

Bob captures this sense of wonder and awe without apology or over sentimentality. For a thoracic surgeon involved in transplantation today, this story reminds me that the initial transplant road was rocky, uncharted and exhilarating for those with the right stuff. I am grateful to be reminded of these surgical pioneers who changed the world. But also, I am reminded of the ongoing debt we owe our patients and donors for their trust and perseverance as we navigate together through uncharted waters.

Rosemary F. Kelly, MD
Professor of surgery, transplant surgeon,
Department of Surgery
Division of Cardiothoracic Surgery
Surgical Director of Lung Transplantation
University of Minnesota

FOREWORD

In *The Transplant Web*, Dr. Maxeiner shows us how people first weaved their lives together to open a new world: the life-saving transplant of vital organs. Since 1985, significant progress has been made in science and in medicine, and in the willingness of individuals to say yes to organ, eye, and tissue donation. However, the sobering reality remains that more people need a transplant than will ever receive the gift of an organ. According to the United Network for Organ Sharing (UNOS), thousands of people wait desperately for donor organs, and every day dozens of them die.

I hope that those who read this novel will be inspired to become organ, eye and tissue donors—a generous decision and a powerful legacy. Join me! Go to DonateLife: www.registerme.org.

Susan Gunderson
CEO LifeSource
Minneapolis MN

Dedication

To the realistic and forward-looking men and women who desire, at the time of their death, to donate tissues and organs for transplant, this book is gratefully dedicated.

Especially to those who have told their families and signed their donor cards!

PART ONE

January 15, 2014

Emerita!

Long ago my professor in surgical pathology clarified some common Latin words. Emeritus, for example, had two parts: "E-" meaning you're out of it; and "-meritus" meaning it's about time! He never bothered with the feminine gender.

But today the word applies to me, Dana Garrison. Professor Emerita.

Perforce.

In a dozen ways over my career I became The First Woman To ... Well, a lot of things. For fourteen years I held the first Martin Stern Professorship of Surgery. For my last ten I was the possibly beloved Chairperson of the Department of Surgery. If I was not a pioneer in transplanting human organs – I'll leave that to history – I was damn sure a vital participant. I should write a book.

But not about me.

In 1985 a tsunami swept over my surgical world. A single new drug threw open the floodgates for successful transplants. As if overnight, every major surgical center gained the know-how to salvage a live organ from a dead patient, implant it in a dying patient, and coax both transplant and recipient to survive. But transplants are no cake-walk. They challenge every dimension of hospital care, and test every corner of the human heart. And in those early days especially, they raised a hot mix of moral and ethical questions that could not wait for someone else's answers.

Here's what really happens. When a patient's ailing vital organ eventually fails, and a donor organ must be found, lots of folks show up. Both lay and professional, they weave themselves into a tight web of mutual concern. Grief and hope and duty may grind them up as individuals, but their common dedication holds them together until the day the transplant works – or fails. The real story of organ transplants is the way these lives weave together in an all-or-none common effort to save one single life. These stories – these lives – are the warp and weft of an ad-hoc social fabric I think of as the transplant web. So how shall I write my book? I could tell how Sandor Brovek sold the regents on a once-in-a-lifetime gamble to build a new transplant center. I might discuss his creation of our transplant program (it thrives today in the university's modern center). I would surely describe how he "did" our first cardiac transplant. All true.

But no heart. No humanity. I can't tell our story without me in it. Without Horace Potts the businessman, and Martin Stern the developer. Without the woven web of our own first year in the new world of transplants. I am haunted still by the unsatisfied ghost of Karen Sondergaard. By the crashed arc of Lance Rudd. And I must do homage to the bit players, critical cameo roles crucial to the weave. Driven by duty, by ambition, by love, all these lives come together to forge for one dying person the gift of a new life.

If my story shows you the web, you will know the truth about transplants.

Dana

New Year's Day, 1985.

Six-forty-five a.m. Five years lie behind me now in post-grad surgical training. Today I become Chief Resident. Top dog. I'm twenty-nine years old.

I slip into an empty doctors' lounge, pull a Styrofoam cup from the stack and draw a steaming hot coffee. One sip, then business.

"Whatcha got?" Pete strolls in, draws his own coffee, and watches me clip a new gadget to the belt of my white slacks. It's a silent pager that is supposed to signal me by vibrating. I haven't tried it yet.

I nod and pick up my hot cup. "Happy New Year, Pete."

We are no longer peers. I watch him for clues. Did he hope to *be* Chief, and not play second to his female competition? Will we work well together? I lay out my first orders. "We have a couple of chest tubes to come out today, okay? Check the films first, and if they look right, pull the tubes."

Pete never says much. He lofts his cup to me and sips.

"I'll start rounds in ICU. You can catch up with me there."

I raise the hot cup to my lips, and exactly then my new pager goes off. The damn thing explodes against my belly with the shock-force of a mugger's assault. I jerk back, coffee sloshing out, scalding my hand while I grope for the shut-off button.

Pete dissolves, laughing.

After five years of slavery, I've achieved the top rung; and look what I get for it. More than my fingers burn.

I press the speaker button, and a quiet voice announces: "Dr. Garrison. Call Station 21."

Pete frowns. "21? That's the medical ward. Do we have anybody over there?"

"It's on my way to ICU. I'll find out."

On the slick vinyl of the hospital floors, my winged heels make no sound. By design. Part of my persona. Standing tall, I make 5'1". But I wear flat heels and rubber soles—silent wheels for a girl who moves fast and covers a lot of ground. Five-foot-one? Big deal. I can't make it more, but I can make it count—look good, do the job right, and be ready. When the time comes, step up and take charge.

Today the time has come. Chief Resident. Most of it, I hope, will be routine.

I sail in to Station 21. At the service desk, the nurse straightens up as if stung. "My God, Dr. Garrison, I didn't hear you come in!"

"I was just outside. Trouble?"

"That's for you to say." Cool eyes and even cooler words. "I am a nurse: I can only suspect."

I've seen "attitude" before. Is it resentment? Of a woman as physician? I'll take your orders, but I don't have to like it. I simply nod. "I'm listening."

She stands and offers a chart. Under her starched white cap her blond hair shines. She is taller by a head than I, and her expression gives nothing away. "Mr. Potts came in five days ago with a small MI. He did okay in CICU, and transferred here yesterday. But today he has a pain in his abdomen, his blood pressure is down twenty points, and I don't like the way he looks."

We both know she should call the patient's own doctor. Not someone else, like me. Certainly not a different service. Protocol.

"Where's Dr. Kanju? He's your medical resident."

"I've paged him twice. No answer." Her words are defiant.

But why call a surgeon? Especially a new chief resident fresh out of the chute? Why take this personal risk?

I skim the chart — the essentials, MI, ECG, enzymes. All the usual stuff. Nothing about a belly pain. Why has this nurse made herself vulnerable?

Aha! "The chart says he has an aortic aneurysm."

"That's why I called you."

"He had no symptoms."

"He has them now."

Oh God! Not me. Not today. Routine? No way. If this nurse is right, her patient is dying. Today. Now. Unless I can save him.

I whip through what I remember about recent case reports. The abdominal aorta weakens with the same sclerotic changes as his coronaries. It blisters out as an aneurysm. No prob. Unless it leaks. And right now it leaks. Soon, the dam breaks and it's over — unless...

Unless some brave soldier, some surgical resident on emergency call, dares to attack this fire hose, clamp it off, cut it out, and replace it. Now. In all the literature there are only a recent handful of successful cases. Am I that kind of soldier? Every week I operate on blood vessels. Ream out arteries. Bypass obstructions. Sew in replacements.

Sure. For vessels in the limbs. But the aorta is the big gorilla. Unassailable.

I hug the chart and center myself. Can I do it?

Yes. I have to do it. Now is the time. Step up, Dana girl. Take charge.

"Let's look at him."

The patient lies curled on his left side in a private world of pain. A fine sweat moistens his brow. His cheeks look ashen. Gray lines of hurt hover around his eyes.

"I'm Dr. Garrison, Mr.—ah—Potts. I'm a surgeon. I've come to see about your pain. Let me look at you."

A thin, rapid pulse. My palpating fingers, gentle as I try to keep them, make him wince. Deep down in the left abdomen, where he hurts, I feel a sinister fullness. Enough.

"We have a problem to deal with, Mr. Potts. Forgive me for being direct, but I must. Do you know about your aneurysm?"

"They told me not to worry about it right now."

I nod. "That's because of your heart damage. Soon after a myocardial infarction no one wants to put you through an operation. If we can, we avoid doing any surgery at such a time."

Potts faces me square on, eyes locked on mine. His voice is level. "But...?"

Here it is. No turning back.

"But your aneurysm has begun to leak. To bleed. The only way to stop it is... is to remove it."

"Operate?"

"Yes, sir. Just as fast as we can get you to the OR."

Potts studies my solemn face, and turns to the still figure in white beside his bed. His nurse, his ally, Miss Sondergaard. Validation for the young doctor with the terrible message.

I wait. I can add nothing to this bare and unrelenting script.

"It's... fatal?... Always?"

I nod. "Affirmative. 99%."

"You are just a girl, Dr. Garrison.... But you must be good to be here. And you are very definite. What choice do I have?"

"You're an intelligent man, Mr. Potts. You need what this hospital can offer, and right now I am it. Trust me."

Potts's gaze flicks through the windows to the winter day, to golden sun and white snow, and then to the gray TV screen—that will show no bowl games today. His big game has already kicked off in his hurting belly. "Bleeding inside? That's why I hurt?"

I nod.

"It won't quit?"

"No, sir. Not without help."

"I have to trust you, Dr. Garrison. Let's go for it."

At Sondergaard's desk, I recite crisp and urgent orders. "Keep trying to raise Dr. Kanju. If he doesn't respond now, call his staff doctor. We need the cardiologists here every step of the way. If the Potts family comes, call me. If they don't appear, don't wait. Don't wait for anything. I want ten bottles of red cells ready, and two of those bottles pumped into him within one hour. Dr. Pete will come help with that. Get started with everything now. I'll write my orders and call my crew for the OR."

But I need to say more. In a gentler voice I speak directly to this tall nurse who has dared to violate routine. "Miss Sondergaard, sometimes we doctors forget how crucial a good nurse can be. I promise you I shall not. Not after today."

I settle the chart on the desk and begin to write.

But Sondergaard's soft words challenge me. "99% ? It's 100% with a ruptured aneurysm. What's the hedge?"

Good question. "That," I said, "is just in case... In case he has something else."

Karen

At three o'clock, the end of her shift, Karen Sondergaard smoothed her white skirt and pulled on her overshoes. Heedless of the mid-winter ice, she set out across the physician-only parking lot for her tiny, but lucky-to-have-it apartment in The Annex.

Dr Garrison's words sang in her heart. *Good nurse. Crucial. I will not forget.*

She hates overshoes. Clumsy. But better than mucking up her every-day soft-soled whites.

And what had she done? She broke out of normal procedure. Mr. Potts was in trouble, and she broke the rules. He needed help and she made it happen. On her own authority, as a professional person.

She relished the feel-good flush that blossomed from Garrison's words. But in them Karen read more than approval. She saw an endorsement of Karen's own radical view of hospital nursing. She has no issue about routines — meds, bed baths; they're fundamental. Do them right. But the nurse is capable of more. Physicians don't see what nurses see...

She lengthened her stride. Easy to be angry.

Physicians write their orders and go away. Nurses see what goes astray. And she, if she could... if she had the authority... if they would treat nursing as a profession....

Because often a doctor's orders lead to mix-ups and delays. And ruffled patients: strange procedures, unexpected shots, transportation surprises, missed meals. In her world, the head nurse would step up and smooth out those up-and-down challenges. Be a professional. Make things right. Example: her service to Horace Potts. She saw him in trouble, yes... And the right people didn't respond... no... and she — woops!... broke... look out!

Her overshoe slipped on the ice and she almost went down. What's this? After five years on hospital vinyl, has she forgotten how to walk on ice? No way. Growing up north of Bemidji, she learned all about blizzards and wind chill and whiteouts.

And she walked on figurative ice today for Horace Potts — broke rules, stuck her neck out, without any slip! And she met a physician who saw things her way. Maybe an omen? Maybe, at last, something good?

Her little apartment was cramped, but thank God it was warm. She tossed her purse onto her cot, the virginal sheet stretched so tight the bag bounced. She shucked off her uniform, balled it up, and pitched its wilted starch toward the closet. She stared at her two diplomas, hanging behind the cot as lifeless as yesterday's news. From her mirror, her own face stared back — sober, with lean planes and strong bones. Fine new lines showed around the mouth. Fatigue? Or was it aging! A thin strap hung off one shoulder.

Well, it was New Year's Day. A person should celebrate. She forced a smile. The other girl smiled. Pretty teeth. She should smile more often. Their hands rose in an imaginary toast. "Here's cheers!" She watched the words move on the other's lips. "Happy New Year to you, Karen Sondergaard!"

And suddenly, without knowing she would, she wept.

Dana

A few strokes of my scalpel open the abdomen. All looks innocent. Clean serosal surfaces, no blood: good. Normal loops of glistening small bowel: good. But what if I'm wrong? Pete helps me drape them out of harm's way. Right or wrong, now comes the truth. I slide a gentle hand down into the pelvis, low in the left side.

Aha! Behind the thin membrane lining the belly cavity, there it is: the thickened mass I felt — or thought I felt — an hour ago. In my own belly, a hard ball of tension releases its grip. This is what I came for.

Does it matter that no one here has done this procedure before? Not even Brovek? No. It's right that I'm here. I'm giving my patient a chance. If I get all the vital steps done right, and in their proper order.

Number one: back off from the clot. Don't mess with it. If it should burst, I could only watch the patient expire in a two-minute bloody flood. My first step must be to control the aorta upstairs, to isolate the aneurysm from the blow-out forces of normal blood pressure. So I shift our exposure higher, behind the stomach. By blunt dissection — like working a finger between a foot and a shoe — I burrow a tunnel through the loose connective tissue between aorta and spine. I'm above the aneurysm now but below the vital sets of arteries to the kidneys, the gut, the liver. Through my tunnel behind the aorta, I pass the jaw of a surgical clamp, the other jaw passing easily in front. Now I close the clamp; its steel jaws shut down on the aorta in a grasp as gentle and as tough as a mother tiger's.

"That's big, Pete. He can't bleed any more now. Let's let everybody catch up."

Blood volume has been restored, red cells flowing through IV's in both arms. The cardiogram monitor shows a stable pulse. All the machinery is in place and working. "We're okay, Dr. Garrison." The anesthesiologist nods across the ether screen.

"Catch me up too, Dana. Looks like you're well started." A new voice.

"So far so good, Dr. Rudd. Thank you for coming."

I knew he would. Six feet and two inches of Ivy League polish, Lance Rudd has always backed me up. Often in the wee hours — or holidays, like today. Staff surgeon, mentor, my immediate boss. "Just to make sure you're okay, Dana."

My first gunshot wound to the heart, just a year ago. "Just in case, on your first one."

Well, this case is a first one too—even historic. But also it is my first go as Chief Resident, my first time to stand alone, to operate on my own authority. *You need what this hospital offers, Mr. Potts, and I'm it.* With every contraction of his damaged heart the long handle of that critical aortic clamp surges, and in sync I hear the echo of my own words: *Trust me, trust me.* Dr. Rudd, in new gown and gloves, elbows in beside Pete. *Trust me.* My obligations settle on me like a mantle. I square my shoulders and go to work. The aortic clamp is secure; I can attack the aneurysm. Most of that doughy mass, that I dared not touch until now, is blood already lost. As I slice into it now, gobs of dark jelly burst out, and fresh burgundy clots in a thick flush of mahogany gravy. I grub handfuls of it into a basin. Rudd sponges up the liquids with gauze, while Pete's sucker gurgles and rushes as air and old blood whistle up the tubing.

Most of it gets cleaned up before I go to the aneurysm itself. I cut into the front wall. It's leathery, like the tongue of a shoe, but flabby and calcified. It crunches in the scissors. I cut a lot of it away but leave the back wall. A couple of vertebral branches need a stitch to stop back-bleeding.

I pause for a big deep breath. "That about does it, guys. Let's sew in the graft."

"Good job, Dana. Do it, and I'll go home."

The graft is a Y-shaped tube of woven Dacron. I match the single end to the aorta, cut off above the aneurysm. I pass the first stitch, its small curved needle passing out-to-in on the graft, in-to-out on the aorta. The fine blue suture glistens in the light as I tie the knot. Dr. Rudd's good left hand exposes the work, and his right holds proper tension on my advancing suture line. All the way around it goes, end of vessel to end of graft, to the tying of a final knot. Next come the two lower ends of the graft, to be sewed end-on to the severed right and left common iliac arteries. Like pipe-fitting, with sutures. Done. Knots tied. Now, comes test time. One by one I loosen the lower clamps. Sometimes a suture line will bleed. Even spurt a bit. A couple of stitch holes ooze, and stop. Good. Finally, the top clamp: the mother tiger. I unlock it, watch the suture lines. The big pump is connected again; blood flows again full bore to the pelvis and legs. All is dry. Now, at last, the clamps come out.

I draw a long breath. "Thanks, Dr. Rudd. I can finish up with Pete, if you want to slip away."

I look up to smile at him across the table, and my heart freezes. Over Rudd's shoulder looms the giant figure of Dr. Sandor Brovek, his green surgical mask no bar at all to his black scowl.

My pulse pounds. Sandor Oliver Brovek, my superego. Professor of surgery, terror of medical students, taskmaster of surgeons in training, the ruling brain of surgical research: the Chief. Why in the name of sense has he appeared here?

From high on his platform riser behind Rudd, he burns his twin lasers into me. "I might have been called about this case."

My mind reels. No one ever calls The Chief at home. The last resident who called Sandor Brovek on a holiday spent the next rotation assigned to the TB Sanitarium. Why should this case be any different?

"I'm sorry, Dr. Brovek. I would have called you if..."

"Do you have any idea who this patient is?"

I ice my pulse. *Who this patient is?* Every patient is a precious life.

"Or his importance to this university? To my — to <u>our</u> — transplant program?"

Importance?

"Did he have an aneurysm? Was it leaking?"

I get it. If there is extra heat here, it's not about me; it's about politics.

"Was all this rush really necessary?"

The Chief is angry. Okay. Stay cool, Dana. Stay cool. Do your job, and maybe survive.

I rest my hands on the drapes, raise my eyes to him and speak in careful syllables. "Yes, sir. On all counts. We had every reason for quick action, and we took it."

The hovering giant is not appeased. His glare burns over me like falling ash. "What did the CT scan show, Doctor?"

He is boring in, and my own anger flares. He's the boss, the big man, but he's out of line. I clamp on my iciest control. "With all due respect, Dr. Brovek, this case has gone smoothly so far. But I still have an incision to close."

Dr. Rudd prevents disaster after all. "Come on, Chief. Let's change clothes and I'll tell you about this case. He's doing fine."

For a long moment Brovek lingers on his platform, a raptor poised to pounce. I force my attention to the field of brilliant light and the demanding task that still lies beneath my hands. At last Brovek steps down, follows Rudd. His words roll back over his shoulder.

"Grand Rounds tomorrow, Rudd. I want this whole story laid out under the lights. And if this lady doctor's ducks don't line up, her feathers are going to fly."

Brovek

New Year's Day. Evening.

Staring through his golden brandy at the hearth fire's flickering colors, Sandor Brovek sits in his recliner and twists the snifter's crystal stem.

That damn lady doctor. With her first breath as his new Chief Resident, she took on more trouble than she knows. Horace Potts, for God's sake! His essential man. All his hopes coming to ride on the rookie scalpel of a hen medic.

But she is not chicken. He has to give her that. How many ruptured aneurysms have ever been saved in this world? Or here, in his own surgical program? None... Well, maybe, this one... He'll have to assign a junior resident to search the literature.

He checks Lotte, in her chair opposite. A fuzzy ball of green yarn rests on her lap. Usually she sits content, knitting, clicking her needles. They make a soothing, happy rhythm. Dear Lotte. A shell of herself. Dementia victims are not always so easy to care for. Count your blessings, Sandor.

Yes. Blessings. Like the new drug cyclosporin! For patients with end-stage organ failure, new hope. And a huge plus for us academic surgeons, too. New procedures. Research. Floods of new journal articles. Expanding programs. It'll be a race. All the major centers hot on the mark to do transplants. To make them work. To report successes. And get famous....

And the others can start today.

He agitates the snifter and slugs a bolus of fire.

But not me. A case or two maybe. But not a program. We're too small.

Balancing the snifter in his left hand, he reaches to the log basket and tosses a new stick of split birch onto the fire. He watches its narrow edge blacken and smoke and catch flame.

Only five years ago we doubled our campus. Two buildings meshed together. Old U, New U. And we grew. New cancer programs. A heart program. Now come transplants, and again we're too small.

Lotte's needles go quiet. He watches her pull yarn into her lap and begin the click-click again.

I pushed the regents, and they saw the need. Agreed. Do it, Brovek. You're in charge.

He shakes his head. Frustrated.

But they cut my legs off. It's gotta be all one campus. Can't they see? We haven't got a square inch to build, hell, anything. We're a whole city block right now. Curbstone to curbstone. Where can we go—up on top?

Lotte's ball of yarn falls off her lap, unwinds a few turns, and sticks to the nap of the carpet. He can just reach it without getting up. He fingers it back and picks it up, rewinds the loose yarn and gentles the ball into her lap.

"Thank you, Sandor," she whispers.

The smartest thing he's done is pick Horace Potts to be the savior. Solid in the town, smart about finance. A straight dealer. Right off he identified a new site, their only possible place: that little church across the street. Time to strike, to move, and suddenly Horace is...helpless. Out of action.... Buggers.

Brovek? Transplants? He can hear how they will whisper about him at the national meetings. Brovek? I guess he's reported a case or two. But he never built a program for transplants. Probably didn't see it coming.

He slugs the brandy, welcomes the fire on his tongue, the burning in his throat: because he *does* see it coming. Transplants are the greatest surgical frontier since...hell...

since Lister. He leans across his knees and fires a mouthful into the flames. Hot and yellow and blue, they flare up and fall back. Lotte made him quit cigars. But he can still spit.

That hen medic. Damn her. He'll boil her in oil tomorrow.

He pours a new brandy, throws it back, lets it burn. It is a pain he can handle.

No. Be fair, Professor. She did everything right. For a rookie, remarkably right... But still.

Lotte's ball of yarn has fallen again; it's stuck to the nap of the carpet. He pulls it loose and puts it back gently on her lap.

If only everything else was so easy in his tangled world.

Dana

January 2, 1985

Seven-thirty in the morning; it's my second day as Chief Resident. Facing my first Grand Rounds—the one, that is, that's mine. I'm wide awake and strung tight. How can I ever be ready for an angry Dr. Brovek?

Laden with x-ray films, I push through the doors into a deserted Keaton Amphitheater. My elbow finds a light switch, and I unload the films onto the viewer. First check: be sure the view-box works. Nothing shouts "sloppy prep" louder than putting up x-ray films on a dead view-box. I flick its lights on and off a couple of times.

I tick off the other necessaries: the same old movable blackboard on its squeaky wheels? Check. Chalk? Yes. Pointer? There. The pivotal lectern stands front and center, ready to anchor and expose the appointed person in charge. Today: me.

Nine years and counting: medical student, intern, resident, and now at last, Chief Resident. A lot of learning has osmosed into my heart and brain right here in this old lecture hall. And now, as I turn on the ranks of room lights, the memories come alive. Lectures in the basics. The liver, a chemical factory. The heart is a pump. In more conferences than I can count, I have seen patients brought in by gurney or wheelchair, to be gawked at from these curved rows of seats that rise in tiers to the entry level above. In my own bottom, I remember how those stone-hard seats kept me from drowsing off. Keaton has earned its reputation as a place to learn.

People begin to enter up there at the top level, and pick their way down the steps to find places. Students with clipboards. Residents in white coats. Staff surgeons in their auras of authority. A few nurses interested in certain cases — we think of them as *cases*, but must remember they are *persons*, individual and real. I see the nurse from yesterday — Sondergaard, isn't it? Lance Rudd finds a place on the left — my right — fifth row. Curious how we settle, in church, or lecture hall, on "our own" seats. Dr. Brovek always arrives late; he'll enter down here at the lectern level, glare at me, and settle in the third row left of center. Whence, today, he will fire his artillery straight at me.

The clock hand races straight up to eight o'clock, and I call for order. A case with a complication comes first, a minor wound infection. Discussed. Repented. Then a case — without the patient — of breast cancer. Is radical surgery still justified? What is the place for conservative surgery? What about the lymph nodes?

Dr. Brovek barges in, brushes past me, climbs to his seat.

My residents report a couple more ordinary cases, and at last the next case is mine: Mr. Horace Potts. My palms are wet.

Pete presents the basic facts: the patient's age, history, admission for MI, his standard medical treatment, and then, suddenly, abdominal pain. I describe my exam and my decisions: yes, an aneurysm; and yes, it is bleeding. Yes, we need to operate. Right there the dreaded professorial voice cuts me off. Strong. Muscular, really. His question booms big in Keaton Amphitheater.

"What did the CT scan show? I didn't hear you mention it."

Here we go.

I grip the lectern and condemn myself. "I did not order one."

"On what basis, then, Dr. Garrison, did you rest your diagnosis of aneurysm?"

"It had been discovered by the medical resident on admission exam. Confirmed on palpation by two staff physicians."

"X-ray? Ultrasound?"

Hoping to project a confidence I do not feel, I speak in full voice to the entire theater. "No, sir. The patient was admitted for a fresh MI. The aneurysm was an incidental finding. In that acute setting no studies were done."

"'MI'? Say 'myocardial infarction,' Doctor.... So... You accepted the unsubstantiated diagnostic impressions of physicians other than yourself"—he leans toward me, scowling—"physicians who, unlike you, Dr. Garrison, had no personal stake in that diagnosis." Not angry, like yesterday. But intense; on the attack.

A personal stake? For sure, Dana. Like, my rep here in the hospital. Like my accreditation for the specialty Boards. He could scratch me from his program, if he chose, even within this conference. Like, right now.

"I did rely on the opinion of others, Dr. Brovek. As we all do. But I also made my own examination."

He sits back, giving me room to hang myself. "Tell me exactly what you found. I know that you rushed into surgery, with no objective imaging to verify an aneurysm—much less one that is bleeding."

"I found a gentleman in pain, a new hard pain, in his abdomen. On exam I found deep tenderness low on the left side, and a feeling of fullness. Not a mass, really, but not normal, either." I step out beside the lectern to show the area on my own belly. I stretch up tall, all five-foot-one of me. I hope the tiers of students behind the Man are on my side.

"Dr. Garrison, I won't ask you how you distinguished that finding from diverticulitis or from left kidney disease. You must know something I don't know." He steamrollers past his own sarcasm. "My interest in this case is the protection of standards in my department. I am interested in process here, so that patients are subjected to surgery for well-founded and logical reasons. I do not want them going to surgery on hunches."

Hunches? The bastard! It's like he has a dagger in his hand.

"Do you know, Dr. Garrison, the surgical mortality figures for patients with recent myocardial infarction?" He's raising the blade. "They are sky high. Do you think it's okay to take that kind of risk when you haven't even a proven diagnosis?"

His question hangs in the air like a black cloud. Time for the defense, Dana. It's your turn.

"Dr. Brovek, your points are real. I weighed the same issues yesterday. I believe in process. I believe in logic, not hunches. But sometimes a decision has to come from a range of chances—odds, if you will. Even a dangerous course of action may be right if it is the least dangerous." I fight to keep my voice steady; the last thing he wants to hear is a female screech. "A CT scan on a holiday would take at least three hours. The aneurysm had been found and agreed on by four examiners. I saw for myself that it was leaking. Not just his acute pain, but also signs of blood loss and impending shock. He was pale. His pulse was thready and fast. His blood pressure had dropped. I had little doubt about what was happening: a rupturing aneurysm."

"A little doubt? You admit to that?"

No one else exists. Keaton Amphitheater melts away. My whole self fixes on this implacable giant, and I will not back off. "Of course I had a little doubt. How could I not? But there the patient is, and his problem hasn't gone away."

I move to the shelter of the lectern and proceed in my defense. "Now, let me, as I did on that day, consider factors of risk. With recent damage to his heart muscle, would surgery and anesthesia add risk? Yes. In some unmeasurable way. Statistically. But hemorrhagic shock represents real risk. Immediate risk. It will cause further damage to his injured heart muscle, and continued bleeding will certainly become fatal. I made the judgment that this patient's most serious risk came not from anesthesia and surgery, but from bleeding. The least risk for him right now required that we treat his shock and stop his bleeding. I decided to get him to surgery just as fast as I could."

I stop for a deep breath.

"All on your own?"

"I conferred with Dr. Rudd."

"And when he arrived, you were...?"

"Waiting for him. The aorta was clamped. The bleeding was stopped."

I watch the emperor. Thumbs up?

"Never in shock?"

"Stable throughout, sir, after blood replacement."

"I saw you sew in the graft. Good job."

If the professor is the person I think he is, he has to accept what I have done. And if Mr. Potts recovers, he will be a historic success. A reportable case. The professor sits immobile, wheels turning. Finally, he says, "Dr. Rudd, I know you were present at surgery. Do you have any comment on this case?"

Rudd glances my way—did he wink? "Just to say, Dr. Brovek, that it was as well performed yesterday as it was defended today. I think Dr. Garrison's first case as your Chief Resident is a tribute to the quality of your graduate training program."

Bless his heart.

The conference is over. Students and nurses in clinical coats and white uniforms chatter and jostle their way up the steep aisles to the exit doors. At the lectern I begin to gather my papers. But here comes Dr. Brovek.

Judgment time? The axe?

He rests a massive arm on the lectern and bends down close. "Dr. Garrison, one more question." His voice is a guttural whisper. "I want to know exactly how you felt, going in to that operation."

Not an axe! A personal question! I open my heart. "Dr. Brovek, I was worried sick."

He nods. "Good for you. You should have been."

Stern

Same day: January 2, 1985

From 33,000 feet the land below looks snow-covered and serene. But that is not Martin Stern's world—Martin Stern, the big-shot developer; he will soon deplane into disorder. Screw it. He throws back his forbidden martini, chews up the olive. Damn his sick liver. Damn the new year—that he'll never see the end of. Damn those two tough words they've tied to his tail: *sclerosing cholangitis.* What the hell do they mean, anyway?

The doctors tell him everything they know. Sure they do. But it's like, nothing. His bile ducts are turning to scar tissue. Why? Don't know. Why me? Don't know that either. What to do? Well, really, nothing.

What it means, Martin, is: you're dying. With sclerosing cholangitis.

Four damn years since that man Rudd took his gall bladder out and pinned the bad words on him. And every year he gets worse. Sicker. Weaker. He can't even get it up anymore, and Lila Mae has given up and gone home to mother. And the worst of it is, he doesn't even care. Dr. Rudd won't say it, but Martin Stern knows. Like this plane that's heading down, his flying is about over.

But he's not done! Not yet.

He crushes the plastic glass under his heel and jams his seat-back upright. First thing tomorrow he checks in with Dr. Rudd for—what else?—more bad news.

But if he's not dead, if he's going to live a while, then by God he'll move! He'll hit up the bishop for a sweet property he has his eye on. A little red-brick church. He wants it, and he wants it now. And he's loaded to fire off his crazy Barnum-and-Bailey offer that's so far out that nobody—not even a bishop—will refuse it.

Because he is not dead yet! Martin Stern still dreams. And to make that dream come true, he'll work right up to his last gasp. The Stern Towers, his master stroke, his crowning achievement. And he's never seen a better site than this can't-miss block by University Hospital. Yes, it's a church. But he'll get it. He'll buy it. He'll put out his crazy offer like nobody ever heard before. He'll nail the bishop and get the site. In a rush he'll raze the church. He'll pour foundations in winter, slate the roof in September. And when the city sees a dying man cut the ribbons on his glistening new super hotel, they'll remember him. Martin Stern? He was a *mensch*!

Karen

The moment the conference ended, Karen Sondergaard slipped from her seat and exited the top level of Keaton Amphitheater. Heart pounding, she found the adjacent stairway and took the first step down. Her moist palm dragged against the varnished handrail. Yesterday she had broken out of channels. Not like her at all. But she did it for the sake of a patient. Now, in more violence to her Norwegian reserve, she would do it again—this time for herself.

In Karen's uplifting moment yesterday, Dana Garrison's good words had reached deep into her core. Warmth. Respect from a physician who saw the real and sentient person inside her white uniform. Now, in the dark stairway, she felt unsure. The grimness of her Nordic mother hovered, disapproving. But Karen Sondergaard was starved for affirmation. She needed another touch of Dana Garrison as she needed to breathe.

On the bottom step she waited at the Amphitheater door. When it jerked open, the massive silhouette of Sandor Brovek blocked the light. If he saw her at all, he ignored the specter in white and powered his way on down the dark hall.

When the door opened again, it was Dana Garrison who appeared, a tiny figure with a purposeful set to her head, and strength in her square shoulders.

In a cloud of self-doubt, Karen stepped down. Probably she shouldn't. A bad time. Dana might have surgery to get to. Nurses shouldn't—she mustn't.... But she spoke out. "Dr. Garrison... Dana... It's me... Karen Sondergaard? From yesterday?"

She wanted to run; she wished she could hide.

But Dana Garrison changed the game. "Karen? It's you?" She laughed. "Will you just look at the fine mess you got me in!"

Karen held back. "I wasn't sure you'd remember me."

"No?" Garrison sobered. "I suppose not. Why would I remember a nurse who should have dinked around calling a medical resident, and let her patient bleed to death—but didn't. No. You just stepped out of line and saved his life. Why should I remember you?"

Karen's heart thumped. She felt on firmer ground. "I couldn't stay away this morning. He gave you a hard time, didn't he?"

"Dr. Brovek gives everybody a hard time. I expected even worse."

In her pocket Karen's fingers found the address she had written up there in Keaton. Her apartment in the Annex. Dared she try to make a friend? "I wasn't sure you'd even talk to me—Chief Resident and all."

"Nuts to that. But thanks for coming to see the show. I hope it was worth your time."

"Oh yes, it was, Dr. Garrison."

"Dana."

Encouragement? She felt the note in her pocket, flattened the creases. "I wonder... would you ever..."

"What?"

Karen took a big breath. "Would you ever, like, just meet? We could talk... Maybe get to be, like, you know, acquainted?"

Garrison laughed. "Love it, Miss Sondergaard. Love it. Like maybe five months from now, when I get out of prison!"

"Karen."

"What?"

"Karen. That's my name."

"A nice name."

"You have to eat, don't you? Even in prison?"

"Have to feed the fire, yes." She patted her electronic pager. "But only where Bozo here can talk to me."

Out came Karen's hand, with the note. "I live in the Annex. I eat there. I cook meals. Come over there tonight and we'll talk."

Garrison took the note. Eyed it. Added it to her pocket. Raised her eyes to Karen. Locked on. "Are you lonely, Karen? I am, sometimes."

Karen's eyes stung. Lonely? Was that the name of her aching? Her emptiness? She couldn't admit weakness — at least, she couldn't have, yesterday. But today Dana has called it by name. Loneliness. Her feelings tumbled softly out of her release. "On the wall in my apartment is my new Master's diploma. No other living soul has seen it. Or wants to. Does that make me lonely?"

Dana's gentle hand touched her arm. "It'll do." Her words sang with the clarity of bells. "If Bozo lets me come, I'll be there."

Brovek

At war with himself, Sandor Brovek powered out of Keaton. That tiny woman had talked him down in front of his own conference. In his head he liked her spirit. Good stuff. But in his gut he didn't like it. Not one bit. And the gut won.

Booming into the dark hall, he nearly ran bang into some nurse standing there like a spook in the dark. He dodged away and forged on, fists clenched. Trying to decompress, he counted his steps. To the left lay his office; he turned right.

The halls grew brighter, and he found himself crossing onto the shiny tiles of New U. Ahead of him would be the staff lounge, and beyond it the operating suite. Again he turned away, double-stepped up a stairway. Forgot to count. Began to unwind. Longer strides. Looser. Slower. Better. He found himself in the main entrance lobby. Shiny marble, modern art — where do they get that stuff? And the inevitable gift shop; Auxiliary ladies in pink smocks. Not today! He escaped to the great double doors of the hospital's main entrance. He shoved his way through to the outside, and there he stopped. He could stand alone and inhale the icy air of this January morning.

Enough. That rookie Chief Resident wasn't his biggest problem. Let her go. Across the street stood the little red-brick church. There stood the key to his future. He glared at it. The only place in the whole world where he could build his dreamed-of transplant center. The site that he and Horace Potts had come down to — had had to dream up, almost.

And Potts had to get it for him. Buy it, take it, steal it. Horace Potts, lying at the edge of death in Brovek's own ICU.

Only two weeks ago Potts had spoken with some hope. "The church belongs to the bishop, Sandy. I know him from prep school. If he says No, we're done. But if he'll sell it — and it is a troubled parish — he could sell it to anybody. Then we have a chance."

But that was then.

Brovek gazed at the silent church, its dark double doors closed against the world. The dingy parish house adjacent, paint peeling from its shutters. The empty playground tramped down in dirty snow. And in his mind he built his dream. A fine hospital, a great square building with two towers. On the left would be research labs, with PhDs and grad students and dieners working elbow-to-elbow to understand immunity. On the right, a phalanx of operating rooms where a whole host of players would issue streams of scientific papers to be presented at the national meetings and published in the leading journals. His young surgeons would fan out to appointments in the nation's best universities and transplant centers. "You trained under Sandor Brovek?" "Oh, yes."

"Good morning, Dr. Brovek."

What? Who? The words wrenched him back to reality. An aged priest came limping up the steps, puffing a cloud of steam the color of his eyebrows.

Brovek drew his own icy breath. There was nothing for him to say to this priest. All he could do was wait for Potts to recover — if he could — and then negotiate. Be silent and wait. How he hated waiting!

He wiped his lips with the back of his hand. "Good morning, Father."

He held the heavy door and followed the priest inside.

February 14, 2014

Well, what do you think, Russell, about the way my story begins?

That's a hot fire you've lit under Dr. Brovek. But the big case was about an aneurysm. When does transplant come in?

Later in the calendar. I want you to meet the folks who will be warp and weft when we begin to make the web. The persons who might die, and the professionals who keep them alive, find donors, do the legals, harvest the organs, sew them in, and coax them to survive.

But you're writing a story. Who is your central character, your hero?

It's me, of course! Dana! But in this story I need you, the reader, to be patient with me. My transplant web was woven from multiple strands – many lives – that converged around a single patient. I want you to know them as individuals. Like me. I'm one of the strands. As I lived my story in 1985, these strands were real people. I knew them. People I cared about, and still care about... and grieve for, some of them.

Okay. As your story grows I'll meet people who will be warp and weft to weave your web... But... wow... That's a lot of double-yoos....

But what?

Well, Brovek and Lotte, for example. You knew Brovek very well. You maybe met Lotte a time or two. No way did you know how they were together at home. That roaring fire, the birch logs, the ball of yarn. You invented that story.

What did you just call it?

A story.

Yes. A story. Not a history. Not just facts. In my story I want you to see a truth: that many lives must weave together to make a transplant work for one.

Stern

January 2, 1985

In Lance Rudd's examining room, Martin Stern, the big shot, stands bare-ass before a full-length mirror. Despite the cold damn floor, he's comfortable with himself. The scar on his belly looks good. Hell, it's an honorable battle scar. Slender hips. Flat butt. His apparatus still looks like himself, even if it's — well — listless. He's too damned tired all the time. He pulls down a lower lid and squints at his eye. Is he getting a little yellow?

Well, why not tired? That's why he's here.

He takes one of those damn paper gowns, holds it up and shakes it out. Front or back, either way makes a problem. He spreads it across his front and settles his behind on that damn scratchy paper. For Dr. Rudd, Martin Stern waits.

Mostly, the man is okay. For a doctor. Not a pussy-foot, anyway. After the gall bladder operation, he laid things out plain. Not cancer, but bad. Bile ducts shriveling up, turning to scar tissue. *Sclerosing cholangitis*, he called it. So what's to do? Tell me what to do; let's fix it. But it's not that easy. Turned out, there's nothing to do. No fix — except no booze. I keep my appointments like a good boy, and every visit I'm worse; and every time there's still nothing to do. So why keep all these appointments? Better tend to my own business. Big business. Like this afternoon, when I go to hit up the bish —

"Hello, Mr. Stern. Good to see you again."

He could be a pretty good-looking guy, in his white coat, Dr. Rudd. If he wasn't so fancy. Creased flannel pants, and loafers with tassels on them. Tassels, for God's sake. Probably he didn't think I'd make it. "So here I am again, your bad penny. You should maybe trade me off for a new model."

Quick look, but no laugh. "Good idea, Mr. Stern. Let's come back to that. Are you feeling about the same?"

"Anybody else I say Yes, I'm fine. You, I tell. I got no go-go. I don't care about schmuck. I can't get it up anymore. Lila Mae got bored. She left, and I don't even care. Maybe I'm running out. What do you say?"

No answer. Rudd grunts, pokes fingers, looks at papers and grunts again. Like always. Then he stands back for a long look. Just looks at me, like *Is he worth a bid?* and I can't tell what he decides. This is something different. And he says, "Dress up, Mr. Stern. We'll talk in my office."

In his office? That's also new. Always he talks right here. Dress up? For what? More bad news?

Stern climbs down. So today it's different? He crumples the paper gown, tosses it away. If something's new and different it's gotta be something bad.

He shrugs into his clothes. Last time, Rudd said I was over the hill. He lifts his zipper, cinches his belt. What is it this time: over the cliff? He jams his necktie into a coat pocket. Rudd's always the same. What's different today? He ties his shoes, shaking his head, and follows Dr. Rudd's steps into… into… what? How bad is it going to be?

There he sits, the doctor, like poker-faced behind his desk. Serious diplomas framed up on the wall behind him. So, yes already, he's an expert. But what's he going to say? And why so formal? in his own office, for God's sake? Am I done? Kaput?

"Mr. Stern, thank you for coming. In the last three months your liver has gone a long way downhill. Your lab tests today show even more damage. That is why you feel so tired. Do you know what is happening?"

Do I know? Yes, I know. For four years I know. Straight talk. Always bad. Never an upside. So now, this time, it's over. Forget Stern Towers. Give up. Fold your tent. Don't waste your time this afternoon to proposition the bishop. Do I know?"I am a developer, Dr. Rudd; I build things. In my world I'm a very savvy guy. Supplies don't arrive, money runs out? I've got problems to fix... I fix them. But my liver? I don't know the score. But I got things to do. I need to know. Like, how long?"

How can he look so happy? Like he doesn't care?

"In a lot of ways, you're good. Strong heart. Good lungs. Normal kidney function. It's just your liver that's in trouble. It's also a vital organ. For four years it has been damaged. And now, finally, it is failing. But you know all that."

"I know all that."

"Until now that meant the end for you."

What's this? *Until?* His eyes narrow; he leans over his knees, perches at the edge of his seat. Until now? A new game? With new rules? All his life, sharp practice. All his life, negotiation. It's what he knows. What he's good at....

He settles his behind into the chair. "What's in your mind, Dr. Rudd?"

"We do have a new possibility. A new procedure—very difficult, very expensive. It's succeeded in Pittsburgh. We are preparing to offer it here. To remove your bad liver. Find a good one and transplant it into you. Give you a new liver."

A new liver? Where does he go to get a new liver? WalMart maybe? And Rudd? His goy doctor? Those long fingers again? Rooting around his insides?... But he said difficult. He didn't say impossible... Expensive, he said. Like, what isn't?... Insurance? Who's counting? Hell, who bothers? Nothing wrong with me except my liver is killing me. And I can get a new one? What's to lose?... Go for it.

He hitches up on his chair, appraises his doctor sitting there behind the desk. His rescuer. Bringer of a new day. Martin Stern doesn't have to lie down and die, after all. Stern

Towers is maybe... yes... it is still in play. He'll hit the bishop this afternoon... make the offer he can't refuse... And maybe Lila Mae... ? To hell with Lila Mae.

To Dr. Rudd he says simply: "When?"

Rudd laughs. "There's lots we have to talk about before we get to 'when.'"

How does such a big-shot doctor manage to look so innocent? Like he's got nothing to hide. "So talk."

"There's risk."

"I'm dead already."

"There's expense. Very high costs."

"Big buildings cost. I build them. Some money rubs off, maybe. Keep talking."

"Getting a new liver for you is an entirely new possibility... much to consider..."

Yah-dah-yah-dah.

"... new questions..."

Who needs questions?

"Procurement... Chances for selection—"

Chances? Stern snaps to focus. Procurement he knows about. Livers are short? Hard to get? "No problem, Dr. Rudd, getting a liver. Supply and demand? That's my favorite sport. I remember when steel was short—"

"No, no. You have it wrong. It does not work that way at all."

Doesn't work that way? What other way is there? Aren't we partners here? How else do we find a new liver? He's talking...

"Finding a liver for you is not a market thing—no buy-and-sell at all. If you get a new liver—and that is a great big *IF* – it will come as a gift. A free gift for you, from someone you will never know. Some grieving person who gives permission—*gives*, Mr. Stern—permission for doctors to salvage the liver from a dead person. And then perhaps that liver may be assigned to you. There's more, but that's what you need to know right now."

Transparent is what he is. You wonder what he thinks, look at him. Earnest. A touch angry with me. "So tell me, what do I do to get my donated liver. Be a good boy?"

Dr. Rudd looks at his gold Rolex. His smile comes late and lasts too long. He's supposed to be my partner, and he's angry with me.

"We enter your name on a registry for liver patients. Donor livers go to people on the list in a formal selection process. If a liver becomes available, someone else may get it. But if it is assigned to you, it means Now. These salvaged organs die within hours. You must come into the hospital immediately to receive the transplant."

Stern spreads his hands, waggles his fingers. "Enough already. You offer me a deal I didn't know existed? Sign me up! You want me to learn something? I learn it. You get a liver? I'm here. What's my chance?"

"If we find a liver for you and transplant it successfully, you are 2 to 1, maybe 3 to 1, to celebrate a first anniversary."

Years of commercial pokering mask his face. Odds like that? They're a burst of hope. Three to one? Yesterday they were zero. "So what's to say, Dr. Rudd? We're partners. I move here. I stay in reach. My turn comes, I'm here. I don't worry. You look out for me, and whatever you say to do, I do."

He's on a roll in a new game. Stern Towers? Yes. Proposition the bishop? You bet. Right now. Today.

He strides out of Rudd's office, too fast, too bouncy.

Hell, why not? What's to lose?

Rudd

Lance Rudd watched Martin Stern as he soared away on his wings of hope; he felt something like those wings going a-flutter in his own Ivy-league chest. He's about to register his own patient—a real live *maybe* — for a liver transplant.

Is he ready?

His first concern is risk. His own. From diabetes. It rules his days. Blood tests, injections, diet, exercise. He grew meticulous before he grew up—before he knew what *meticulous* was. But he hid it from his friends. He felt ashamed — still feels — ashamed of his genes. So he has kept his diagnosis from public knowledge: only Brovek knows. Diabetes? He can handle that risk. No bar there.

But is he ready? After months of constant study? Poring over journal articles. Reading everything about hepatic surgery. Operating in the dog lab. Doing the surgical steps even in his nighttime dreams. Martin Stern will be his big chance to step up in the surgical world. A *maybe*, of course. A donor liver will be, as he said to Stern, a pure gift.

But yes, he is ready. For whenever his chance comes.

So, back to reality. To now. For right now he has a lecture to give.

He gathered his notes and dropped down the stairs to the warren of passages that led to Keaton Amphitheater. New U to Old U. Corridors of time, reminders of tradition. And somehow reminders as well of his troubled, old, personal decisions. About bad genes. About no kids. So no marriage. Single guy. Behave... Usually, no problem.

He pulled open the door to "the pit" and entered the rostral level of the old lecture hall.

Like an empty church, it slept in thick silence. Curving rows of seats rose to the entry level above, and his heart stirred. Echoes of lectures past whispered in his memory. The fragrance of learning. The thrills he had felt here as a student, when new and vital insights would strike home and light up the expanding lattice of his knowledge.

He hopes he can strike light like that for these neophyte doctors, his students. Like himself two decades ago, they dedicate these prime years of their lives to the study of a noble profession. They offer up their *now* — their leisure hours and their very major debts — for the sake of a hopeful future. As he stood at the lectern he felt again his own emotions of so long ago. His eagerness. His stress.

And here they came, spilling down the steps like otters, piling into seats, notebooks in their laps. He has coined pet names for some of them. Thomas, the class doubter. From the highest row he would make the keenest observations. St. Joan, her arms piled high with books, her eyes on a distant star. And Tony and Cleo, arriving last, and hand in hand. And suddenly his own surge of desire stirred in his loins. Urgent. Unexpected. Unfamiliar. Not you, Lance; not now. No way.

He tapped the lectern and began. "Last week we reviewed immunology, and antibodies, and the ways our bodies reject foreign materials. In bacterial infections, we very much want those immune reactions to succeed. We want to be rid of the bad agents. But sometimes an alien substance in our body can be a good thing. For blood transfusions we do cross-matching, simply to *avoid* triggering an immune reaction. But if that desirable foreign substance is living tissue, the immune response has too many triggers. We can't avoid it. For decades, science has searched for ways to control the immune response. Some methods didn't work, and the alien tissue was rejected. Some agents worked too well, and the recipient died. We dared to try renal transplants in humans only because failure of the graft left the patient no worse off than he was before. But it was a dismal story.

"Now comes a remarkable breakthrough. A drug called cyclosporine can strike the right balance. We can reduce the recipient's immune response enough to allow both graft and host to survive. In the last few years, from Pittsburgh, Dr. Thomas Starzl has reported successful liver transplant in humans. It is a world-change for transplants, and a sea-change for us. Because of cyclosporine — and years of prior experience — we expect soon to undertake human organ transplants right here."

"No disrespect, Dr. Rudd. But how will you know how?"

It sounded like Thomas, high up in the seats. He grinned and waggled his fingers. "Good question. First you apply the formal disciplines of good surgery: know the anatomy; know the procedural steps; handle tissues gently; minimize blood loss. Those are standard precepts with any good surgeon. In transplants, the key technical step is to unite the patient's blood vessels to the artery and vein of the new organ. We sew blood vessels every day. Is it a new technique?"

He expected no response.

"The technique won Alexis Carrel a Nobel Prize in Physiology."Silence.

"In 1912. We use the same method today — but with better thread. May I ask who dared to ask that good question?"

Pause. A hand lifted from a row below Thomas.

"Thank you for the cue. How do we know how? We must know more than technique. I mention also scholarship: we study and learn even as you do. We read and keep up with research papers and journal articles. We might travel to other centers. Dr. Starzl's, for example. And for a new procedure like a transplant, we will also devote hours to the dog lab or anatomy lab.... Just so you know."

He rattled his sheaf of notes on the lectern. "Now let's get personal. You have responsibilities. Because you, even as a student at an unhappy bedside, could become as important to a successful transplant as any operating surgeon. Whose job is it—don't skip this point—to propose the salvage of tissues from your patient? That this dying person become an organ donor?"

No one spoke.

"Take it in steps. Question one: is this dying patient a possible organ donor? If your answer is Yes, then comes question two: has the idea been raised? Why not? Red flags and whistles! There is your cue. Go to the senior person in attendance and inquire. Throw the ball and make him field it. Or her. The saddest, poorest reason to lose an organ donor is to fail to ask. We must not—not ever—forget the immeasurable value of multiple tissues—skin, bone, eyes, and organs—from one solitary donor. These priceless gifts can help dozens of other patients on down the line. Somebody has to speak up."

No one spoke. He hoped St. Joan would find something to say. He wished he had brought a jug of water. He pushed on.

"The actual asking for the salvage of organs should be part of a program in your hospital. There is a strict legal definition of the person in the family who can give consent. Is it the relative grieving by the bedside?"

"Could be, Dr. Rudd." It was indeed St. Joan, from the third row. "But only if they are the next of kin."

"And who is the next of kin?"

Joan nodded. "Surviving spouse, maybe. Then the oldest child. The succession is in the notes."

"Ah, yes," Rudd chuckled. "The printed notes. The precious backup to a tedious lecture. You must know the sequence. But, is next-of-kin the only person who must agree?"

Joan again, in her honeyed mezzo. "You want everybody to agree. All the family."

"Yes-yes-yes. We want everybody to agree. But families may split on this issue, debate and disagree. But we need to harvest the organs now. We may have to press hard to get permission. Is there a downside? Could we press too hard?...

"The answer is yes, we could. This whole business of salvaging organs from the recently dead is a new idea. People may be spooky about it until they understand the great value. So we need to build public understanding and wide support for organ donation. We don't want to cause hostility and objection. From today's grieving families will come tomorrow's attitude toward the donation of organs. It's up to us today."

"Hold it, Dr. Rudd." From his seat high above, Doubting Thomas floated his challenge. "A donor organ is too hard to come by. You say you have a legal okay. But you let somebody else, some sob-sister relative, veto it? I couldn't be so wimpy."

"Why is that wimpy?"

"Suppose I have a patient in the next room. He needs an organ—liver, kidney, whatever. I want to get it for my live patient, and that dead one doesn't need it any more. Not to fight for it is wimpy."

"You're helping me write my lecture. Let's call this your No-Wimpy Rule. Write it down. If you care for a patient who needs an organ transplant, you must not also care for a dying patient who might be a donor. If you care for a child who needs a liver, or a young mother dying with heart disease, you must not be in the same universe as a patient dying from a head injury, with a healthy liver and a sound heart. Not in the donor's universe and especially not in his family's.

"If I need a donor organ for my patient, I will not treat a patient who must die to provide it. I'll say it again. If I need a donor organ, I must not care for a possible donor. I may appear only after a declaration of death and the legal consent."

Pretty good discussion, Rudd thought. Good way to teach. But Thomas was not through.

"You're saying that the doctor who needs an organ can't ask for it, and the doctor who asks for it can't use it. No wonder there's a shortage."

"You're right. Always the limiting factor is to salvage organs from dead donors."

St. Joan nodded to Lance. "The government ought to do something about that."

"They're beginning. Last year we got the National Organ Transplant Act."

"What about ROPO?" Juliet's voice played the question like music.

"The Regional Organ Procurement Organization. I'm glad you know about it. Their people are expert in the art of gaining permission. And they allocate donor organs to go where they can do the most good. Which brings me to my next point of the day. When is a body dead? Does it die all at once?"

He let them think about that. No one spoke.

"When the heart stops, does everything stop?"

No answer.

"The answer is yes; everything stops. But not all at once. Some tissues live longer than others. Example, anyone?"

Juliet stirred. "A live baby after the mother dies."

"By C-Section. Good."

Another voice: "Skin and eyes."

"Yes. But solid organs are different. Liver, heart, kidneys. These tissues have high metabolic needs. When the circulation stops, they die fast. So how can we salvage a liver, say, after the heart stops?"

Thomas: "Take it before the heart stops."

"While the patient is still alive?"

Joan: "Oh, no!"

"In history and in law, we have always defined death as a stopped heart. But to salvage live organs for transplant, we must have a beating heart. How can the patient be dead with a beating heart?

Thomas: "Find a different definition for death."

Rudd: "Like?"

Pause.

Thomas: "Brain death, naturally. If you keep the ventilation going, the heart doesn't quit."

Rudd: "Right on. Good. But brain death is a new concept. We need to think about it. As important as it is, it is also a treacherous concept."

Rudd feels the energy coiled before him. The students lean forward in their seats, pencils down.

"Why do I say 'treacherous'?"Joan: "It's spooky. I saw one yesterday: unconscious, breathing on a respirator, but pink skin, warm, normal blood pressure. Dead? How do you know?"

Rudd: "That is the key question." He took his lecture position again behind the lectern, and triggered the pencils. "We have very few absolutes in medicine. But about brain death, here are two. The absence of brain function must be *total*. And it must be *irreversible*. You must accept those two absolutes and stay absolute in your obedience to them."

He paused while they wrote.

"The first absolute is *total:* that the brain has no function—none—at any level. Don't cut any corners on 'total loss.' It means there is *no* brain activity, not in the higher centers, not in the brain stem. If he breathes, if he rolls his eyes—even if he can do nothing else—his brain is not dead. Total means no reflexes—none. It means silence on the electroencephalogram, a flat tracing. We're not talking guesswork here. We are talking a formal, legal, and irreversible decision: a declaration of death. You do it once, and you must do it right."

He paused. "Now let's look at the other absolute—"

"What about those vegetable cases that live on respirators?" Unidentified voice. Male. "They're totally out of it, can't do anything. They might as well be dead."

"Yes. But are they dead?"

"Not by what you say."

"And not by any legal definition. Those cases are tragic. They raise all kinds of problems, and they go on and on. But the questions that come up concern life, and treatment, as they do for any living patient."

"They ought to die."

Lance fell back. Was it judgmental ignorance that he heard? Or a truly suffering sensibility? He said only: "They will die in their own time. And at that time they will receive a proper declaration of death."

Move it, Lance. Don't let him argue. Get back on track. "The second point? Does anyone remember the second one?"

"I don't remember the first one." The same voice. Insolent?

Nobody coughed. Nobody stirred. Students sat silent, watching. Careful, Lance. Keep them on your side. What... Ah...

He pretended confusion. He ruffled through his notes, seized a page, flourished it in apparent relief. "Thank God for good notes! The first point? Oh, yes, here it is!" And he sailed on. "About brain death, right? <u>Total</u>. That means ALL the brain is dead. The brain stem too. Nothing works. Not a shred. Not a reflex. Not a twitch. That's point one—whether we like it or not—*total*."

And he went on. "Now: Point Two. <u>Irreversible</u>. What? Can a brain with no action come awake again?"

Juliet's voice came confidently. "Anesthesia, Dr. Rudd."

"Yes, and other drugs on and off the street. Another reason?"

"Concussion."

"Still another?" He waited. "Very important this time of year."

Faces lit up. "Hypothermia!"

"Right on. Low body temperature can shut down the brain. Cold water immersion? Exposure? Coma? Keep the patient on the respirator, let her warm up to normal body temp for a day or two. Does she wake up? If not, do the checks for brain activity. If there is still none—none at all—then can come the declaration of brain death. Total loss, irreversible loss: brain death."

"That makes a long wait for all those donor organs." Thomas again, from on high.

"Yes, it does. But keep sharp in your thinking. Vital organs are retrieved from dead bodies. Never from patients. Donors of vital organs must be dead, and 'dead' has to come first. Stay precise about that, and you'll keep organ transplant on the right track. Questions?"

Buzzing in the sounds of release, his students went rattling up the stairs, balancing their books, pulling on their coats. Good kids. Steeped, all of them, in the explicit sexology of medical education. St. Joan, with her books, climbing the stairs in what he sees now are very tight white slacks. Perhaps she needs a different ID. Tony and Cleo have paused up there, at the top level—paused to touch lips before going separate ways. Do they feel the stormy passions of, say, Cyrano? Do they understand true love, as in the poems of Elizabeth Barrett? He hopes so. For them.

But for himself? No. Bad genes; no dreams. This afternoon, Lance Rudd feels only empty.

Fr. O'Leary

In mid-afternoon the old priest stepped out of the hospital into the January cold and shuffled back across the street. His breath came short as he labored up the seven concrete steps to his empty church. Schoolyard deserted. Attendance scant. Two years since he was cut in half by the new freeway. His parish but a shadow of itself. But Kevin O'Leary was called to the priesthood to labor for Christ. To be a priest. After each morning's Holy Mass at eight, and coffee with a soft egg, he makes his migration to the hospital. Thank God he still can find ministry there, and many souls to welcome him.

His Roman collar usually opens the way, though sometimes it seems a barrier. So he has modified his old formula, a prayer and a blessing. He tries first simply to make contact, to be present. To say little and listen long. To hear a person's murmured confidence with understanding and with sympathy. And sometimes an Our Father before his final blessing.

But now, in mid-afternoon, he needs to go home.

And home is first his church.

He hobbled down the center aisle, bowed to the altar, and grasped the altar rail. As his stiff and hurting knees bent to the velvet cushion, his reluctant groan lifted like incense to the silent apse.

"Well, Father in heaven, it was a good day and full. May you bring your healing power to all who suffer there in the hospital." His eyes rested on the shining red glass of the vigil candle.

"Especially your servant Horace Potts, who told me today..." Near it, in the tabernacle, the sacred host—

"...his hope for my frail old parish."—a simple unleavened wafer—

"But he's not able yet, poor man, to call upon the bishop."— consecrated by himself this day—

"Perhaps I should tell him ..." — -the symbol and reality of his invisible God —

"But I'm only an old priest...." — -and he released his cares at last into blankness, into simple, silent adoration of the sacred presence.

Karen

Karen set the lid on her chicken stew, turned down the heat and checked the clock. Five-thirty. Garrison won't come. How could she have had the gall to proposition Dana, a big-shot doctor? Nurses don't —.

But she did. Out of her need.

She riffled through her closet — not much to choose from — and picked a simple dark skirt and white blouse. She slipped them on, pulled her combed-out blond tresses into a neat ponytail and tied it up with a red ribbon.

At six o'clock a sudden jangle almost made her drop a plate. Door bell? She didn't have one! No. Her awful little alarm clock. Had she set it for — for tonight? No. Surely not; it's for morning, Dumbo. She punched it off.

Dana'll come if she can... She said she would... She's not done after eight hours, like nurses are. She works whenever they need her. Day, night. She'll come if she can... Maybe... When she's through... If Bozo lets her. What would it be like...

Six-thirty. She checked the stew. Starting to go dry. She poured in chicken stock and turned off the heat.

Different strokes. Her own schedule is plain vanilla. Eight hours and done. Five days a week. Forty hours. Dana's? Can't count them. She doesn't even get eight hours for sleep — not hours she can count on. Working twelve hours a day maybe. More, sometimes. An eighty-hour work week? *Uffda.* How does she keep up? Like most of the docs in training. How do they? Maybe they aren't so unforgivable, considering.

Seven o'clock. From her window she looked out at the snow-covered parking lot two stories below. No... No Dana tonight... Forgot?... Doctors give orders, nurses... take them. Maybe they can't blend, can't be friends.

No. Not tonight, anyway.

Nearly eight. Forget it. She snatched up the cold stew and stuck it into her tiny fridge. Nothing new about disappointment. She pulled off her skirt and blouse, tossed them on hangers in the closet — saving them for what? — and shrugged into her bathrobe. What will you have, Karen? Peanut butter?

Then, suddenly: a tap on the door!

Dana stood a couple of steps out in the hall. "You said 'whenever I get through'? Is it too late for you?"

Oh never! Karen thought.

"Not on your life," she said. "Come in." Karen looked down at her cotton robe and scuffed slippers; they would have to do. At least her hair was okay, still tied back with that crimson ribbon. "You must be beat! Come on in."

Dana flashed a smile. For a moment she looked around, nodded to Karen, and dropped with a sigh into the only cushioned chair. She didn't wear a winter jacket. Just her limp white clinical coat with a stethoscope curled in the pocket. Karen saw none of the panache Dana had showed in her conference this morning. What she saw now was Dana spent, in acute need of some TLC.

She poured glasses of cider for them and retrieved the stew. She put it on the stove again, turned the burner to medium, and sat on her other chair. In the small space their knees nearly touched. Hesitant, they sipped their ciders and eyed each other across the amber rims.

"I'm glad I went to the conference this morning. Dr Brovek was pretty tough on you."

"He hoped to slay the dragon lady today. He's not ready for women to be on top." She sipped. "Or should I say, at the top." She smiled. "Anyway, I'm still here."

"I'm glad."

"He'll learn."

"You need some dinner."

In heavy silence they nibbled at a couple of salads. But the spicy aroma of Karen's reheated stew awoke their juices, and they began to tell about themselves. Where they came from. How they happened on University Hospital. When their plates were empty, Karen poured strong coffee into a pair of white pottery mugs. They sipped slowly, relaxing into confidence.

Karen yearned to share her constant dream with Dana, that nursing should be a truly professional career. In the hospital world of conflicting needs, graduate nurses should function on their own authority. She explored that subject — without a good answer — in her Master's thesis. But share with Dana? Not yet. She wants no controversy. Not yet.

"My dad was a doctor," Dana said. "He took me along on his calls, sometimes. I remember watching him try to fix a hand after a farmer tangled with a corn picker." She centered her mug on a paper napkin beside her plate. "I think he always wanted me to be a doctor."

"What does he think about your picking a tough specialty like surgery?"

"He doesn't. The doctors' disease got him. He had a fatal coronary at fifty-eight. I was in my first year of med school."

"Oh, how sad." Karen took her empty mug the couple of steps to the sink, set it down. "He would be so proud of you."

"Oh, I hope so. I've got to be good, Karen. A better resident than the guys, just to stay even. "

"You're already better than the guys—especially when it comes to manners." She sat down again at the table. "At least you knew your father. Mine died when I was eight."

"Oh, that's too young, Karen. That's hard."

"I remember only that he was tall. And unapproachable. I don't know what he wanted for me... if anything."

"What did he do?"

"He was a Lutheran pastor. He left my mother with four children and a tiny pension and a shack of a house out on the prairie. She still lives there." Karen's eyes stung. She rose to the stove, snatched up the coffee pot. "And she's like a hermit."

Coffee twisted from the spout and swirled in the two mugs.

"But she would be there for you, I suppose, if you needed her. My mother died when I was little."

Karen thumped the pot hard on the table. "Enough of the sad stuff. What about the men in your life?"

Dana's throaty laugh bubbled across the cup at her lips. "That's not more sad stuff? My men all wear stethoscopes!"

Karen laughed, and stuck pointy fingers in her ears. She crossed her eyes. "One of these guys? For me, they're no good at all!"

"Maybe some day." Dana swirled her cup, watched the little whirlpool rise to the rim. "I have my hands full with Dr Brovek. He hates having a woman for his chief resident." She set the cup down. "He could fire me tomorrow, if he took it in his head. I've got to be about flawless, just to keep my job!"

"In my book, Dana, you're better than a fine doctor because you're also a woman!"

"A spent and tired-out, well-fed and grateful woman."

Dana relaxed her body into the good chair. "Lift your feet, Dana." Karen stood and slid her own chair under Dana's legs. Good legs. Lean and strong. Flesh-colored pantyhose. Nothing like her own dreary arctic white.

But the shoes?

"You're not all that tall, Dana. No heels?"

Dana laughed. "Never. Remember Cyrano's white plume? Low heels are my trademark. They say Hey! I'm who I am; I'm me."

"Yes, you're certainly you. Nobody else."

"And my low heels are silent, too. That's how I snuck up on you the other morning."

Karen studied her new friend. "That was only yesterday, Dana. Take a rest."

She went to the table, put her leftovers in the fridge. At the sink she spritzed the few dirty dishes, and her heart sang. Too many nights she had stood here alone, dumped food in the garbage, swished dishes with dead hands. Tonight her soapsuds smelled of fresh lemon, and her glassware gleamed. She found herself humming a tune—something she hadn't thought of in years. *Klappe, Klappe søte*, a Norwegian patty-cake song!

Dishes finished, she reached up over the sink to pull the bead-chain light switch. And her insides came alive. Her skin tingled. A couple of quiet steps put her at Dana's side. She knelt down and took her hand. But Dana Garrison was asleep in the sleep of exhaustion.

Dana

Valentine's Day. February 14, 1985

I'm working on a feisty old guy with a blocked femoral artery. When I first saw him in Vascular Clinic, he had actually brought me a valentine. "Fix up my big toe, Doc, and I'll take you to fiddle music we kin stomp to." Bless his heart.

It's his foot and leg I worry about; his toe is dead.

With Pete, my fellow resident, assisting, I make a simple incision in the upper thigh. We dissect clean a bit of the normal femoral artery. In direct connection to the heart upstairs, it carries a strong pulse. I am about to cut a hole in it.

Because downstream, above the patient's knee, this artery is blocked. His leg muscles cramp, his foot is cold, and his toe has turned black. In a tunnel under the skin, I'll run a tube graft of Goretex from this good part of his artery near his groin down to the popliteal artery below the obstruction. His pulses will pound through the graft and make his hind leg happy again. Except for the toe.

Vascular surgery is getting better in 1985. I wear a magnifying lens, for more precision. I choose from a range of special vascular clamps and forceps that allow temporary shut-off: they squeeze vessels closed without crushing them. Yet the clamps are absolutely secure—like my mother tiger six weeks ago. Needle holders and tissue forceps are fine-tipped, for precision. We use tiny new curved needles that carry their own built-in synthetic sutures. I suppose only scissors haven't changed much.

And now, attaching the graft to my patient's femoral artery, I mean to restore his circulation. So he can go stomp to fiddle music.

Always I worry about risk. Infection. Mishap with anesthesia. Bad arteries in the limbs go with bad arteries elsewhere: stroke, or heart. Can happen any time.

But worry doesn't help. My goal is technical perfection. First, of course, I put small spring clamps across the artery above and below; now I can cut my small window. I size it to match the synthetic graft. In the fingertips of my left hand, the tissue forceps dances counterpoint to the slender needle holder in my right palm. It sets up the first stitch as I pass the needle first through the graft, outside-in, then through the artery, inside-out. Tiny, precise stitches. Tie the knot, seven throws. Take the needle again, pass the stitch, pull it snug as a continuous stitch, and go again. Rhythm. Precision. The vessel and the graft match perfectly; I run the suture all the way around and make a good secure knot. Pete clips the threads.

Before I take off the arterial clamps, I put a new clamp on the graft (high-tech plumbing-101!). Now I open the distal arterial clamp, clean up any back-bleeding at the suture line. There is often a tiny spurter that will stop with finger pressure and patience. Next, off comes the proximal clamp. The full force of his blood pressure comes jamming into the native artery and the clamped graft. Halfway home.

Placing the distal end of the graft is essentially a repeat procedure, to the popliteal artery at the knee. Done.

Pete is good help, in exposing the field, keeping it dry, holding tension on the running stitch, closing the wounds. But the guttural sigh I hear couldn't be Pete—it comes from behind me. I turn in time to catch the rolling gait and broad back of Sandor Brovek, as he pushes through the swinging door, out of my operating room.

My face flushes hot. "How long was he standing there, Pete?"

He sees my angst and loves it. "Ten minutes, maybe."

Brovek isn't convinced about me. I know that. He never gives me the collegial chuckle he sometimes shares with the guys. And at every conference he gets on me about — well....

Enough self-pity. What he wants is the same thing I want: perfection.

"What's wrong, Dana? You grumbling about something?"

"No, Pete. It's nothing. Let's get done here."

I put in a skin stitch, snug it up and tie the knot. Cut the thread. Start another....

The hell it's nothing. For half a year of right now, I will live or die on Brovek's front burner. My future, my career — my whole life — are in his hands.

But it's in my own hands, first. It's mine to make right.

I feel a new steel settle in my spine. Five more months. Whatever it takes, I'll give. Like, every beat of my heart.

Karen

Karen's diplomas — the old BA degree and her new, hard-won MSN — hung in her apartment, alone and unseen. Now, suddenly, Karen found her labors to be well known to the Director of Nursing!

"I have watched your progress, Miss Sondergaard. You have a fine record here, and your new Master's degree is a wonderful achievement. I offer my congratulations."

Karen bobbed her head. Nothing in Prairie Falls has prepared her to be interviewed by a figure of such authority. But here she is, summoned from her duty station by special messenger. Is she in trouble?

Settling to the edge of the offered chair, she rested her nervous hands on her knees. Shoulders squared, she kept her back straight and looked directly in the other's eyes.

"You have a fine record here as well. I wonder about your plans. Do you wish to continue with us here, as a member of our nursing staff?"

Well, yes. Of course she does. And more than a member. Why else had she sacrificed so much to earn that advanced degree?

"I believe so. Yes."

Reticent by nature, she moves always in the taciturn gray shadow of her pinched Nordic mother. She knows the nursing routines; she serves them every week for forty or more long hours. But she dreams of change. Nursing should be more than beds and meds. A nurse might be an ally to her patient, an advocate in the hospital system. Mr. Potts, as an example, recovering now at home! But to help Mr. Potts she had exceeded her authority.

Do you feel satisfied with our policies here? With the way things go for our nursing staff?"

Karen studied the director, who sat comfortably, hands relaxed, eyes intent. Not defensive. She had asked an honest question.

"No, ma'am. Not entirely."

"Ah?" The director sat back, nodded. "Tell me more. Where are we deficient?"Karen shook her head. "I did not say you are deficient. That was not my word... ma'am."

"What would be your word, then? Please be free. Tell me your thought."

Dare she speak? Would she ever have a better opportunity? ...Yes, Karen. Dare.

Quietly she hinted at the idea she carries always in her heart. "My word might be 'limited.' Like, we're missing opportunities."

"In all our reporting district, this hospital has the lowest incidence of medication errors, the second lowest infection rate, and the fewest readmissions."

Karen's energy rose. "Yah. You can be proud of that."

"What 'opportunities' do you think we miss, Miss Sondergaard?"

"One of my patients is in the hospital because she was losing weight. Yesterday, for an x-ray, she was on 'nothing by mouth.' No breakfast. The procedure was delayed. When they wheeled her back, even her lunch tray was gone. I could not get a new tray."

"That seems rather minor. NPO for a necessary test."

"Yah. You think so. It was not minor to her family. Their mom needed food and had none. All day, nothing. And I couldn't help. If you wanted angry people, there they were."

"What should be different?"

"The nurse should have authority to make things right for her patient. She's not going to break anything — she knows the rules. And she won't hurt the patient, nor the system either, because she is a professional person. But your system does not give her the authority a professional person should have."

"Interesting. Of course, many nurses nowadays are men."

"Even men can be professional."

"Some day you should tell me more, Miss Sondergaard."

She knows a kiss-off when she hears it. "Please call me Karen." She stood up to leave.

"But I asked you here for a different reason."

A different reason? Now what? Am I in trouble?

"I have studied your record here. Four years. Steady. No problems."

"It's five now, ma'am. Five years last month."

"All the better. Please sit down again."

Karen settled to the edge of the chair.

"Your good record. Your new Master's degree. And our interview today... I like everything I see in you."

"Thank you, ma'am." I'm maybe not in trouble, after all.

The director sat forward, clasped her hands on her desktop. "I want you to accept a promotion. I want you to be the head nurse on Station 21. Starting next week."

Head nurse? No more night shift? Her heart leapt. Authority? Yes! To teach... to set goals... to promote her profession. To step up and make a difference... But head nurse? Was she up to that? Could she...?

The director opened her hands. "Do you accept?"

And the little girl from Prairie Falls burst out: "Oh yah!! You bet!!"

Fr. O'Leary

Father O'Leary thinks he's tough enough. He ministers to hardship and suffering almost every day, and those poor souls are never ready. People don't think of trials and illnesses as normal parts of living. So when trouble comes along, we have to learn the hard way. Learn about courage, and acceptance, and about clinging to belief.

But today he felt shaken beyond acceptance. For the beautiful Mrs. Herold, admitted today to Intensive Care, life had turned exceptionally tragic, the sight of it enough to disturb even an old priest like himself. She lay in the oxygen thing, eyes closed. Young and handsome, even in duress.

Surely she wasn't aware of his presence, nor of his blessing. She could only breathe.

He blessed her two youngsters also, confined and unhappy kids. Not in ICU of course — they were not allowed to come to her bedside. ICU rules. He shook his head. Hospital rules may be necessary. But they can be so harsh. They do a lot of hurt sometimes, to people who already suffer. And Mr. Herold, too. The devoted husband, barely able to speak — and clearly not open to any approach by clergy. Not yet.

Fr. O'Leary respects that. People deal with confusion and grief in their own time and in their own way. The Herolds are a church-going family, so someone said; but they were so torn today that he held back his words, said nothing at all. Often his best help lay in simply offering for a few quiet moments his caring presence. As he did today, with respect to the human agony in a family that is losing its heart. For poor Mrs. Herold, he was told, there is no hope at all....

Unless there be a miracle.

Karen

Karen stares at the clutter of charts on her desk. How little she knows about this hospital she works in. Uncountable numbers of everything: people, patients, pills — and everything run by pen and paper. Maybe she can't keep up with it — nor catch up to it — but she means to try.

As head nurse she will set her own priority, and first on her list is to assure her patients get proper care. She'll study those charts, and she'll see who of her nurses are on top of things, and who need attention. Keeping good charts, with timely and legible notes, is a pain sometimes—how well she knows! But good charts reflect performance: procedures properly done, meds given accurately and on time.

That done, she wants also to observe her crew for the other side of nursing: the heart. She'll watch each one's manner with patients. She believes in TLC; it is not a gimmick: it's a gold standard. From her own years with patients, she knows the aura of healing that should arise from the gentle starch of nurses. And she wonders whether that concept, so deep within herself, will be something she can teach.

Right now her new RN has to give a pain shot to last night's emergency admission. A Mrs. Carson. Karen slips down the hall, waits by the open door to watch the newbie's way with a needle. She is alone with the patient, a doctor in scrubs having just left the bedside. Mrs. Carson is in tears.

"Nurse!" A harsh voice. Male. The same doctor, now at her desk, beckons her with an imperial wave. "You don't look busy. Can you help me?"

His surgical mask hangs loose, its strings flirting with his wiggling pen as he writes on a chart. He doesn't look up. Karen strides back to her desk, gives him a closer look. Green scrubs; paper booties; a hood on his head that could go with a bank robber. His too-small lab coat leaves bare wrists sticking out. But she doesn't dare giggle. Surgeons always take themselves too seriously, and this one already shows a head of steam.

"I'm Dr. Rudd, nurse. I just saw your patient in 2110—the woman with a ruptured appendix. I want these orders seen to right now before we call her to surgery. Can you do that?"

Karen faces him. She stands almost as tall as he. Her blood surges, as scalding as the coffee she hasn't taken time for. And she wonders, as she always does, if ever there will be a man who is gentle—who can look past her uniform and see the person inside.

"I am the head nurse, Dr. Rudd. Yes. I can do that."

She stares at his back as he marches away.

How many times in her life has her Nordic reserve hidden her anger and saved her dignity? Her courtesy might be only façade, but every doctor deserves that much. And in a confrontation, if she were to let it happen, she knows who would lose.

She checks his written orders and sets to work. Lab tests now; IV antibiotics stat; a pre-op shot. Fine. But she herself will add the dimension she believes most often forgotten: an understanding ear.

"2110," indeed. Here comes the hero, racing in to operate on this scared lady, and he can't even say her name.

Rudd

Lance Rudd storms back to the surgeon's dressing room. He chose academic medicine to avoid stress like this heavy load today. The three majors he had listed already made a heavy schedule. But sometimes you have to extend yourself for patients, and today that's what he did. And now, on top of all that, this damned emergency crops up.

The woman has already gone too long with her bellyache: she, with her medical doctors. Her appendix is probably ruptured. Bad deal. But he can't change that. He'll bite the bullet. Squeeze the case in. Cinch up his belt, measure his glucose, maybe suck an orange or shoot up his secret insulin. And then go to surgery and do his best.

Regrets. On top of the press, he'd also been a mean bastard to that nurse. Good looking gal. Not cowed by his rant, either. Steady blue eyes that never flinched. Cool.

But women are in quarantine — or, rather, he is. Locked out. Insulated even from saying a nice, plain "Hello." That's the way it would begin. Talk. Get acquainted. Date a girl. Marry a woman. Spawn kids that inherit bad genes and live and die with diabetes.

Let people wonder why he's alone. It's his secret. He has locked it up inside; no one else need know that Lance Rudd... Lance Motherwell Rudd...has a fatal flaw.

"Ready, Dr. Rudd. Room Two."

A gastric resection. Bad ulcer. Constant pain. Curing something like that makes all the hassle worth the game. "Coming, Mizzoh. Thank you."

He grins about Mizzoh. That crusty old supervisor runs a tight ship in the surgery department. Makes things hum. He'd never dare treat her like he did that nurse this morning. What was her name?

He pushes through the double doors into surgery. Room Two. Here he comes....

Sondergaard. That was it.

Karen

Evening.

The old bulb cast a yellow light on the dark window, and shined on down to Karen's sink. Dana wouldn't call these few square feet a kitchen, but they do the job.

She elbowed Karen away from the dishes and stole the Chore Boy. "It's my turn. Go sit down." Karen, she thought, was acting pretty bitchy tonight. Something was eating her.

"Okay. Go ahead and wash, if you feel like it." Karen snatched up the dish towel. "But I'll wipe."

Dana swabbed a dish, quietly. Maybe she'd hear a clue. "I sure do like our pattern these nights. You're a good cook."

"And you're a good eater."

Dana smiled at that. Big appetite? Oh, yes. Guilty. But Karen? What's wrong? She never eats much; but tonight she just picked. "I'm glad there were no calls for me. No interruptions. We've talked about everything under the sun, except us." She turned to her friend, who was dabbing her towel at a dinner plate. "But you haven't told me about today: Day One as Head Nurse."

Karen stiffened. "Don't ask... Just, don't ask..."

Dana's hands went still. Yes, Karen is hurting. "What is it, love? What's the prob?"

"Who said there's a problem? It's just the same-old same-old.... Tell me instead about you. You're so uppity; you must have had a good day."

Dana dipped the dish in the suds and swished it. "An ideal day. A good case. A valentine from a patient! And a long hot shower." She wanted to tell about her admirer with the black toe; maybe later? "And now... a good dinner with a good friend." She studied Karen as she talked. Get a clue? "And now look at me. Where else do I get a chance to clean up dinner dishes?" She waved a soapy plate. "These sessions with you are a God-send for me. A wonderful break. Everything else is business."

Karen bit off her words. "But you like your business. You're top dog in your business. You write your own ticket in your business." She slumped on the kitchen stool and turned away. "And I have to eat shit." She twisted her towel into a cable.

Dana splashed the lasagna pan back into the suds, hoisted her lean buttocks up on the counter, wiped her hands on her thighs. She took Karen's towel. "Tell me about it."

Karen squared her shoulders, punched her words. "Your life is surgery. Being the best. Being independent. Mine is nursing." She took the towel back and twisted it tight again. "And the best isn't good enough. I want to make it better."

"Karen, the radical? Are you a troublemaker?"

"That's not my nature. No. I want other people to see what I see. A nurse is a professional person. She ought to have the authority of a professional person. I want a nurse to be able to stick up for her patient. Be an ally. A protector."

Dana jumped at that one. "Protector? From what? From me?"

"Don't pick a fight with me, Dana. You know how I feel about you. But a lot of doctors are not like you."

"No. That's true. Most of them are men...." Wait, Dana. No joke. There's something deeper here. "Tell me what happened today."

"One of my patients came in with a ruptured appendix. You know how sick she was with that, and hurting. And she got carted off to surgery scared and alone."

"I'm sure your nurses took good care of her."

"Yes, Doctor. Certainly, Doctor."

"Where was her family?"

"Who knows? She was alone. She thought she was going to die. And nobody told her any different."

"I bet you did."

"I tried."

"But you still feel bad."

"Yes, I do. Bad in two ways. Nursing should do better. Patients need something better. I haven't figured it out yet."

"You're head nurse. You can do something."

"Do what? I don't really know what I want."

Dana turned back to the soapy dishes. "What's the second way?"

"The doctor. He was a jerk. Rough on me and rough on his patient. And he was the only male person I saw to talk to all day long."

"Just curious, Karen. Which doctor was it?"

"Dr. Rudd. The pig. He was just plain mean."

Dana bit down on her reaction. Gentle Lance? Her mentor and friend? "I heard him say he was booked tight today and then had to squeeze something in. He must have been under pressure."

Karen snorted. "He could still treat me like a human being. And his patient like someone with feelings."

"Bad, hey?"

"He told her he had to operate or she'd die. He never even said she'd get well."

From her seat on the counter, Dana's heels tapped a hollow beat on the cupboard door. She said nothing.

"You doctors have no idea what feelings patients have. How distressed they are. We nurses see that. See it all the time. But we have no power." Karen threw down the towel and dropped into the padded chair. "Jesse Jackson talks about empowerment. I keep thinking about that."

"Good for you. Think some more. What would you do with power? If you had it."

Karen glared at Dana. "I could find out in a hurry, if I had it. But I can't change the system. Nobody listens to nurses."

"But maybe you can!" Dana pushed herself down from the counter. "I thought you were a bundle of ice, once." She slid the other chair near, so they faced each other, knee-to-knee. "And what happened? You reached out. You offered me friendship. You made things different, Karen. Better, for both of us."

From Karen, her first faint smile. "I was driven, Dana. I couldn't admit it then. But you nailed it. Lonely. Thank you, Dana."

"I was lonely too. And too busy to know it. Thank you, Karen."

"Know something funny?"

"What?"

"That first night you were here? I thought I was falling in love with you." Karen clasped her hands in her lap. "But the Lutherans won. I won't settle for less than a man."

Dana whooped. "Less than a what?" Her laughter echoed in the tiny room. "Hey, Karen, I have to be twice a man to be here at all!"

She jumped to her feet, clutching at Bozo. His antic vibrations in her groin no longer shock her, but he has caught her by surprise.

"Dr. Garrison," Bozo crackled. "Call Emergency Room."

She took up Karen's phone, dialed, and spoke across it. "Reach out again, Karen. Develop your idea. It could be a whole new career. But you'll have to reach out."

Then into the phone: "Garrison here.... On my way, thanks."

Then to Karen, as she hung up the phone: "And Karen, give Dr. Rudd another chance. As men go, he's a good one."

PART TWO

February 14, 2014.

You make me wonder. Were you and Karen ever... in love?

Love knows no boundaries, Russell. Wonder on.

I don't really think so. You must have been just friends.

Don't shortchange friendship. It can be life-changing.

Just asking. I've always wondered. Because pretty soon after that, you and I... got acquainted, should I say?

Indeed you should. And here we are now, a quarter century later, my whole career later, and we're still... well... we're writing a book together.

So let's talk about the book. You made a point about improvements in surgery – how your instruments got better. I suppose everything gets better over the years.

Look what's happened since then. Ruptured aneurysm today is a recognized hot challenge but not a pioneering groundbreaker. In fact, aortic aneurysms are more a management problem. Physicians check for them routinely now. If they find one, they measure it, follow it. If it gets bigger and threatens, we go right after it. That way, when it isn't bleeding, its repair is only a standard elective procedure.

Still a huge one, though, isn't it? As a layman, I'd think so.

A major operation always; but low risk. Even more progress: some centers are handling aneurysms with no open surgery at all. You remember that femoral artery I told you about?

Your valentine patient.

That one. In the upper thigh we stick a special needle into the femoral artery, and through it we can slide a compressed tube-graft up-stream into the aneurysm. There, it's supposed to open up and become a new aorta. If it works, we don't have to open the belly at all.

Sounds like coronary arteries and stents.

Same idea.

And now, finally, are we getting to transplants?

Didn't you notice? We're already there.

Danny

Saturday, March 9, 1985

"Be careful, Danny!"

"Yeah, Ma." He is always careful. A darned good rider.

"Wear your—"

Sure, Ma. He always wears his helmet—except today it's at school. He'll wear it home. She'll never know.

He's eager to get there on this Saturday morning. He's into a neat term project, to program his own computer game on the school's new MacIntosh. He's building the gate to his Crystal Castle. He's got the drawbridge to go up and down— pretty cool! And now he wants to add a portcullis. If nothing goes wrong, maybe he can get it done today.

In the gloom of the machine shed, his father and little brother are bent deep into the big John Deere. When he revs up his Honda, they look up and wave their tools at him. Out he goes into the sunshine, circles the yard and roars off to town. He checks out the malt shop, but nobody's there yet — it's too early. He shoots off a couple of backfires, just to be sure. At the Lutheran Church he makes his turn, starts down the hill, past the hospital, toward school. Nearly there.

There's a pickup coming up the hill, loaded down to its springs with firewood. It's in the right lane, coming up, and he can pass it, going down. Plenty of room. But suddenly a car darts out from behind the truck. Head-on! Now! Danny hits his brake, not too hard, and dodges into the driveway of the hospital, then hauls left, leans into a sliding turn. No sweat — until he hits the sand. Loose sand they've spread over the patchy ice so nobody will skid — except a motorbike in a tight turn. His knee scrapes concrete; his wheels slam a curb. Danny launches, airborne. He sees the ground whirl away. He sees the sky. He sees the old elm tree coming at him. Then he sees nothing.

Dana

Tuesday, March 12, 1985

4:30 a.m.

Not Bozo. It was her bedside telephone, strident, merciless. Dana struggled awake. Who...? Her clock glowed 0430 in green numbers. Who would — ?

Dr. Brovek's unmistakable voice rasped. "I need you in my office, Dr. Garrison. I am here now. Can you come?"

"Yes, sir. On my way." She knew not to ask questions. Her feet thrust themselves into her winged shoes and away she went. From behind his big desk his black eyes bored into her. He made no greeting. "We have a cadaver donor for Mrs. Herold. We need to go out there and get it. Right now. Get it back here ASAP. Can you handle that?"

His question struck her like a blow to the stomach. Nothing polite about it. Not "could you do it for me?" His blunt question dug deep: "You are my Chief Resident. Are you *able* to do it?"

Her mind raced. Get out there, somewhere. Cut the heart out. Bring it home. Do it fast. Do it now. *Can* she handle that? She knows the procedure. Last week she helped Lance with a harvest. Those organs had gone elsewhere — not the point. Her personal code is the point: *Be ready. When the time comes, step up.*

"Yes, sir, I can. Other organs, too? Or just the heart?"

Brovek nodded. "I thought you'd say that. It's a kid off a motorcycle. He ruptured his gut, so we'll take only his heart. You fly out there right now in the University aircraft. I'm sending a support technician along to help. Bring a good heart back here, Dr. Garrison, and we'll plant it in Mrs. Herold this afternoon."

In the jolting taxi, but afloat on Brovek's trust, Dana clung to the seatbelt and reviewed her charge. First, remove the donor heart, intact and undamaged. Ice it to preserve its life. Then start the race against the clock — before the salvaged organ fades away beyond recall. Four hours at most. She must carry out her mission without a wasted moment.

But where? Where is she off to like a bird from the barn? She always keeps a tightlipped presence with Brovek: no soprano gab. But maybe, this time, she could have asked?

5:45 a.m.

Her taxi squealed to a stop beside a small Cessna aircraft, three wheels, single engine running at idle. Behind and below the high wing was an open door. She seized an offered hand and swung up into the plane. Like St. Joan, on a sacred mission.

"Hey, Doc." A laughing baritone. "Let's go break a heart."

Flippant words. Out of place. She flared at them.

But he had already taken the pilot's seat and was working the controls. A large box occupied one rear seat, and a young man in a scrub suit and trench coat sat in the other. She settled into the co-pilot's place and scrabbled around for the seat belt. She glared at the pilot. A cartoon of an airman, in brown leather and an actual white scarf! Like Snoopy! Unaccountably, her anger vanished. His weathered face flashed a smile, and her own overworked, hard focus splintered. "Go break your own heart, cowboy." She shot the words in a mix of serious and sass. And don't, she said to herself, mess with my heart.

"Name's Rusty, Doc." He flicked through a series of switches, checked with the tower, taxied the aircraft to the runway. "I'll teach you to fly, going out." The engine roared; they accelerated down the strip and were airborne. "And you teach me surgery coming home. We're playing MedEx, and I don't like the weather. We'll take an hour to get there, then your thing, and then we run home. And we'd better be running ahead of it."

My thing? Like stopping for groceries along the way? This guy needs some punching down.

She checked him out again. One hand rested on his dual wheel; the other, in his lap, steadied a coffee cup. The leather of his jacket looked good on him; it went with that tough brush of rust-colored hair. Ah, yes: Rusty! What would his real name be? She checked him again and looked straight into those cool green eyes. Neat.

She tried to cover. "Does your flight plan have a name on it?"

"Sure does, Doc. Some little place out there called Hangarville. Ever hear of it?"

Hangarville? Couldn't be! That's where she grew up! Followed her dad at the hospital. Saw her first operation. Held his hand when he died. And stood by the graves, her mother and father, side by side. She never meant to come home this way.

She watched Rusty at the controls. Good profile, strong nose, rugged features. The leathery skin that some redheads are lucky to get. His hair looked tough and wiry — or would feel like that if she dared to take hold of it — as thick as a scrub brush and the color of copper. She remembered his flash of white teeth and the green eyes that, despite his first crass words, had sparked her. Watch out for this one.

And at once she chided herself. She has no room for — for — anybody. Today, she is a solo operation. No support troops. Do or die. Today she has to prove to Brovek: Yes! She does have the grit, the smarts, the cool, to make a surgeon. Salvage the heart and take it home. Truly a sacred mission.

Go break a heart indeed.

She'd never sat in a copilot's seat before. She studied the dials — they meant nothing to her — and watched her wheel move as Rusty's did. Watched the snow-covered fields slip away behind. The flight was smooth. Nothing much to look at. Rusty? What a name.

The engines cut back, and the plane tilted down. In the sunshine she could see fields below and then the town itself. Yes. There was the tall Lutheran church at the top of Hangar Hill. Her hometown. They had hardly stopped moving on the tarmac when an ambulance drew alongside. She slipped her belt and climbed out of the seat.

Far off on the western horizon she could see the weather front, a flat line of heavy gray drawn across the sky.

Rusty waggled his fingers at her. "Weather coming, Doc. We need to beat it. Don't get lost in there."

Lost? In Hangarville? No way. She might know a nurse or two. And — oh — she might even know the dead boy's family!

No. She would not get lost.

Jack Herold

7:00 a.m.

He rose from a ragged shallow sleep, lit a cigarette, splashed his face, lit a dry cigarette, took three deep drags, stubbed out the butt, and set out to the hospital's Intensive Care Unit. If Millicent had died in the night, they would have called him. Maybe she's better.

He had the flu before she did, and got over it. Francine and Eddie had it first — they brought it home from school. What, five weeks ago? Six, maybe? They got well. But Millicent? Not. She was last to get it, and the flu hit her hard. She didn't get better. Couldn't breathe. Pneumonia, they thought. But she got worse, and they decided to blame her heart. Myocarditis, they called it. Three days ago — it seemed like forever — he rode in the ambulance to bring her here, to University Hospital. And it's the same routine here. Intensive Care Unit. Short visits. Oxygen prongs in her nose. Food by the teaspoon. Blue lips. Mostly asleep. And every day, weaker.

He watched her on the pillows now, breathing, but barely. Maybe she knows he's here. She doesn't respond. Surely she does know he is lost without her. Only a month ago she sang the soprano solo in church. *I know that my redeemer liveth. The Messiah.* Maybe she sang her heart out. She gave him goose bumps that day.

Would a little redemption right now be too much to ask?

She's no better. He can see that. Yesterday they told him her heart is failing; she cannot recover. Her only hope is to replace her bad heart with a new one. A transplant. Then this other guy came on. Brovek. And everybody stood back.

I paid attention to him.

Your wife needs a transplant. Okay. We have no donor for her. No way to get one. Just have to wait: wait and hope. Maybe none will come in time. Difficult, Mr. Herold.

But what about an artificial heart? I've read about that.

Too experimental, the big man said. Too many bugs. I don't recommend them.

Jack Herold stares at his comatose wife. Experimental? How could he stay alive without her? What about Francine and Eddy? They need their mother. But no donor heart? Okay. Then try the artificial thing! Experiment! Give her a chance; keep her alive until a real one comes along!

And here he is again, this morning. Dr. Brovek. Fast feet for his size.

Jack Herold, desperate, is faster. He steps in front of the big doctor, blocks his way. "Millicent is damn near dead this morning. You can't just let her die. I want you to try that experimental thing. Do it. And don't wait too long."

He expected anger. He didn't care. But Brovek's voice was soft. "We have a donor, Mr. Herold. A couple hundred miles from here. We will harvest the heart right now, this morning. If we can get it here by noontime, it could be beating for your wife by the time the sun sets. Cross your fingers or say your prayers, and excuse me. I have work to do!"

Rusty

7:30 a.m.

Rusty ran through the pilot's checklist for his layover, made things right for the airplane and drifted into the airport's small office. No layover was dull if he had time for paper and pen. So far he's the University's airplane pilot. His real goal is university teaching — English; Creative Writing.

That's one good-looking chick, Doc Garrison. Yes, sir!

He fed a couple of quarters into a machine and retrieved a Dr Pepper. Popped it, swigged it, found a table and chair and sat down.

He wasn't there yet with the University. Flying pays the bills, and gives him time to write. And mail out stories. And file rejection slips. And feel lonely. Most of his old buddies have spawned kids and slipped out of sight. That's a normal story line, he figures, like the sun going down. But where does that concept leave him? A straggler? Or a misfit?

He hauled out his Sanford fine-point pen and yellow legal pad. *Dullsville*, he wrote. *Nothing ever happens here.* He grinned. Except a kid dies, a glamorous lady-surgeon flies in from the big city, scrounges the kid's heart and flies away.

But not into the sunset. He empties the Pepper and crushes the can.

In the next hour or so, he'll take off again in the advancing edge of a mean-looking weather front. The end of that story he can't write yet.

Dana

7:45 a.m.

"Welcome to Hangarville, Dr. Garrison."

They have a Greeter! The eager OR nurse, sturdy and round in gray scrubs and green paper boots, dances ahead of Dana to the nurses' locker room. "I remember you when you came here with your father. I often scrubbed for him... your wonderful dad."

Dana offers a quick smile and moves briskly to don her own scrubs and boots. She cannot be "old Doc's girl" today. "After I meet Dr. Bockman, I would like to speak briefly to your nurses."

"Well..." Only slightly put off? The good nurse points the way. "Dr Bockman is already at the scrub sink. Danny is on the table being prepped. We are all, I think, quite ready for you... Dr. Garrison."

Dana pulls on her hood and surgical mask and approaches the operating room. She greets three nurses in OR scrubs, caps and masks. On the operating table, heavy surgical drapes leave only Danny's chest exposed under the bright circular light. At his head, a nurse anesthetist gives her attention to oxygen and ventilation and blood pressure — everything for an operation except anesthesia. Dana speaks up for all to hear.

"You know that our patient is dead. We intend to remove his heart here, and transplant it into a patient at University Hospital—a young mother barely clinging to life. Our job here is to save this heart. We must have strict attention to sterile technique: absolute asepsis. Think of this case as being like any standard thoracotomy, and we'll get along fine. Thank you."

She turns to the sink and begins to scrub. "Dana Garrison, Dr. Bockman. Sorry we can't ignore the clock today."

"No problem, Dr. Garrison." He completes his scrub, bends his elbows, lets the water drain. He stands behind Dana, drying with a sterile towel.

Dana works a black-bristled stiff brush under the running water, sudsing the dark brown germicidal soap in her familiar pattern, nails, fingers, hands and wrists, and finally the forearms, taking plenty of time. "I appreciate your help, Dr. Bockman. You have already put a lot of hard work into this patient."

Bockman grunts through his mask. "Yeah. Right here in this room. Sewed up his gut all right; but couldn't help his head."

"If you hadn't fixed his gut, though, we couldn't save his heart."

"That celebration may be easier for you. I knew Danny."

"Whoops! I didn't mean to be insensitive. But a lot of bigger places probably don't yet do what you did. You recognized brain death, asked for the organs, and here we are. Thanks to you."

They hold out their arms for their sterile gowns.

Brovek

7:45 a.m.

Sandor Brovek paced the length of his office. He flipped some technical pages about heart surgery. Hell, he knew all that. He'd done all those procedures before. Except... well... except what his Chief Resident should be doing right now. He hasn't yet cut a heart out. But he's about to, and sure as blazes he's ready and eager to sew one in!

"Mizzoh!" He barked into his phone. "We'll have that heart here in an hour or so. You ready?"

"I have your room scrubbed and ready, Dr. Bro. I have Myrna standing by — she's thrilled to be your scrub nurse for this... this... this what? This first one!"

"Good. I was going to ask for her."

"I'm ahead of you. When should we be ready?"

"Can't say a clock time. But when Garrison starts home, we'll move. Set up your instruments. Put the patient on the table — let the anesthesiologist keep her happy. Prep her chest, drape the field. I'll scrub and get my gown and gloves. I might even take up the scalpel."

"While she's still awake?"

"Until the last minute. Once she goes to sleep, there is no turning back. She'll wake up with a new heart, or she won't wake up at all."

"She'll have a new one."

"I'm glad you're running the shop down there. I'm counting on you today."

"We've been doing this for a lotta years, Dr. Bro. I'm here for you."

Dana

7:55 a.m.

In a way, she remembers them all. Danny's people herd themselves into Dana's pickup consulting room, in silent contact of elbows, fingertips, concerns. The room fills with them and with their familiar odors of honest sweat, grain dust and the animal barn. Her heart swells. Shy, respectful, suffering, the Hovelunds hook thumbs on their clothing or rest their hands on chair backs and look at the floor.

She wishes somebody would sit down, but they stand, eight of them, silent, like a knot of sheep. She tries for eye contact; but at the edges of their new life without Danny, and in the enormity of this precise moment, they are silent and unseeing.

"My name is Dr. Garrison. I've come from University Hospital to…to…"

To what? Cut the heart out of your boy? Unreal! In this same room, she used to wait for her father to finish his Sunday rounds!

She clears her throat and tries again, directly to Danny's mother. "This tragic accident took Danny away. I am truly sorry for your terrible loss. Dr. Bockman did all anyone could do for Danny, and his fine care gives you… and us at the University… a chance to make something good out of his death. Danny's head injury was fatal. He is legally and actually dead. But his heart still beats. We can rescue Danny's heart and transplant it to a woman whose heart is dying. She will live again. You have given your consent to a great gift. Thank you. Do you have any questions for me?"

Danny's mother sobs softly. Dana imagines those last three agonizing days, the family clinging to hope. Then losing

Danny. Then accepting this revolutionary idea, and giving his heart away, that someone else may live.

Danny's father — a *Trojan Seeds* cap tucked into his bib overalls, his bronzed face dark against his bone-white brow — says simply, "I don't see nothin' good in this except what you say to do. So just go do it."

"Thank you, Mr. Hovelund. Thank you all. Time is important. I will not see you after the... after I... I must move fast."

But she pauses in the hallway for a necessary Kleenex. Through the open door comes Danny's father's voice. "Hey, Bernice, you think that could of been ol' Doc's girl?"

8:05 a.m.

Her scalpel draws a red line down the midline of his chest. The boy is dead, but he bleeds. Spooky.

She splits the breastbone and spreads it wide.

In full view within its pericardial sac, Danny's heart beats in 16-year-old vigor. She incises the pericardium and lays it back. Now the heart lies bare and unprotected, clenching and loosing and clenching like a great fist. She sees the two major veins that enter the right side of the heart: the superior and inferior venae cavae, the size of garden hoses. And one great pulmonary artery, that rises on its way to the lungs. Arching from the top of the heart comes the thoracic aorta, even bigger and more daunting than the aneurysm she dealt with on New Year's Day. Behind the heart she knows, when the time comes, she will find the pulmonary veins, inaccessible and multiple, returning blood from the lungs into the right atrium. She'll bypass those, simply by cutting away the patch of heart wall that includes them.

It's like a three-dimensional puzzle. Dr. Brovek will follow the identical procedure to remove Millicent Herold's dying heart. Except that she is alive, and these same preserved vessels will be blood-filled and alive, their circulation driven by a heart-lung bypass pump. When he lifts the heart from her open chest, the same cut-off great vessels will be there, and each will receive its match in Danny's transplant.

She takes on the vessels one at a time, teasing and trimming filmy bits of extraneous tissue, so each vessel is clean — just as she did with the femoral artery on Valentine's day. Now she is ready.

"Okay, Dr. Bockman?"

"Looking good."

"Here we go." She slides a clamp across the inferior vena cava, another across the superior: click, click, closed and locked. Now, when she cuts the heart free, even dead blood will not spill. In a steady sequence she applies the other clamps, one to each vessel. All circulation to the heart is now blocked.

Dana glances up to note the time. The critical clock begins to run. It is 8:50 a.m.

But the heart has not stopped. It struggles on, trying to pump, moving no blood, burning its energy. A no-no. Into the heart's own circulation she injects her special solution of potassium chloride. Danny's heart shudders, twitches a couple of times, and lies still.

Moving steadily, she cuts the isolated vessels, frees the heart, takes it in her hands and lifts it out of Danny's chest. Immediately she begins flushing it inside and out with iced salt solution — all the chambers, again and again, with volumes of the icy saline, to rid the heart of unwanted blood cells and to cool it down nearly to freezing.

A chill runs in her own spine. Is it the ice water? Or the enormity of what she has done? For the briefest moment, all urgency falls from her mind. In her hands she holds a live human heart, an engine of life, a heart moving from tragedy to hope. For a moment she lifts it above the empty cavity of Danny's open chest—not as a trophy, but as an offering.

Then urgency returns. A harvested heart has a four-hour shelf life! She packs the iced heart into a series of sterile bags, and nestles the bags into a mound of crushed ice in her technician's insulated box.

"Thanks, Dr. Bockman. Saving this heart is a fine achievement, and you made it possible. Thanks for welcoming me back to Hangarville!"

Dr. Bockman stands by Danny's body. "Good job, Dr. Garrison. Good luck." Holding now a large needle and heavy suture, he will do the necessary minimum. There will be no healing.

Dana strips off her gown and gloves, snags her clothing from her father's old scrub nurse, nods her thanks. Leading her technician with their precious box, she presses on outside to a waiting ambulance.

And the gathering storm.

Jack Herold

9:15 a.m.

Jack Herold inhaled a long breath from his short cigarette. He was too damn tough to cry in front of his children. As Millicent's gurney moved away down the hall, he shepherded Francine and little Eddy into a family waiting room. Vinyl-covered sofa and three straight chairs. A couple of folding chairs leaned against the wall. A small sink with hot and cold faucets fit into one corner. No windows. A prison.

"How long, Dad?" Francine pulled Eddy down to sit with her on the sofa. Eddy snapped himself loose, and curled up with his back to Francie. But he stayed close.

"The longer the better, Honey. Let's settle down and be good waiters."

"Is Mom going to die?"

Jack dropped to a chair. "I don't know."

"I've got nothing to do." Eddy squirmed on the cushions.

Jack and Francine were good buddies. He never lied to her. "Some day she'll die. Everybody does, some day."

"But not now, will she? She's so sick."

"That's why we're here, Francie. To get her well again."

"She's supposed to sing again at Easter. They're rehearsing already.... Who's that man?"

Eddy quit squirming and stared at the black-suited figure in the doorway. Jack stood up and let out his breath in a long sigh. The last thing he wanted was another visit from that Roman-collared priest.

"Here you are, Mr. Herold. Family all together, pulling for your wife and mother. I'm glad to see you together."

"We'd be nowhere else, uh—O'Leary isn't it?" God, I hope he doesn't plan to wait here with us, he and his holiness.

"Yep. You remember me." His eyes danced under his white eyebrows. "Properly called Father O'Leary. I won't wait with you, Mr. Herold. Waiting is no fun at all." He brought his hidden hand into view. "But I did bring a little something to help you pass the time... If I may?" He handed a couple of magazines to Francie. *American Girl* brought a large smile. Eddy came out of his sulk to seize a proffered coloring book and small box of Crayolas.

"Do I hear a thank-you?" Jack prompted. But Fr. O'Leary was already gone. He hadn't really even come in.

Jack watched his kids settle down, and settled again onto one of the hard chairs. Waited. Checked the clock. Longed for a cigarette. Finally he stirred. "Francie?"

"What, Dad?"

"Can I look at one of your magazines?"

Dana

9:30 a.m.

A gusting wind whips her short hair and plasters Dana's thin coat against her body. Rusty's aircraft rocks, its engine rumbles, the wind howls. No flippant words this time. He gives her a no-nonsense haul into the cabin and turns to his controls. She checks the box, strapped and belted into its seat. The technician, pale, looking small, bends to his seat belt.

She sinks into the co-pilot's seat, straps her belt. Never before has she felt the need of one when the plane is still on the ground! She looks across at her pilot. She's ready.

Rusty holds her in a steady gaze. "It's rough, Doc. We have a decision to make."

"We do? No! Let's go!"

"Planes are grounded all around this area. Nobody's flying."

"We are! We have to."

"No, we don't have to. If this were a normal mission, I wouldn't even ask what you think. I'd hangar the plane and go find a hamburger palace. A storm like this is too dangerous."

"Is it possible to take off in this weather? Can you do it?"

"Barely. This is a weather front. Severe turbulence. A couple hours from now it'll blow over. Then we can go."

"That's too late, Rusty. Can you fly now? Get this plane into the air?"

"One burp more wind, I'd say No. As is, it's a maybe. If we don't turn over first."

"This mission is urgent. Life-saving. We can't quit."

He does not argue. Quietly he states his opinion. "I understand, Dr. Garrison. My advice is still that you abort the mission."

For a moment she pictures Brovek's towering rage. Sees Mrs. Herold, laboring to breathe. Weighs her own values. What would it mean to fail? To let Danny's heart die in its icy box while she sits safe at a counter, eating hamburgers. Or the other way to fail: to fly, and crash, and die. Four lives lost, and a salvaged heart, in a quixotic effort for life. Conservative coward or dead hero; which one are you, Dana?

She looks deep into his earnest green eyes.

"No. I can't do that."

"We're risking three lives here, if we fly."

"We're losing two hearts if we don't."

The engine's roar and the wind's howl are an even match. The little plane is buffeted in the wind. Could she die? Yes. Face it. She could. Along with her pilot and her technician — and Millicent Herold.

"Can we make it?"

"Maybe. If we're lucky. We won't know if we don't try."

She turns to her pilot, his hands resting on his controls. Their eyes meet, each of them searching deep. She has known him for a thousand years.

"We've got to try, Rusty. Let's head for home."

The engine's deep throat blends with the wind. The plane lurches, bounces. She is tossed against her belt, caught, pulled back and bounced again. The harsh bang of the runway gives way to great swerves and dips of ragged flight.

But her part is played. She folds her hands and sits back to watch Rusty make his magic with the airplane.

Brovek

9:45 a.m.

"They are airborne, Dr. Brovek. A little over an hour they should be here. If the storm doesn't stop them."

"Okay, Mizzoh. Let's proceed."

What storm? Deep in the subground level of New U, the Staff Room, where he waited, and the Operating Suite where he headed now, all is steady and silent. What's all this talk about a storm?

Dana

10:45 a.m.

Heavy plumes of snow course over Dana's side window. The plane lurches in the wind, tosses her against her belt and catches her to be tossed again. They are starting down, and somewhere ahead she makes out a faint floating blur of light. She watches Rusty, hard on the controls, fighting for stability. Crack! The wheels hit ground. The plane bounces, twists, bounces again. A blur of light passes her window at a frightening speed—the same one? The engine's roar fades a bit. The wind screams. The plane stops, or seems to, slues in a hard spin and tilts sidewise. In the scream of the wind, the wing lifts. Dana hangs by her seat belt. Turning over?

No. The seat comes back under her, and she slams into it as the plane bounces twice and settles down. She checks the box, still safely strapped in its seat. The technician, white-lipped and trembling, gropes for his belt release. Rusty speaks quietly into his microphone, then falls back in his seat, letting tension drain from his shoulders.

Flashing lights of the University ambulance pulse red through the cabin.

"You okay, Doc?"

"No broken bones, and I've got the heart!"

"You surely do, Princess; and your coach is here.'

She steps down to the tarmac, and the wind smashes into her. Her eyes sting with the lash of icy wind. She looks at the plane. The valiant thing stands well off the runway, tilted at a rakish angle over a broken wheel. She follows the technician into the safety of the ambulance, with the heart of Danny Hovelund, heading for home.

As the great door of the ambulance swings shut behind her, she catches a glimpse of her pilot, bareheaded in the storm, only his flight jacket against the cold. He raises his hand to her in farewell. Or is it in benediction?

The ambulance moves off, casting its own screaming siren into the raging wind. She huddles in her flimsy coat, and rubs cold hands together. Somehow in the rush she has left her gloves on Rusty's airplane.

Brovek

11:15 a.m.

Sandor Brovek, wholly obscured in hood, mask, gown and gloves, stood by the draped body of Millicent Herold. He tapped his fingers in a rapid tattoo on his scalpel handle. He hated waiting.

The intercom spoke. "Twenty minutes, Dr. Brovek. Ambulance on the way."

"Okay, Mizzoh. We'll start."

He nodded to the anesthesiologist, who bent over his syringes and murmured something soft into Millicent

Herold's ear. Injections made, monitors checked. He found Brovek's eyes and signaled okay.

In minutes Brovek split the sternum, laid open the chest. With Pete assisting, he incised the pericardium. The failed heart still beat, but barely. Flabby. Dilated. Pale. Its day was over.

First step was to connect the heart-lung machine to provide vital circulation to the body while it has no heart. The machine receives blood from the venae cavae, saturates it with oxygen and removes carbon dioxide, and then pumps the good blood into the aorta above the heart. Extracorporeal circulation. Brovek set the necessary tubes into the aorta and the two big veins.

This much was their standard procedure for open-heart operations; he and a pumped-up Pete whizzed through the steps. They closed the vascular clamps and switched to the machine. At once the patient had better heart-lung function than she had struggled with for the past four weeks.

As if on cue, Mizzoh busted into the room, an ice chest in her arms. "Here we go, Dr. Brovek!"

"Perfect timing. Myrna, get that heart ready for us. Keep it cold. Mizzoh, tell Dr. Garrison to scrub in here and see this thing through with us."

With clamps in place, all was in order. With a scissors he severed the aorta just above the heart, then the two venae cavae where they entered the right atrium. Close to the heart he amputated the pulmonary artery. All clamps secure, the field had no bleeding. The heart, however, was still attached to those pesky pulmonary veins. He cut into the atrial wall, cutting out a patch to remain in situ, with the open-ended veins looking up at him. Dr. Garrison, he was sure, had done the same maneuver with the donor heart. The parts had damn well better match! He lifted the dead organ into Myrna's ready basin.

Careful hands passed the icy heart. He set it gently into the pericardial sac, exposed the back wall and sewed the atrial edges all around. They fit.

"Good job, Dr. Garrison."

"Thanks for inviting me in. It makes a full circle."

How could he not like her attitude? "You've earned it." Damn her.

He irrigated the open chambers, ridding them of residual potassium chloride and any hiding air bubbles. Now the pulmonary artery stumps. He placed a couple of running sutures to go from back to front on each side. Good. Next, the aorta.

In the open cuff of the donor heart lay the aortic valve, and in two of its three cusps the opening into a coronary artery. When the aortic clamp came off, warm blood would flood those arteries and bring new life to the dormant muscle. Again he ran two careful sutures around to join the two vessels.

He tested the suture lines, opening the various clamps in turn, to check for any bleeding. Seeing none, he took the clamps away. The heart chambers filled with blood. From the pulse of the pump machine the coronary arteries writhed on the surface of the heart, and the cold muscle blushed red. Seconds passed.

This kind of waiting he can stand — if it turns out right.

A few muscle fibers fluttered. Then others. A quick twitch. Suddenly the heavy-muscled ventricles came together like a great fist. Then...nothing.

Dana and Pete watched, rapt. Myrna stretched up on tiptoe. The anesthesiologist, who never looked over the ether screen, watched over the screen. No one breathed.

Another contraction. Then another. Now a burst of regular beats. A rhythm.

"Danny's heart is beating," Dana breathed.

"It's Mrs. Herold's now. But it's beating. Let's try her without the assistance."

He clamped the tubes to the heart-lung by-pass. Could the new heart carry the load? It looked good. Beating well. The anesthesiologist looked up from his dials and gauges and nodded a Yes. They waited.

Brovek jittered his fingers. Waiting was the hardest part.

The heart beat steadily. All measurements stayed on track.

Enough. "Take out the by-pass, Dr. Garrison. I'll help you with that, then you and Pete can close."

He watched her apply a clamp, withdraw the aortic tube, tie up the restoring suture. Quiet hands. No wasted motion. Good.

He stepped back, stripped off his gown and snapped his gloves away. "Thank you, Myrna, everybody. Our first heart transplant, and so far it's a good case."

"A wonderful case, Dr. Brovek. Like clockwork." Garrison's voice.

Would a man say that? No. Clockwork is human work, mechanical. If it's done right, it works.

But a heartbeat? That's more like a miracle.

Dana

4:30 p.m.

Dana twists the shower to hot-hot-hot and revels in the sting and the steam. She soaps her dark hair, plays with the thick suds that splash her shoulders and stream down between her breasts. She captures hot suds in her hands and rubs them around on her smooth skin and flat tummy. A fantastic day. Harvest and implant, done. Real danger, seen, accepted and survived. And not least, Brovek's surprising gift this morning: his deep confidence, totally rewarded.

She steps out and towels off, the nubby fabric brisk on her skin. She feels alive again, cat-lean and resilient, ready for action. Not bad for five-foot-one and the first day of her period. She puts on her usual scrub suit and clinical coat — they don't pay her much, but they do provide the laundry. She steps into her flat shoes, fluffs her hair and checks Bozo. He's no longer her attacker, only her constant companion. But he still startles. She clips him to her belt. Back in business. Dana Garrison, in charge.

In the brightness of the ICU, she checks out the long series of beds on each side of the room. She finds Mrs. Herold in a bed near the nurses' station. Not quite awake, she is quiet and stable with her new heart. Except for her wristband, she would be anonymous, a generic patient under her multiple connections — fluids, oxygen, suction tubes, a catheter, and a tumble of wires that will monitor her every breath and heartbeat. She is, for now at least, stable.

At the nurses' station, Dana checks the chart. Dr Brovek has written orders — unusual for him. She checks them against her own that she wrote in Recovery Room. No conflict.

For a moment she stands as if suspended, the chart weightless in her hands. She gazes unseeing into the far reaches of this hi-tech space... seeing the presence, the spirit, of Dr. Sandor Brovek. He piled responsibility on her today. And she came through for him. For what she did today she deserves stars, even from him. Even as a woman doctor — what he calls a hen medic. Today she lived up to his expectations. Probably exceeded them. He has to give her that. Skill? Obvious. Judgment? Yes. Stamina? What she has done today would make an athlete cry, and she is still ready for more.

She closes the chart, checks the ventricular contractions marching in a steady parade across the heart monitor. She nods, contented.

And she'll throw in a star for courage, too.

The professor holds his crew to near perfection. And today in every way she has lived up to that. Surely she has met his standards...

Hold it!

She pops the chart down on the desk.

His standards?

What about her own standards? Where does Dana Garrison rate herself? Doesn't she have her own scale of value, her own measure for ability, integrity, devotion?

She sweeps her eyes around the glaring white cavern of the ICU — a super-focus, high-tech, special-purpose micro-world. And suddenly she knows, knows in her heart, knows in her marrow, that this ICU, this technology, this hospital, is *her* world. She knows every tube and wire. She understands every machine that hums or breathes, every red eye that blinks. Hers is the brain that sets the checkpoints for every nurse. She defines acceptable values and redlines the levels of alarm. This specialized world exists for patients like Millicent Herold. And Millicent Herold, with her pulsing transplanted heart, is alive in it because of Dana Garrison. Ingenue? Wannabe? No ma'am. No more! She is master here, not servant! In her 61 inches, she commands this room. Under its high ceiling, all the technical knowledge and necessary skills, as formidable as they are, are contained within her grasp. Today, she has taken charge.

Has she convinced Sandor Brovek that she can be — or is — a surgeon? Oh, yes, she hopes so. Because she herself on this day, on this monstrous wonderful day, has risen to the mountaintop.

Today she has convinced herself.

Rusty

4:30 p.m.

Not counting the mounting snow, Rusty had two problems to face: the Cessna's damage—that part was easy—and the haunting presence of his passenger.

He arranged for the airplane to be towed to shelter in its unheated hangar, and there he shivered the afternoon away in a careful check-over: every strut and bolt from prop to tail light. Damn lucky to get by with only a broken wheel.

Like other pilots he knew, he didn't think much about disaster. Better to think positive: fly right, stay safe. Easy to say. All afternoon he suffered visions: his plane down; twisted wreckage; three frozen bodies. And four deaths. Their flight had been that close to failure.

So he clung to his attractive antidote: his female passenger. While he worked on the plane, her sleek, slight figure kept him company—but always just out of sight.

It had been too damn dangerous to fly. If it had been up to him, he would have sheltered right there in Hangarville. But it wasn't his decision. On an emergency medical mission, she had to make the call—as long as they had a chance.

And she listened to him. She heard him out, took in his opinion, found her own. He watched her as she counted up the chips—go-or-no—and worked it through. Then came the moment that zapped him. She had looked into his eyes, all the way to the bottom of his well, and simply given him her trust.

It was his first taste of a strong woman.

He cracked open the hangar access door. A blast of wind set him back, peppered his eyes with icy flakes. He slammed the door. He'd be crazy to go out in a blizzard just to hunt up a woman. He'd had plenty of women.

But this one? One taste wasn't enough. He wanted the whole meal.

Dana

5:30 p.m.

From her new perch on the mountaintop, Dana understands her flat tummy demands to be fed. The cafeteria line, all too familiar from her three months of foraging here, offers the same old food again. She selects something innocuous and carries her tray off to find a table.

"Karen! What a happy surprise." She joins her friend with a huge smile. "I've missed our sessions lately."

Karen looks up, briefly, and nods. "It's been a while. You're too busy setting records and being first." She raises a forkful of salad to her lips; she does not smile. "Congratulations on today."

"You know about it! A pinnacle day! Best ever!" Her meatloaf isn't bad; more oniony today.

"The story is all over the hospital. First heart transplant for your Dr. Brovek. Were you in on it? I suppose you had to be."

Dana studies her friend. Spotless uniform, as always. She admires how Karen can do that, from her tiny space in the Annex. But why does she look so troubled? "Having headaches, again?"

"No. Not lately. You know what bothers me. You've heard it often enough."

"Yes. The nursing thing. You don't usually blame it on me, though."

"It's your case I'm upset about."

"The heart case? I wasn't even here for half of it."

"And I wasn't in on your bloody heart case at all. But I've reached out about it, Dana, like you told me to. The word gets around. Stories come to me, because nurses know I care." A trace of a smile crosses her lips. "I'm sort of a gossip person."

If that's true, it's thanks to me. Reach out, I told her. Get involved. And she has this empowerment thing in her mind, that we've fought over. And haven't come together on. Not yet, anyway. "You're not a gossip person. You are a person who cares."

But she is upset. Something about our heart case today. Something bad for... for somebody. Bad enough that she can't care about me and my day today. "Damn it, Karen, don't be a grouch. If something's wrong, fix it. Is that it?"

"Yes, damn it, Dana. But you wouldn't understand."

"Leave me out. It's your problem. Is there something to do about it, whatever it is?"

Karen sets down her fork. "I don't know..."

"Let me in, Karen. I'm your friend."

"Well... I have an idea, but..." She shrugs, stays silent.

"But you're too chicken to try it out. Get a life, Karen. Reach out. Do something."

Karen shoves her chair back, snatches up her salad plate. "Thank you, *Doctor*. It must be nice to know all the answers. Don't choke on your meatloaf." She storms away.

Dana sags. From mountaintop to the pits in one quick slash. She shoves her uneaten meal aside. She knows now why it's bad to soar too high. There's nowhere to go but down.

Well, she sure as hell has lost her appetite. She'd better hitch up and ride on over to ICU. Maybe her patient—her thrilling, pace-setting, triumphant patient—has awakened to her new life.

She pushes her chair back, reaches for her plate. But a strong tan hand pushes her fingers away and takes her dinner. "If you don't eat this, Doc, I sure will."

Rusty? What...?

And there he is, that red brush, those dancing eyes, her hot-shot hero-pilot, settling into the seat that Karen just deserted.

"How did you get in here? How did you find me?"

"I have a U security card. Even star surgeons have to eat. And I've crashed gates since I was ten years old."

Her laughter bubbles up—she didn't know she had any left inside. "I suppose nothing you do should surprise me."

"I'll keep on trying, if it's okay with you."

Oh, it's okay all right. Better than okay. But she'll have to set the rules.

"I want to hear your story, Doc. And get acquainted."

She watches him take up her used fork and make quick work of her meatloaf.

He steals her crumpled paper napkin, wipes his lips. "I'd say let's go out somewhere. I'd take you to Mario's; it's not far. But that blizzard says we chickens better stay inside."

"I say that, too."

He looks up, surprised. "Chicken?"

"Don't count on it. No, Rusty, I always stay right here inside the hospital. And I will, for another three months. Working. I can't go outside at all." He might as well get the truth right up front.

"What? You *can't* go out?" He scrunches down, peers under the table. "You got chains on or something?"

He's a writer, she remembers. With a comic streak. "Not on my ankles, Rusty. On my honor. I'm indentured here for my education."

His eyes dance. "Then you gotta have a nest of your own— you know—a hideyhole, a niche… around here somewhere… where you can—"

"Where I can what?" Her words are a gentle snub; his uppity comedy is gone.

"Okay, Dr. Garrison. You live here. You work here. You have different rules. So I wonder: do your rules allow a male person, like me, for example, to come calling on an indentured slave girl?"

"Like, for example, me?"

"None other, Doc. I have a serious intention to come calling on you. To crash your gate. Because I got hooked today. I want to learn more about a certain brave, very professional and… and extremely desirable…woman."

She's lost. The feelings stirring in her insides are strange to her. Alien? No, natural and real. Does she want more? Oh, yes. But can she make it work? Keep up her total commitment to Brovek's program even with this male hunk hanging around?

There has to be a way.

Step up, girl. Take charge. "Okay, Rusty. If you mean me, it's a go. Here's Rule Number One."

"Shall I take notes?"

She was primed, but he moved. Okay. She can play that game! "If you need notes, you flunk the course."

He grins. "Rule One?"

"Don't call me Doc."

"Easy, Doctor. Number Two?"

"We may meet together in this hospital, but only in its public spaces."

"I get it. We can't go out—I'll get rich on the gas I'll save! And I can't come in, except for those public spaces. I'm warming to those already. Okay. One and Two. There's gotta be a Number Three."

"My work here has to come first. No exception. My call. Every time."

Too severe? Too high a fence? Will her rules drive him away?

Rusty's eyes no longer dance. Solemn-faced, he stands up, takes the messy dinner plate, shoves his chair square to the table. "That's pretty much to ask, Dr. Garrison. Show me where we dump plates."

Yes, too severe. Inside, black disappointment. She rises to her feet. "Follow me."

He tosses the plate onto the moving carrier and turns to her. "I threw you a curveball, Doctor. I had to see if you could take an inside pitch. And you did: you hit a home run. Now, can I get on base with a walk? Show me one of those public spaces where we can go and... you know... like... get acquainted."

Karen

6:15 p.m.

In her dudgeon, Karen out-storms the storm to reach her Annex apartment. In her conviction for her new plan, and in the intensity of her anger, her mother's gray shadow has boiled away. Now in plain slacks and a no-nonsense shirt, she marches back to the hospital, brushes snow from her clothes and walks directly to the ICU. Maybe she's breaking a whole codebook of rules, but she doesn't care. She scouts the ICU waiting room. There are no children.

The rumors had reached her in late afternoon. Upsetting rumors. Then she heard the story from a nurse who'd been there. Bad stuff that fed her anger. And then Dana—her dear, tolerant friend—didn't listen. She erupted instead into an angry challenge that still hurts. Now she is too disturbed to think. She needs to cool down. And she needs to know the truth.

In her uniform she could go right into the ICU. But that is not where her answers lie. She means to find Mr. Herold. But it won't hurt her to slow down a bit. For a girl—no, damn it: for a professional woman like herself—to go ballistic will not help her cause. She steps into the empty waiting room and sits down to cool off.

And rate herself. She has come a long way in two months. Timid, introverted, then. If she had not been so freaking lonely, she could never have reached out—Dana's word—to find a friend. And now with Dana's support and counsel she is fleshing out her radical idea for nursing. She is ready to move ahead.

Only two months. But she knows her target now; she knows her plan; she needs only a trigger. And if today's stories are true—her anger flares anew—that trigger has fired her off today.

But cool it, Karen. First, get the facts. Talk to Mr. Herold.

And that's why she is here by the ICU, where she has no business. Out on a long limb. And still wound tight.

A man comes in, nods to her, stands adrift, can't pick a chair, doesn't seem to care. He pulls a magazine from his coat pocket, rolls it up, raps it on his knuckles, looks for a wastebasket. She has known that cover for years: American Girl!

She rises to her feet. Musters her professional bearing. Speaks quietly.

"Mr. Herold? My name is Karen Sondergaard. I work here."

Dana

6:45 p.m.

"Come on, Rusty. There's lots of long hallway from here to ICU. I want to check a patient." She sets off in her quiet, ground-eating pace. See if he can keep up.

He can.

"Are you a smoker? Redhead like you shouldn't go near a cigarette."

"Oh, I'll go near one — if there's a pretty girl smokin' it. But I'd never burn one in my lungs. I bet you don't either."

"Haven't got time! But no. I never have smoked. My dad did. Not me."

"Hangarville, eh? I heard about him today. A fine doctor, said the man at the airport. That why you picked to be a doctor?"

They were passing the entrance of Keaton Amphitheater. Dana stopped. Pulled open the door. It was pitch dark in the two-story auditorium, but she triggered the rostrum light.

"Look in here, Rusty. I have spent a lot of hours in this place. Studying. Lectures. Presentations. Medical student. Intern. Grad student. Now, Chief Resident. I do the presenting."

He peers in at the silent auditorium, its rows of seats rising into the dark.

Dana sags against the doorframe. She's gone full bore since 3 a.m. Raced the clock. Faced the weather. Dared the gods for her own life and three more. Operated on two hearts, and discovered her personal high, her mountaintop, her own confirmation as a surgeon. And now, Rusty. A whole new game. But she's running out of steam.

Rusty looks back at her. "Years of your life spent here? How many?"

"Eight years and counting. I'll be through at last at the end of June."

"Three more months."

"Three and a half. Meantime I'm chained in this hospital to a job that demands 100 percent and takes 110." And feels like 150.

Rusty peered down at her five-foot-one. "Then what? After all that. Will you rejoin the human race?"

She hasn't seriously thought ahead. Even her times with friend Karen are unplanned, always hey-let's-do-it squeeze-ins. But tonight, now, a new relationship — or a chance for it — has popped up. Her first whiff of romance since college. Even in her exhaustion, that's front-burner stuff. And inside she hears a voice of caution. Careful, Dana; words carry consequences.

"I don't know the future, Rusty. After July I'll have to go out on my own."

She studied his leathery face. His steady gaze. She flicked off the light, let the door close behind her. "A surgical practice isn't just a job, you know. It's a way of life."

She moved on toward ICU, Rusty tagging along behind. He acts pretty cool, but through that front she sees sincerity. She likes that. It is her own style as well.

He caught her elbow, pulled her around to face him. "Come on, Dana, get real. In this surgical practice you're looking at, what do you hope for? Suppose all your dreams come true. What then?"

Dreams? She's been too busy to dream. Hope? She'd rather lie down to sleep, thank you. Her mountaintop was only an hour ago. But right now, in the shadow of Keaton, Rusty has challenged her to look past Sandor Brovek, to imagine a life beyond.

She studied his face, strong in repose. His moist lips. His green eyes, steady on hers. She inhaled the sweet man-fragrance of him. She has known him only — not even! — eight hours! Actually more like three hours today, where together they dared death to achieve their mission. Now, tonight, more heroics: he has fought a blizzard and crashed her gate to find her.

And she is too tired to think. Can he see how tossed she is?

Her words surprise her. "I want to teach and do research. I want to build a transplant program. Right here at University Hospital." The words sounded presumptuous to her, and she blundered on. "But that's not my decision, you know. That's up to them."

He laughed, took her hand. "That's a shoo-in. Nobody could help wanting you."

She is losing control. She retrieves her hand. "Come on, I have more hallways to show you."

New U appears ahead, its corridor shining in bright lights.

"Wait up a sec." He touches her hand again, turns her to face him, his calluses hard against her scrubbed skin. "Straighten me out a little."

She comes to full stop. Straighten him out? She's too beat to straighten anything out. She watches his lips move, making wonderful words.

"I guess you don't have a man in your life — you don't have time. But I don't hear you say it will ever be any different. Will it?"

Any other time, that might be a fair question. Tonight it is too much. "I don't know."

"Guess. Can you make time for me?"

Again that little voice. Like Nancy Reagan's *Just Say No.* You are committed. You have a job. End this right now... Should she?...No! Not with this man! Even bone-tired, she feels something real here.

She crosses the line. "Yes. I want to."

"Then I'm here. I'll meet you tomorrow; you say the time."

She touches his arm, shakes her head. "There's the rub. I can't promise a time. I'm always on call."

"I don't count? I have to play for last place?"

"Yep. After every other job in my job-jar." And that, Pilot, Stranger, Man, is how it is. Take it or leave it.

"First time I ever thought 'last place' was a winner."

"Well, it's last in priority, not in desire." The word slips out, and her mind is gray. She leaves it in the air. "If I get a break in the action, I could call you. Quick-draw-shoot-fast. If that's enough for you — and I hope it is — then yes, I'll find time for...for us."

"Good enough for me." He seems taller, as if she has lifted a burden. He produces a scrap of paper, braces it against the wall, and writes his number. She watches the curve of his body, the grace of his motions. With gut certainty she wants to know this man — but not now. ICU is waiting.

He puts the note in her hand. "Call me. Day or night. I'll jump in here before you can hang up the phone."

She drops it into her pocket. "Thank you, Rusty, for accepting my... my rules. Now I have some patients to see, so I'll say good night." She touches a finger to her lips, then to his — and pulls a hair trigger. He wraps her in strong arms, gathers her in, places a no-nonsense kiss on her ready lips. Surprised by her own quick fire, and too tired to care, she meets him with abandon, mouth, limbs, body, hungry for the strength of two.

And between them, a bomb goes off.

Rusty tears his lips away, pushes Dana back like a hot rock. Clutching his groin he dances in front of her like a man betrayed.

Dana doesn't know whether to laugh or cry, but laughter wins. It wells up out of her shoes, out of control, her shoulders shaking with it. "You just got your first lesson about me." She unclips Bozo from her belt. "Meet my vibrating buddy—my radio pager!"

"Dr. Garrison," Bozo squawks. "ICU, stat."

Oh God, not Mrs. Herold?

She moves off fast, but his voice pursues her into the bright lights of New U. "You are one hell of a woman, Dana. I'll be back!"

And he, too, is laughing.

Potts

7:00 p.m.

In the full dark of night, as the winter wind still drove the roiling snow, Horace Potts summoned a taxi. Ten weeks after his ordeal, and healed at last, his untended commission to secure St. Luke's for Brovek has begun to irk his conscience. Frustrated and angry, with himself and with the weather, he determined not to end the day before he conferred with the professor.

This morning, lured by the beautiful winter day, he had called at the cathedral to see his old friend the bishop. A social visit. Plus a nibble at the availability of the church. And there the winter storms came on. Outside, the raging blizzard; in his heart, bitter frustration. Marooned at home, he burned to touch base with Brovek. And tonight, watching and waiting for the storm to abate, he had even let his dinner go cold.

Now, in a growing fit, he threw down his napkin, shoved his plate aside. The wind still whined against his windows.

But the weather had to be better by now, didn't it? He notified Brovek, bundled up and went out to a waiting cab.

Brovek welcomed him into the den, where the lovely, tragic Lotte received him. As regal and straight as a young tree, she extended a cool hand as if she were a duchess.

"Good evening, Horace." Her voice was rich and slightly accented. "Tell me how your dear Catherine is these days."

Well aware of her tragic dementia, Potts was prepared. "Well, Lotte, you know Catherine passed away last year. And I do miss her."

"Horace and I have some business to discuss, my dear." Gently, Brovek guided her to the love seat nearby, and settled her knitting on her lap.

"Thank you, Sandor."

Potts moved at once to the fireside and dropped himself into the deep leather chair that he had often enjoyed on happier occasions. Impatiently, he sniffed at the fragrance of the wood fire and scowled at the split logs stacked alongside, with melting snow puddling on the hearth. When Brovek offered his special golden Courvoisier, he seized the crystal snifter, swirled it once, and threw back a fiery swallow. It didn't help.

"I called on the bishop this morning."

"You're well enough for that?" Brovek settled into the chair opposite. "I'm glad, Horace."

"Well, I thought I was well enough — this morning anyway."

"I guess it didn't go well. What happened?"

"He was very gracious. Old school chums, you know. Did I remember, and all that. After a bit, I mentioned St. Luke's Church. Oh yes. That wonderful little red brick house of God, a lovely place. So we talked about it. Yes, the parish had been split by the freeway. Father O'Leary's little church. Through no fault of Father O'Leary, St. Luke's was indeed a failed parish. Yes, he could sell it. In fact he had it appraised last year, the whole shebang—church, playground, school and priest's house."

Brovek leaned forward, rapt. "And?"

"Well, you don't hurry a bishop. But I was riding in high hope. I said I would like to buy the property. He nodded, said he would look kindly on the University as a buyer. I told him our intention. Yes, indeed. He would look kindly on a new hospital. Truly an extension of God's work there."

"Damn it, Horace. Get to it."

"But the property is already sold, Sandy. He accepted somebody's offer the very week I damn near died in your hospital."

"No!" Brovek stormed to his feet. He crammed a new log into an already robust fire. "How come nobody knows about it?"

"He stressed this with me. 'Selling a property,' he said, 'may be easy. But closing a parish church requires preparation and diplomacy. It needs a thoughtful, careful shepherd. Surely,' he said, 'as your bishop, Horace, I can count on your discretion?'"

"Nuts." Brovek dropped hard into his chair. "If he's a thoughtful shepherd, he won't be stupid. We'll make a higher offer."

Potts shook his head. "You won't go higher than this one, Sandy. Whoever this guy is, he walked into the bishop's office with a certified check for one million dollars."

"We can beat that."

"Don't shoot 'til you hear it all. That was just for an option; they would negotiate the purchase within two years. If they can't agree, the bishop keeps the money."

"Usually there'd be a strike price."

"Not this time. Instead of that, a condition: the bishop had to sign the deal that same day. One million bucks, in the bank right now, with two years to look for another deal. He couldn't lose. Even a bishop can't let that money walk away."

Brovek frowned, poured brandy, sank back in his chair. "Something strange there, Horace. Who is this guy?"

"Don't know."

"What does he want to do with the property?"

"Build a hotel, he said."

Brovek slammed his open palm on the cushioned arm. "The bastard! He could do that anywhere."

"Yes, Sandy. I know. He could; we can't."

"You're sure we can't."

"Yes, I am certain. You are authorized to expand the hospital, not build a satellite. I looked at every parcel of land that touches us. Examined mortgage docs, and even searched titles. I spent weeks on this. The church is absolutely our only chance."

He watched Brovek lie back against his leather cushion, hold his snifter to the firelight, swirl the golden liquid before slitted eyes. This is the reason he braved the blizzard to come here tonight. The professor is thinking; he doesn't see a thing.

The fire crackled, spat sparks. Brovek flared awake.

"St. Luke's means our future, Horace. It opens the way to our new hospital, and a new transplant program. All of it. My life's work here at the University will be measured, up or down, by whether we get, or don't get, that building site." He turned to Potts. "Something is different about this guy. Somewhere he is vulnerable. Find out. I want him out of our way."

"Investigate?"

"Damn right. There's something screwy there. Find out what it is."

Potts stood up, reached for the bottle of brandy and poured himself another dollop of fire. This is why he came. The professor could always see a way, and set a course for progress.

He twisted the crystal stem, swirling the brandy; he held the glass to his nostrils, inhaled, then sank back into that capacious leather chair. "It's ironic, Sandy."

"What is?"

"If I hadn't had my coronary at Christmas time, I would have been first to approach the bishop. But I fell into your hospital, you saved my life, and when I finally made it to the bishop, I'm too late."

"Yes. Tough. Ironic, all right. But in one thing, Horace, you're wrong."

"Wrong?"

"It wasn't me that saved your life. It was Dana Garrison."

"Don't I know!" Potts gazed at the fire. "I wonder, Sandy, if you really know how good she is."

"I've watched her. She's very skillful. Five years in my program. She's learned a lot."

Potts settled back in his chair. No. He doesn't see her this way. He is Professor. Chief Surgeon. Head of everything surgical. He won't like being challenged, but—and one more bit of brandy won't hurt—here goes. "Have you ever been cut on, Sandy?"

"Have I what?"

"Been cut on. Like, surgery."

"Why the hell ask me that?"

"Well, I did have surgery. Not so long ago."

"In the nick of time, too."

"And I learned a basic truth: it's dangerous to lie down in a hospital."

"Easy on the brandy, Horace."

"No, really. The moment I lay down, as a patient, I was, like, well, prey. Technical machinery came and aimed itself like weapons. The techs wouldn't look at me–not in the eye. They mumbled things—stuff I couldn't understand—directions, maybe. And then they say 'Okay?' Everybody—I mean, even the nurses—they all say 'Okay?' Always: like, doubledy-diddley-boom: Okay? Like, I have your pain shot now, okay? They're not asking if it's okay. It's code for 'Do what I'm tellin' ya!'"

He wonders if he is babbling. For almost two years now he has lived alone. "Just once in a while, Sandy, somebody in the scrub-suit crew ought to stop and listen to you, as if a person had feelings."

"Nobody did, Horace?"

"Glad you ask. Garrison did. She'd come in on her rounds and check the chart, feel my pulse, maybe look at my incision. Whatever."

"Hell, that's routine. We all do that."

"There's more. When she was through, she wasn't done. For another moment, she'd stay there, simply be there for me. Maybe touch my arm. Oh, you can smile if you want. But I was lying helpless at the bottom of the trench, and I felt the healing power that flowed through the hands of that young woman."

The fire flickered, burning down. Lotte Brovek stirred in her chair. Brovek tipped the decanter again into his snifter. Potts declined. Brovek grinned.

"Actually, Horace, I am very high on that girl. Today she played a central part—an essential part—in our first heart transplant."

"Sandy! Superb! Congratulations."

"Too soon to say 'successful,' I suppose. But it's a winner so far. And it cements our potential—we have to get that church!" He held Potts's coat, pulled it up on his shoulders. "Our transplant service should be the biggest and best thing in this university. Hell, Horace. Even greater than the football team!"

They laughed together, and Potts, feeling revived, pulled on his overshoes and slogged into the wind and snow to his waiting cab.

PART THREE

April 23, 2014

You had a great admirer in Horace Potts! He thought his Dr. Garrison was top drawer.

It was mutual. He had an admirer in me. A man of integrity and courage. And smarts. He was key, you know, in what happened later.

I love to picture you and Rusty in that dim hallway, finding out you were both pretty well sparked.

I remember it well.

One day? That's all it took for you to fall in love with him?

Yep. And even then he was ahead of me.

You were both deprived. Easy to start a fire on such dry tinder.

That's a good metaphor. Good thing I had enough demanding duty to dampen us two fireballs.

Also, you lived in a fishbowl. Private moments must have come hard.

Oh, we found a few. On a different subject, it's fun for me, as an old doc now, to look back at what used to be, at how much our practice has advanced. Rudd's day of pressure, for example. A stomach resection for ulcer? Rarely need to do that anymore.

Why is that?

More effective drugs to control acid. And we can treat <u>Helicobacter pylori</u>. In those days we didn't even know that bug was there.

Dr. Rudd took my appendix out, about 20 years ago. Appendicitis probably hasn't changed very much.

I used to take an appendix out in about ten minutes, through an incision about an inch long. I don't see much advantage in doing it through a 'scope. And I question how much benefit nets out from a CT scan for several thousand dollars, when good old-fashioned horse sense handles appendicitis pretty well. Why are you laughing?

You sound like a grumpy old doc.

Maybe I am! I've plenty of reason, wouldn't you say? But in my story, Rudd was right about a ruptured appendix. You never want that to be your fault.

But your first heart transplant? You don't mind taking credit for it?

That's the day I came of age as a surgeon.

You made it happen.

I was part of the team. And I was thrilled to be there.

And she recovered, that patient. Happy all around, right?

Yes. Cling to the feeling. Other days are ahead that I still regret.

Well, don't waste your time talking to me. Go write your story.

Karen

Thursday, March 14, 1985

Long before dawn, Karen Sondergaard lies awake, counting off a list of her hospital's sins. The Herold incident is the worst yet, a family gripped in fear and worry, left in neglect and isolation. But many more troubled memories come to her — out of wakeful recall, and from dreams, and from deeper than dreams. Missteps. Omissions. Even significant errors that she has seen in her five years of nursing. Not all serious. Not all her fault — thank God for that. But nearly all hushed up, ignored, passed over in the streaming needs of hospital care, like a river that runs against a snag and flows on by.

She can't help herself; she feels obsessed. She isn't like other nurses, who do their eight hours and go home to a life. She wants to make a difference. Like what she tried to explain to the director of nurses: to make the hospital a happier place, simply by better support to patients and families.

She chafes all the more because she can't make a difference. Nobody listens to nurses.

But today? This morning? Has the world changed? Under Dana's frowning challenge she has hammered out a plan. Is it a proposal she can fight for? Is she in a stronger position now, as a head nurse? Is she more credible with her master's degree? Are the Herold kids her trigger to take on the world?

She still feels the anger and hurt she felt on that night of the transplant. The rumors about Jack Herold and his children broke her heart. She couldn't let it slide. This time she acted.

She interviewed him and verified the story. She visited that miserable excuse for a waiting room. On an impulse, she relieved Jack for a few hours and took Francine and Eddy to see *Return to Oz*. A new film. Nice kids, but confused and unhappy.

Now, in the early light of her Annex apartment, she sees clearly the fault line that no one else does: in the juncture of a single surgical case her hospital functioned in two separate ways. Professionally, a supreme scientific achievement. But on the human side, a deplorable failure.

Enough. She throws back her blanket. Karen Sondergaard, Nordic defender, rises to — what? To propose a new program? Yes. To condemn the old? Yes. To risk her precious job? Yes. Risk...Fight...New ideas for a little girl from Prairie Falls.

She calls the director's office. Finally, at nine, someone answers — someone with sleep in her voice, and not enough spine to say No. At nine-thirty Karen faces the same Director of Nursing from the same hard chair where she was so recently anointed as Head Nurse.

"Speak, Miss Sondergaard. What is so urgent that you —"

"A deficiency, ma'am. Last visit, when you appointed me Head Nurse — and I thank you for that; I am thrilled — we talked about opportunity. This time I say fault, deficiency, neglect. We have a problem, and I want us to deal with it."

"This time?"

"Tuesday."

"The transplant day."

"Yes. Our system showed up a major deficiency, and people suffered for it. I am ashamed that our hospital allows such a thing to happen."

"Yesterday" — the director leans forward over her desk — "was a proud and historic day for our hospital. The successful transplant of a human heart. I find it hard to contemplate a *terrible deficiency*."

"Not in the hospital, ma'am. We have a fine hospital."

"I hope, as our employee, you do think so."

"I do. Our patients have serious problems. They are our business."

"Indeed." The director sits back, folds her hands in her lap.

"But patients have families and friends, who come here as visitors. They're in strange country and often under stress. Aren't they our people too?"

"Are they? We give them visiting hours and rules to follow. They're supposed to fit in."

Fit in. Dr. Rudd's uncaring words. She draws on her reserve, as she did with him. Reins herself in; deals with it. "You deserve, ma'am, to be excited about yesterday's heart patient. A wonderful achievement. Have you asked yourself about her family?"

"Should I? They must be thrilled."

"Must they? The patient's husband hasn't slept for three weeks. He has two children to care for, brought along with him because their mother was dying. They watched their mother carried off to the operating room for one last chance to get well again."

"That's the way it works, Miss Sondergaard. Why are you taking my time about this?"

"Because we failed them. You did. I did. Our system did."

"Are you going somewhere with this?" Her hands reappear, her fingers splayed on her desktop.

"Yah. They were boxed in to a little waiting room with no window, no TV, no bathroom, nothing to eat, and no information. Five hours. Not a soul came to check on them. Nobody told them whether his wife, their mother, was still alive. Five hours. I can't defend that deplorable negligence."

"I doubt the story. Rumors are undependable."

Hold on, Karen. Be grateful for all that ice and snow you grew up in. It put iron in your back. Use it. "You don't know me, ma'am. I do not mess around. I sought out Mr. Herold and verified these facts. Please consider them and hear me out."

"You should not have done that."

"Fire me."

The director leaned back in her chair, knitted her fingers. "So you think some nurse somewhere was negligent? She should have brought news reports, when there weren't any, and entertained the children?"

"I do not think any nurse was negligent, nor did I say so. I'm sure several nurses thought about those little kids, waiting so long. But they had other duties. That is my point. Our care system ties nurses to what the hospital does for its patients. No one has authority to be on the patient's side."

"We are all on 'the patient's side,' as you say."

"Tell that to one who's delayed in x-ray and gets no lunch. Tell it to a relative who flies in on a late flight and isn't allowed to visit. Tell it to four-year-old Eddie after five hours in a box."

"You feel strongly about this!"

"It's why I worked for a master's degree."

The director betrays a tiny smile. "I wonder whether I dare ask this question. Do you have a proposal to make?"

Karen grins. Progress? "Oh yah, I do. Appoint a nurse to be that patient's friend. That's her job. If someone feels crossed up in the hospital and doesn't understand, give her a friend in the business. Someone on her side; a personal representative. Settle confusion before it turns to anger."

The director does not quite smile. "Do you know the term *ombudsman*?"

"Yah! It comes from Norway! It's the person I'm talking about."

"My colleagues and I have thought about a plan like this. Thank you for your initiative, ah, Karen. I may get back to you."

Alert to dismissal, Karen arises at once and exits, walking tall. She wasn't cut off. She wasn't fired. She can already taste her steaming cup of fresh hot coffee.

Potts

Wednesday, March 20, 1985

From a tableside window atop the University Club, the businessman Potts and the professorial Brovek look out over the city. Far below and now clear of snow, the streets are drawn in thin, dark lines; traffic is moving again.

Potts makes frequent use of his club. Mingling with the leader of the city, he tunes in to business reports and listens to rumors—and allots generous doubt to them all. And it is here, for any sustained attention from Brovek, that he must invite the professor for a captive hour. Always to this table by the window. Always for a light lunch, a glass of wine. Almost always with their mutual decision that neither one needs ice cream—a coffee will do. And at last they come to what they came for.

"Well, Horace, I presume you have the full story on our million-dollar man."

Potts lifts his cup, sips. His saucer sits half in the shadow of the window's edge. He nudges it into the sunlight and sets down his cup. "His name is Martin Stern. He is an aggressive and well-respected developer. This University Club is his building. The kind of cowboy offer that he made to the bishop is not his usual transaction."

"Okay, okay. So why did he do it?"

"He is dying."

Brovek looks up in surprise. He lifts his cup in a toast to Potts. "Good for you, Horace. Right to the heart of it. Then we can wait. We can begin to plan — that will take several months anyhow. Sounds like good news to me."

"Unless he doesn't die."

Brovek drops the cup into its saucer, shakes his head. "You'd never make a surgeon, Horace. Call the shot. Is he dying or isn't he?"

"Yes, he is."

"Good. He dies, we buy the church. So what's the problem?"

"You, Sandy. You are the problem. He is on your list for a liver transplant."

"We haven't even done one yet."

"Are you ready, as you like to say, to *do one*?

"Ready and eager."

"For Martin Stern?"

Potts watches his challenge emerge in Brovek's mind. Find a liver. Do a historic transplant. Stern recovers. Buys the church. Builds his hotel. And the transplant center dies unborn.

Brovek is silent. Potts's cup lies again half in shadow. He slides it into the sunlight. Waits.

At last Brovek straightens, faces his friend. "Most likely thing is, we'll get no donor. No liver, he dies. Then we acquire the church *post mortem suam*."

"That makes it easy, right?"

"Right. No problem. Okay? Enough. You did a good job, Horace. Shall we go?"

"Not yet, Sandy." Never has he been anything but deferential to Sandor Brovek. Now he has a line to draw. "If, before you get a liver donor, Stern dies? Then yes, there's no problem — except the one for him."

"When he dies, his option dies. We know that. There's no residual interest anywhere. He's done. And then we can deal, right?"

"Right. But suppose you do find a liver. Suppose you give it to Stern. In that case, he lives and you die. Right?"

"That's a little strong. Then we don't get the church."

Potts taps his cup with a fingertip, stares at Brovek.

The professor heaves a deep sigh. "You're right, Horace. Then I die. Might as well." He wipes his napkin across his mouth and picks up his cup. It trembles. He sets it down, folds his hands in his lap.

"If you find a liver for Stern, I want to know what you will do."

Brovek scowls. "Come on, Horace. We're wasting time."

"No, Sandy." Has he ever flat out contradicted Brovek? Ever before? Not in memory. "The ethical question is stuck on you like duct tape. Stern trusts you with his life. You promise to serve that trust. But you have a conflict. Your laudable ambition to build your program runs contrary to your professional code–and your own integrity. Probably the first time ever that your personal interest collides with your patient's interest. When a liver is found, will Stern get it? Might you say 'No, not Stern; he's too sick?' Or worse: be careless with a stitch? Or be a little loose about infection? These are real possibilities, Sandy. I want to know how you'll answer them."

"Hypothetical. We aren't there yet."

Potts drags his saucer closer, out of the sunlight, swallows the cold coffee. Doesn't want to push the professor too far. Rattles the cup back onto the saucer. Pushes it away. "Pleasanter subject, Sandy. Tell me about my favorite doctor."

Brovek welcomes his release with a whistling out of his pent-up breath. "Three months more, she's through. She should be looking ahead for a job."

"How about you? If you expand your hospital, you'll need a bigger staff. Why don't you grab her?"

Brovek laughs. "I've thought of it, Ho; I really have." The sound rumbles up from his great chest. "But fortunately, I've always thought twice!" He tosses his napkin on the table and leans back in his chair. "But seriously, I have considered her in the way you mean. Would she work out? She is good enough."

"She proved that with me!"

"But could we count on her, like, you know, being there? Women are —

"Hold it right there, Professor! Has she missed a day in five years?"

"No. Not one. That's unusual, even for the men. But she might, you know, get married, or pregnant, or something, and leave us stranded."

Potts marshals his data; from long involvement he knows the University's graduate medical programs. He thumps the white cloth with an emphatic finger. "Eighty percent of your residents are married. One is divorced. Half of them have kids."

"But they're guys, Ho. They weren't ever pregnant. They didn't moon around with backaches. They didn't take six weeks off when the babies came."

"Maybe they should have! Do you have any idea — do you even care? — what the rigors of your training do to family life? to wives and children? We should look at that some time. For now I ask you: do you have a sick-leave policy?"

"Of course."

"Has it been tried?"

"Once or twice."

"Did it work?"

"Yes."

"Do you believe Dana Garrison would exploit you or abuse your policy?"

"I don't want to take any chances."

Potts hesitates. Hold back? No. He wants to push his case for Garrison. "You took a chance on Lance Rudd."

"What chance?"

"I know about it, Sandy. Diabetes mellitus. Type 1. He's always had it. He'll always have to care for it. Every day. Diet. Insulin. Blood sugar tests. The whole bit, right? And you throw secrecy in on top—that's another layer of risk."

Brovek's fingers beat a harsh tattoo on the white linen. "Nobody's supposed to know that.'

Potts smiles. "I'll never tell."

"Rudd is a fine young surgeon."

"So is Garrison."

Brovek nods. "Point taken." He opens his clutched fingers, drops his hand into his lap. "Here's a happy report: Millicent Herold went home yesterday."

"Congratulations."

"Historic day."

"Milestone day."

Abruptly, Brovek's intensity returns. He splays his hands on the soft linen; the table quivers. "She may be the best one, Horace: the best one yet. But she's only one in a line of graduates from our program. We are a university center. We stand for progress. Research and training. Expansion is our destiny. Transplant medicine is this century's greatest opportunity. And I mean to lead us into a great future."

"Yes, Sandy. Grow or die. But if Stern gets in your way, you'll have a choice to make. I want you to choose the right road."

"I'm not there yet."

"No, you're not. And that's too bad."

"What's too bad?"

"Too bad you have to think about it. That such a fundamental challenge to the very core of who you are doesn't find an immediate response in your convictions."

"I'm a surgeon, Horace. Not a philosopher."

"You are a professional man, Sandy. It would be too bad if Stern should die before you decide what kind of professional man you are."

Brovek surges to his feet. "Back off, Horace." He shoots his chair backward; it teeters but settles. "That's enough." He crushes his napkin, flings it to the table, marches off. "Thanks for the lunch."

Potts trots after him, catches up at the elevator. Brovek receives him, scowling. "One damn thing more, Horace. Get this straight. We had a bad meeting today. But it's private. Between us. Nothing leaks out. Agreed?"

"Sure. We'll meet again. But if you get a liver for Stern, I will watch what you do with it."

The elevator door opens and Brovek thumps in. "I don't know yet. Don't hold your breath."

"Just remember, Sandy," Potts spoke to the closing door. "Like duct tape, I'm stuck to your shoulder."

Dana

Thursday evening, March 21, 1985

A bit before six on a frosty night, Dana stepped out into the darkness, sucked in a breath of cold air, and picked her way across the doctor's parking lot to Karen's nook in the Annex. It was too long since last time. She knocked.

"Well, you made it, Dana. Come in."

"First chance since the big day. I'm still exhausted."

"Roost right there, friend. Take a load off."

They brushed fingertips as Dana stepped to Karen's good chair and sank into it.

"But I need a Karen-fix — a good talk with my good friend. We're behind on that! And hey, throw in a good dose of that lasagna I smell in the oven."

"It's still winter, Dana. I heated the cider." They clinked glasses, and Karen turned to the stove. But her words came clear. "You haven't even told me about your plane ride in the blizzard. "

"No chance to tell. For sure not that night!"

"Not in the mood I was in. A real snit, Dana. And I'm glad, because... Well, you talk first. I've got news to tell, but it's just nursing level stuff. You go first."

"Nothing bad about *nursing level*, whatever that means. But I can't wait to tell you about the guy that flew my airplane. Rusty Waters. He's cool, Karen. I like him."

"Like him? How do you ever get to see him?"

"He's found me at least once every day this week. I get a break, I call, he comes, we talk, Bozo squawks, he's gone, I'm back at work."

"You're lucky. Where is he tonight?"

"Flying somebody somewhere. That's his University job."

Karen peeks into the oven, turns it off. "So he's away and you can come slumming to my cafe."

"Not slumming, Karen! Your lasagna is nice. But you, my friend, you yourself, are the reason I come here."

"I hope so. Because you have moved me into a new life!"

"New life? Wow! Tell me!"

"You first. We had that terrible blizzard and you were in an airplane?"

"I was. It was weather from hell. We were lucky to make it. We broke the plane! Did you know that? A wheel. But the results were worth the risk."

"The heart!"

"Oh yes, the heart. A thrilling, exhausting day. A great day for Brovek." Her own epiphany is too fresh to share.

"Three months, you'll be done with your training and out of here."

"I guess."

Karen slices the lasagna, dishes up two plates, moves to the little table. "I'll miss you, Dana. Three months ago, I almost...well...I almost came on to you."

"I know you did. I almost wished you would."

"But I didn't. The Lutheran in me said No. Well, I'm good with that, I guess. Especially if you've found a man. But I'm still lonely. So far, those Lutherans haven't sent me even one single masculine male-type person."

"Ooh, that's good lasagna... Last time I mentioned reaching out, you stormed off on me. But reaching out worked for us. You made a friend out of me!"

"Yah! Reach out! Grab somebody by the collar. Like, any man that comes along? But in my narrow little orbit, no man ever comes along."

"You had a shot at Dr. Rudd!"

"But I missed. Good thing, too. I'd have shot him dead that day."

"He's a good man. Don't write him off." Dana collected some melted cheese on a crust of bread. "Your turn. You have some good nursing news to tell me?"

Karen put her plate aside, leaned over her folded hands. "I reached out, Dana. Just like you told me to. In the last few weeks I asked a few nurses, have you ever wanted to do something extra for a patient but couldn't? Well, the stories came in from all over. Patients confused and upset. Families restricted, kept in the dark. And the nurses not free to help. They want something to change — but don't know what."

"That's what you and I have argued about. You can't always blame the doctors."

"Skip who's to blame. Don't worry over that. Go with what to do."

"I like that part."

"So finally I figured out a move I could make. Probably get turned down. But even that would be something. The back-breaker came with your famous heart case. That's why I was in a snit the other night."

"I never saw you like that before. What happened?" "While you were playing Hollywood with the heart, everybody forgot your patient's family — the dad and two little kids. They were abandoned. Stuck in a room by themselves, like a little prison, to wait and worry. No word, no progress report, and not another soul to share with. When I found out about that, I was furious."

"Bad?"

"Like I've tried to tell you. Stuff you doctors don't see. We see it all the time."

"And this time?"

"Well, I was like gangbusters. I didn't just reach out: I attacked the Director of Nurses. You need somebody, I said. Somebody to stick up for your patients...and their families. A staff nurse. That should be her job, to do that."

"That's exactly what you've wanted all along. What did she say?"

"She said Yes! <u>Yes</u>, Dana! I'm it! Starting Monday. With a Norwegian title: Ombudsman."

"Patient rep!"

"A department of one. But it's a new direction. A policy change. And you'll never guess what!"

"What?"

"She wants to introduce me to the medical staff on Monday afternoon. And the nurses, too. Three o'clock. I hope you'll be there."

"Wow! If I can. I'll put a gag on Bozo. Monday afternoon?"

"Three o'clock."

"Have enough cookies for two."

Karen cocks her head. "Two?"

"I'll collar Lance Rudd and make him come along."

Stern

Friday, March 22, 1985

1:00 p.m.

Martin Stern, the big-shot developer, is pissed. Damn near three months on Dr. Rudd's transplant list, and no liver. If it was machinery they needed, he'd have it for them tomorrow.

Except he's so weak he can't dial a telephone. He can't even stay pissed.

And he won't eat the crap they serve him here. Boiled rice! *Chazzerai!*

He was eating better in the hotel, even on the diet the doctors had ordered for him. But last Saturday he cheated. How could he say no to a roast beef chef special, fresh cut, rib-in, red rare, au jus? But he's not in the hotel; he's in the hospital. That's about all he knows.

Three days he can count. Sunday — too confused to argue and too weak to fight. They hauled him back in hospital. Yesterday was all fog. Today he's thinking again — but it's Friday? What gives? Where did Tuesday-Wednesday-Thursday go? All those days in the coma they talk about? Three days then, lying here, not a man, not a person, sure as hell not Martin Stern. Better, he should have died.

But he didn't. He's still in the game.

What else can he remember? The rookie doctor with the pimple on her chin, sticking with her needle, sticking, sticking, trying to get an IV going. That was way last Sunday, five days ago! He should stay alive just for her.

Can he dredge up anything out of those lost days? People? Nobody. Even his doctors he can't remember. Today's smart little nurse was here every day, she says. If he can't remember her, he was damn near dead. But somebody was here. Something. A presence? A person? A shadow hovers at the edge of his mind, a lost idea that he tries to find again.

The little nurse takes his tray away, cranks his bed down a bit. Rest time?

Hell, he's so weak he can't even rest! He turns on to his side, and — oy — his swollen belly shifts like a big bag of seawater. He turns back, and all that weight sloshes around again, pushes up against his chest. He can't take a good breath. He drifts off.

He has a sense of someone hovering, not himself, maybe a person nearby. Like a dream. Something he has to do. Something important. He wishes he could cry, let it all hang out, bawl like a little kid, and have everything come right again. And go back to business.

Business! That's it! The church! He comes alert. He sees now what he has to do. Cover his tracks with the hospital. They mustn't know there are two Martin Sterns. One that blocks them from the church they want to buy. And me, paying big dollars for my new liver. If they find me out, it's over. *Sorry, Martin, your liver got sent off somewhere. Too bad, Mr. Stern, you're too sick. Sorry about that.*

He holds up a bony hand, scaly and yellow, shakes his head, folds the arm down to cover his eyes.

Who around here could finger me? Nobody knows about — hold it! That old priest could. I bought his church. And I've seen him here, tottering around, probably a gossip already, a yenta in pants. I have to get to him.

Yeah? Like how? How get to him when I can't even breathe? I'm done. Nobody cares. There's nothing going for me....

"Do you remember me, Mr. Stern?"

What? What?

"I'm surely glad to see the light in your eyes once again."

Stern shrugs. Like he'd called in an order? Send me the priest. That's a hot one, a priest! for Martin Stern! "Have I seen you before?"

"Each day this week, except you were not awake enough to know."

"Every day? Who's watching your store?"

"Oh, I have more store here than I do across the street. And I think you know about that."

Ah-hah. Stern's blurry thoughts come together. The priest. Father O something. He's the one that knows. "I need to talk to you."

"I'm Father O'Leary. I want to help you, if I can." He draws a chair to the bedside. His white hair and crinkly eyebrows come clear in Stern's vision.

"You know a secret about me, ah, 'Father,' about our visit to the bishop. It's got to stay a secret."

The priest chuckles. "I carry more secrets than I can remember. Many are sealed behind my lips forever and ever, world without end, amen. And I don't know which are which, so I never tell anybody any of them."

Stern knows about secrets. He keeps them stored away, so at the right time he can use them. He doesn't know about "forever and ever." Whatever that means.

"You surely are a better man today. Daily I stood here, not sure you even saw me."

"Why? I'm not one of your people."

"Are you not?"

"Not even close."

"But not too far, either. The Lord has put us together, first at the bishop's house — so we are acquainted. And now in this hospital, where you — well — where you're pretty sick. And waiting a pretty tough wait. No one should have to walk such a hard road alone, Mr. Stern. I think He wants me to tag along, if you don't mind. By way of support, don't you know."

If the old geezer is up to something, let him come. Easier to keep tabs on him. "Tag along, Padre. Be my guest. Not much of a party, though."

"Discouraged, Mr. Stern?"

What a dumb question. Three months, waiting. For what? An outside chance. Nothing happens except I get worse. Itch. Turn yellow. Everything gets smaller except my belly swells up and surges around. My brains walk away, and he wants to know if I'm discouraged. Let me tell him about discouraged.

"Three months I've waited for a liver. Three months I've gotten worse. Three more months I'll be dead. Last month there was a kid on a respirator. That big hospital down the road. She had a head injury. She died. Perfect donor. You know why I didn't get her liver? Why *nobody* got her liver?"

Father O'Leary leaned in, his ear closer to the whispery voice.

"Because nobody asked for it!... Can you believe it? Here we are, desperate, and they didn't even think of it.... 'Don't have a policy,' they said." Careful, Martin. A man might cry, but not a mensch. "Christ, Father, aren't they doctors over there?... When I die with my bad liver, I'll give them my brains."

He hears Father O'Leary's voice, simple, clear, as if speaking to a friend.

"It is hard to persevere, to cling to life when hope seems gone. Imagine the feelings of our father Abraham, doing what Yahweh had commanded. He climbed the mountain with Isaac, expecting to slaughter his son. He obeyed, but surely he persevered in hope. Maybe that is most important—to hope for what we want, while we accept what God wants."

Stern can't move enough air to speak up; he nods. He needs no lesson on the Torah—not from a goy.

"But in this case, we know, Isaac was spared. God provided a ram. At the very last moment. A kind of donor, Mr. Stern."

Stern opens his eyes to the old priest. "You put me in company I wouldn't dare to claim... But if I can breathe.... I guess I can hope for a liver...and maybe...if it comes...maybe some day, Padre, you'll see...who Martin Stern really is."

Dana

March 22, 1985

Friday afternoon.

Dana dropped into a chair, careful not to bang her knees on Lance's desk. "For a man of your standing, friend, you have a tiny cell of an office." She has had no reason to be here before. She scans the array of certificates and diplomas behind him.

"It's too small to add a welcome sign, Dana, but the feeling is there. What can I do you for?"

"Seriously, Lance. Don't you need a little more clout in here? I know how good you are. But patients need to feel it. You do see patients here, don't you?"

"Sure. But I spend more time in the OR, or the dog lab, or the library. I don't need much space."

"Nor need to impress your patients. The old personality does it, hey?"

"Thinking ahead about offices? You'll be out of jail pretty soon."

"Yep. First day of July. At least the snow will be gone."

"It will be a cold place here when you go."

Dana grinned. "If you sweet-talk your patients like that, you don't need a bigger office!"

He thumped his forefinger on the desk. "I'll have you know a patient said Yes, right here in my cubbyhole. Sitting in the same chair you're in! He didn't need a palace to be convinced."

"And what huge procedure did you convince him to say Yes to, dear Lance? Varicose veins? A hernia repair?"

"He said Yes to — well, he'll be my biggest case yet. Brovek knows. But I bet you don't."

"Bariatric surgery, Lance? You going into 400-pound weight relief?" She bounced up and down, testing. "Nobody's broken your chair."

"And you're not able to, Skinny. No. No morbid obesity on my plate. Just a liver transplant."

Dana, serious, clapped her hands together. "Wonderful! A ground-breaker. It will put you on the map."

"Like your aneurysm did for you. I'll be in good company."

She had to settle a bit at that. "If I'm still here."

"If I had my way, you'd always be here... But about my transplant case...we don't have a donor yet. And the patient is running out of time. The medical people are doing their best. But a new liver better come along pretty quick or we'll lose him. He's my big chance. And I don't want to disappoint Brovek."

"No, we never want to disappoint Dr. Brovek!"

"Okay, Dana. Out with it. You must have some subtle female reason to find my tiny office. What gives?"

"An invitation. Monday afternoon. The administration is introducing a new nursing job they'll call a 'patient advocate.' She'll represent the patient if there's any kind of problem with the hospital."

"Hell, Dana. That has nothing to do with me."

"That's what I thought. I didn't like the idea at all."

"But?"

"But the new person is a very dear friend of mine. She cares deeply about nursing and about this opportunity. It's pretty much her own idea, and Monday's announcement is her official send-off. I'm going, and I want you to come."

"Forget it, Dana. Not my business."

"Cookies, Lance."

"I don't eat cookies."

"I want you to come."

"Why me? She's your friend."

"You've met her. She's head nurse on Station 21."

"Oh. That one." He propped his forearms on the desk, leaned on them. "I owe her one."

"She told me."

"No secrets between women! Well, her coming-out party gives me good cover for speaking to her again. Tell you what, Dana. If you go with me, I'll give it a shot."

"Good. Let's meet in the staff room, three o'clock."

"Roger. I remember her all right. A pillar of ice... Sondergaard, isn't it? You call her Karen."

Dana

March 24, 1985

Sunday afternoon.

"What are you laughing at?"

"Me. And Keaton." Holding Rusty's hand, Dana leads him onto the dim and deserted stage of Keaton Amphitheater. "I've come here a thousand times for lectures and conferences, but never 'til now to be alone with a man."

No wonder she feels twitchy and tight in her chest—a delicious feeling. "I bet, in all its however-many years, Keaton has never been a trysting place before."

"Then I say it's about time." Rusty surveys the curving rows of seats that rise up a story to the translucent windows, amber in the daylight. "I remember this hall. You showed it to me before. Transplant night. Our very first walk-about. How come we haven't come here — trysting, is it? — 'til now?"

"We haven't met on a Sunday afternoon until now."

They stand together on the bare stage of the deserted hall. She is ready to match his usual desire, his quick passion. She turns to him and opens her arms. But he takes a quick step back and plants a stiff forefinger on her breastbone.

"Oh-no-you-don't! I won't fall for that again!"

"Fall for what?" She draws away, confused.

He points at her groin. "Bozo. Once is enough with that guy. Clip him around in back. Or better: throw the bastard away!"

Laughing, Dana moves Bozo to a safe pocket. "Consider it done, Cowboy. Now quit stalling and come visit the doctor!"

He grins, spreads his arms, and moves in.

For a decade she has kept a strict but happy focus on her future, on her surgical career. No room for romance. But now? She is losing her heart to this man. She wants him. Her keen edge of passion, long kept asleep, has not gone dull, not one little bit! If she follows her desire, if she gives herself to this red-headed stalwart, can she go back? Stick to her academic discipline? Rule by her brain?

She must!

"Rusty, wait. Let's go sit down somewhere."

"Okay." He releases her, except for one hand that lingers on her arm. "Golly, Dove," he scans the empty tiers, "I hope we can find two seats together."

"I suspect," she laughs, "we can squeeze in somewhere." Is this why she loves him? She points to the other side of the theater. "But not over there. That third row on the left is Dr. Brovek's turf."

"Sacred ground, eh? Let us retreat to a couple of ordinary seats for plain folks. Like ordinary every-day surgeons and their cohorts."

"And hot-shot hero fliers and their co-pilots."

They walk to the right-side aisle, then up three rows, then a couple more, and slip into two seats, together.

"Good place. Should have tried this before."

"Yup."

"Why are we talking?"

"Who's talking?"

Dana's passion leaps out like an uncaged animal that she must keep on a sturdy leash.

"Let's find a way, Dove. I need you. All of you."

"Can't, Rusty. Just can't."

"I'll check out backstage down there. Find a gurney and wheel it out right there, center stage."

"Remember to lock the wheels."

"Or not. We'll go rollin', rollin' — "

"–rollin' on the river! Let's do it, Rusty. In July. When I get out of here."

"Your damn calendar is giving me fits, Dana. Cold showers don't do it for me."

"Tell me about it! I lie in bed thinking about you, and I'm so turned on I almost welcome a Bozo call."

"Almost?"

"You know it. Bozo commands me. But my heart belongs to—"

" — to Brovek."

She punches him on the arm. Lightly. "Only three more months. The last day of June."

"On the first day of July we'll fly away. I know a place—"

"I don't care where, Rusty. Just love me and fly me out of here."

Dana

March 25, 1985

Monday afternoon

What a difference a day makes! Dana enjoys her private joke: walking down the same dim corridor in Old U, yesterday with Rusty, today with Lance. How different can a girl's boys be? She's semi-dragging the reluctant Lance—he really does want to square his conscience—to Karen's reception.

"It's up ahead, Lance. I hear voices."

He slows his steps even more. "Yep. And they're all *female!*"

She wheels on him. "Are you allergic to *female*? Half the world is female. Come on, Lance. Join the race."

"Let it lie, Dana. I made a decision years ago for—for private reasons. I haven't walked beside a woman since—I can't even remember when."

"Ouch! That's two women in your life with no presence at all: one you can't remember, and one you don't even count—me. You're a real builder-upper, buddy."

She turns away, walks, he steps out to catch up.

"You're different. You're a colleague, a professional associate. And, I hope, a friend."

"Count on it. But there's more to a person than his working life. What does he care about? What does he turn on for?"

"I'm not gay, Dana. I'm not anything. I live solo; that is my personal and private decision. Leave it at that."

They move on again, together, with that settled, in no hurry.

She has long wondered about Lance Rudd the man; she dares to probe a little deeper. "Our nurse corps happens to include a lot of women. Have you noticed? As a staff surgeon and single male animal, you offer a constant puzzle. They're alive with guesses and starved for facts. You're not unattractive, you know."

"I don't know about that, yes or no. But gossip is all the more reason to stay out of the mix. I'm coming with you only because of your friend Karen."

"Has she caught your eye?"

He stops again, a shake of head, a small frown. "I owe her an apology, that's all. What I just told you, Dana, about me? That's pretty deep and private. I don't share it with—with anybody. Maybe you didn't listen."

"Oh, Lance!" She seizes his arm. "I'm sorry. It's a part of you that's none of my business. Let's go find Karen's reception."

He takes off in his long strides, and she quick-steps to keep up. "I fought her ideas at first, you know. We doctors are the top of the pecking order, and some of us—shucks, most of us—have a thin skin for criticism."

"But she won you over, right? You're on her side now?"

"We're all on the same side. Or should be. And part of that you're going to like."

"What? Messing around with my patients? What part am I going to like?"

"Instructions. Preparations. Details. I've heard you complain about spending so much time on that stuff…. Puff. Puff."

"Sorry, Dana." He slows his pace. "I don't mind going through the real stuff with my patients: a consultation—what's wrong, how we can fix it, what the risks might be. That's all pre-op, and it's important. Patients have to understand what's involved when they say yes."

"Of course. That's informed consent. Also the patient wants to meet you, and see if you measure up."

"Yeah, that too. But then comes scheduling and preparations, more explaining, more repeating, all that stuff. It's a drag."

"Let Karen do it."

"Is that her plan?"

"Part of it. Sort of the preventive ombudsman. The better your patients understand what's going to happen, the happier they'll be."

"Yeah, maybe. Here we are."

Dana

But where are all those female voices? Dana is stunned. They step into an empty room.

No uniforms. No people. Only the debris of a meeting—a scatter of empty cups and crumpled napkins on a table. "We aren't late. Bozo slowed us down, but what—five minutes? Where is everybody?"

"They moved it up to 2:30, Dana." Karen's voice comes from a chair in the corner. "No warning. Nurses get used to that off-hand kind of treatment." She rises and comes to them. "Hello, Dr. Rudd."

"I'm sorry we missed the announcement, Miss Sondergaard. We had the right intentions, didn't we, Dana?"

"Sure did. Good turn-out, Karen?"

"Couple dozen, I guess. People left to start their shifts at three. A lag right now, but a few more will come after they're relieved. I'm glad you're here.... Both of you. Your attitude toward my work will make a huge difference."

Lance nods a faint Yes.

Dana figures Rudd will hold back any opinion about Karen's plan, so she steps right up. "You have my support, friend. I'm only resident staff, but I'm on your side."

"You're the one that lit my fuse, Dana. I count on you. But our plan is a new thing for Dr. Rudd. Perhaps I need a chance to...to explain it to him...sometime." She lets the latent question hang between them.

"Sure, Miss Sondergaard. I want to hear more about your plan—sometime." He sticks to his own agenda. "I suppose... well...I suppose you remember our, ah, encounter? A few days ago?"

She stands before him, still cool, and even taller. "Should I?"

"I don't know about 'should you.' But I remember that day with regret. I treated you shabbily. I was stretched pretty thin, and I failed to treat you like a professional." There. He's said his piece. He's apologized.

Karen is cast in Nordic ice. "You gave orders, Dr. Rudd. I followed them. No problem."

But there was a problem. Because he made a problem. "But I was...abrasive."

"Were you? In my starched white armor, I felt no wound."

Dana, entranced, watches Rudd. She has never before seen him flummoxed, his apology hanging out there like a floating balloon, and he can't pass the string.

"Well, I...damn...Miss Sondergaard, I don't want to treat anybody like that."

"Anybody?" She hasn't bent an inch. "Who is 'anybody'?"

Rudd struggles. Chokes. Blurts: "Any actual, real person with a beating heart."

"Thank you, Dr. Rudd. Even in my white armor, even as a nurse, I plead guilty to being an actual person. I am grateful to hear a true apology." She still stands tall, is still professional; but spring has come. Ice is gone; she seems warmer by several degrees. "Thank you. You came a long way today...to my announcement party. There may be a cookie or two left over."

Dana thinks skyrockets! Firecrackers! They're standing in front of her, her two favorite people, nose to nose and eye to eye. And neither one knows what comes next. And here goes Bozo? ICU stat!

Couldn't be better!

"Sorry, guys. I gotta go." And on her winged heels, Dana takes off and leaves them alone.

Rudd

3:05 p.m.

Hey! Don't leave me here, Dana. I came to apologize, that's all. I didn't expect to get stuck in a face-off.... This nurse-friend of yours hasn't moved an inch. Eyes fixed, looking right into me. I gotta say something, like...like...Ah!...

"Dana tells me you are going to solve some of my communication problems."

"I do have some ideas, Dr. Rudd. Your transplant patients will need lots of information. Some of it they'll need to hear twice. But they have feelings, too, and I want them to be good feelings...."

Yeah. Whatever. I'd like to just turn on my heel, like the books say, and move on out of here!

"Your attitude toward my work will make a huge difference."

Well, yes, I suppose it will. Dana told me she's tall. She's nearly my height. And wow! She is so-o-o focused on me. Deep blue eyes. Scandinavian, I guess. Longish blond hair pulled back, controlled. "Well, in all honesty, Miss Sondergaard, I am eager to have you take on your new job. I'm all in favor of the 'facts' part. My patients need more teaching than I like to take time for."

"I can help you with that."

Pretty teeth. Great smile, in fact, when she lets it go. But hold it! What did she say about *feelings*? I don't want her messing around with that. "But you're biting off too much if you worry about feelings. Patients have to give in and go along with our program."

That'll fix her on the 'feelings' business.

Oh? No, it won't! What did I say? She's spewing fire.

Yes, I know Martin Stern.... Cool it, lady; you're going to detonate! No, I didn't know Father O'Leary has been seeing him.... So what? I want to know. Big deal. These damn women nowadays. It's all this lib business. And this one, this nurse, wants to be partners? Nuts.... But look at her.... Classic.... Generous mouth. She's a piece of work, and is she ever giving me what-for!

"The 'feelings' part, Dr. Rudd—that's your term—is a big hole in your program and you need to fill it."

Whoever said blue eyes are cold eyes never saw these eyes. Okay. Yes! I'll talk about...whatever she wants. But God! those eyes! She's a princess, and I'm getting a hard on, and I don't need that.... The hell I don't. *Patients'* feelings? What about *mine*? Okay. We'll meet somewhere. Anywhere. And ASAP. "You might teach me something about feelings, Ms. Sondergaard. I'd like to hear more about your, ah, desires. Your office, or mine?"

"I'll be glad to come to you, Dr. Rudd. I look forward to it."

Come to me? I like that. "How about tomorrow morning?"

"Yes. As early as you like.""

Karen

Still 3:05 p.m.

"Dana tells me you are going to solve some of my communication problems."

I'm surprised he even remembers me. My first day as head nurse on Station 21, and he stormed in like a little Napoleon. But up close like this, he has nice eyes. Steady. Deep brown. It's only courtesy, I suppose. But... what's bad about him talking to me? "I do have some ideas, Dr. Rudd. Your transplant patients will need lots of information. Some of it they'll need to hear twice. But they have feelings, too, and I want them to be good feelings."

Holy Joe, he's a good-looking dude. Don't be bored, lover-boy. Let me tell you my plans. "Your attitude toward my work will make a huge difference." He's staying with me. Not looking for escape. No. In fact, he's staring right at me. Right into me!

"Well, in all honesty, Miss Sondergaard, I am eager to have you take on your new job. I'm all in favor of the 'facts' part. My patients need more teaching than I like to take time for."

"I can help you with that." I'll say! We nurses are totally capable of taking on a lot of your job. In fact, we could do some of it better! Like the patients' feelings—if you grant us a little—what's he saying?

"But you're biting off too much if you worry about feelings. Patients have to give in and go along with our program."

Oh, you uppity bastard. You really tee me off. Well, stand back, Buster. Little Karen has big ammo here. "Dr. Rudd, do you know Martin Stern? Did you know that Father O'Leary has been visiting him? Regularly? Giving him hope, and motivation to fight? Somebody cares about him. Without that, he'd be dead by now. The 'feelings' part, Dr. Rudd — that's your term — is a big hole in your program and you need to fill it."

Hey, that felt good! I've just kissed off all my crummy years of kowtowing to doctors. And why not! I've got credentials, and a special appointment. And more important, I have a mission! And he didn't get mad!

"You might teach me something about feelings, Ms. Sondergaard. I'd like to hear more about your, ah, desires. Your office, or mine?"

Okay. We're going to meet. Good. That's a quick start for — hey! For *what?* What did he say? My *desires?*

Easy, Karen. This guy is turned on. To my program? He's too hot for that. God! Maybe...to me? Well, why not? I'm twenty-seven years old, with all my teeth. *Easy,* Karen? No! Not easy. Let's go. "I'll be glad to come to you, Dr. Rudd. I look forward to it."

"How about tomorrow morning?"

"Yes. As early as you like."

Lance

March 26, 1985

Tuesday morning

All through the night Lance's life plan churned in his dream and wobbled in his waking thought. Karen Sondergaard had stirred him up like a can of paint. Excepting only his diabetic discipline — controlled diet, exercise and insulin are absolute. In brief teen-age rebellion, he learned those rules the hard way. But sexual desires? Suppressed and bottled up in his celibate intentions? That part was by choice, by deliberate decision. And yesterday that decision came uncapped like a shaken bottle of Coke. He could have withstood her cool Nordic beauty. But when she erupted in her passion for nursing, she breached his walls.

What in God's name would happen this morning?

To start the day, he had to deal with the two fat legs of a patient burdened with varicose veins. First, in one groin, he dissected and detached the saphenous vein from the femoral vein. Then he passed a stripper—what he liked to think of as the tool of a barber-surgeon: a malleable heavy wire with a knob on each end. He threaded the small end into the saphenous and slid it down to the ankle, where he cut the vein off and retrieved the knob. Delicate surgery? Hardly. He took a solid hold of the knob end and jerked the stripper out, tearing away the full length of saphenous vein and ripping off the vessels feeding it. Next he made tiny incisions at ink marks, to excise the unsightly blue varices that yesterday, with the patient standing, had been obvious.

Then, the other leg: repeat. Tedious surgery. Especially today. But doggedly, like a painter to his canvas, he clung to his discipline. At 10:30 he whipped off his gloves, zipped into slacks, shirt, tie, and white clinical coat, and sailed off to his tiny office.

She was already there.

Cool and professional, she stood as he entered. A fresh rose was pinned at her breast. Moist and fragrant. Like her lips?

He squeezed past her and dropped into the chair behind his desk. A professional visit, Lance, right? Her eyes were unbelievably blue. His brain was a-dither. Why was she here? He struggled, came up with the words that had stuck in his craw yesterday. "Tell me, Miss Sondergaard, about the hole in my program that you need to fill."

Her eyes rested on his face, half smile and half mystery. "Your program does marvelous things, Dr. Rudd. Through mysterious and frightening procedures. When you cut into your patients' insides, you know what you are doing. But they don't. They need to understand."

Do they? He keeps still. What they need is to accept. To go along. They have to give themselves over. "That's where we differ, isn't it. Patients need to go along with the system. Leave the driving to us."

Her face was set, her jaw tight, her eyes slits. No nonsense there. Smooth skin. Her eyes fixed on his. No escaping this lady. This woman. Not that he wants to!

She pressed her hands on his desk. "Go along? Yes. That is the choice they make. You call it 'informed consent.'"

"Right. Normal procedure."

"I see a higher calling. They also need reassurance. Understanding of their stresses. Peace of mind. You don't honor those things in your program."

Her criticism rankled him. The lib thing again. "What would you do different?"

Karen sat back, straight, ticked off ideas on her fingers. "Tell patients and their families what to expect. Where they'll be. How long they'll wait. Answer questions. Be their friend, their champion in this alien hospital world. Be there for them."

Lance tried not to sound bitchy. "Is that all?"

She laughed. "That's just the beginning. I'm thinking big, Dr. Rudd. You plan to start a transplant program. People will come from miles away, and their relatives will hang around in motels, isolated and miserable. Better, they should be housed together somewhere, in a community of support, to share the wins and losses."

"God, Karen, I can't do anything like that!"

"No, Dr. Rudd. You shouldn't have to. But your program should. Expand your team. Let me do it."

She has said her piece. She sat back, hands on her thighs, shoulders square.

He studied her. Good face, too classic to be pretty. Blond hair in a tight bun at the back of her neck. He watched her, said nothing. Has some color come to her cheeks?

He watches her fold her hands in her lap. It was his turn. "To a surgeon, those are far-out ideas."

"I suppose they are."

"Where in the world do they come from? Who dreams up stuff like that?"

He's done it again, triggered her down deep somewhere.

"As a matter of fact, Dr. Rudd, these ideas are around, for one who cares. But the local push comes from me. I've been a full-time hospital nurse for five years—and earned my master's degree during those same five years—because I see what happens in hospitals, and I see who suffers when something goes amiss: and it's always the patient. And I believe in my heart and soul that we need a broader vision; we can do better."

"You're a voice in the wilderness."

"We're not a wilderness. We're an important and vital social system, and we can make it better."

"A system that has a hole to fill?" He throws his small challenge.

She is not afraid to show her flag to the enemy. "Your part of it does."

But he doesn't want her to be enemy. Enough discussion. "Dana agrees?"

"She didn't. Now she does."

"You want me to sign on?"

"If you agree."

He doesn't, and he's glad he doesn't. "We should meet again."

"I hope so."

He was sure of it now. He sees color in her cheeks, in the hollow of her neck. Surely not an invitation — but the color is a good clinical sign!

He stood up. Karen rose to her feet. He squeezed past his desk, stopped beside her. The tiny office Dana had made fun of? Ideal! And Karen did not give way. He inhaled the scent of her rose, saw her face turned up to him, her lips parted in a half smile.

He was lost.

His arms moved of their own desire, wrapping her body, pulling her close. She pressed against him, yielding, soft. Their lips met. Full, unhurried, passionate, their first kiss both foretaste and mutual promise.

Lance fell back to his desk, his hands on his thighs, tried to come down. Her flushed cheeks, her eager breathing: she was turned on too. "You said you could teach me about feelings, Karen. I want to sign up!"

"I think, Lance, that you just did. For my seminar. In a class of one." She chuckled. "And you're the one."

Oh God! He has tasted the strength, the throb of health in that strong young woman. Does he want more? Does he want her? Oh yes, and yes.

He does want more, and he does want her.

To hell with the consequences.

April 1, 2014

What's up, Dana? Have you run into a snag?

You're a published writer. Tell me how to handle this. Tell me what to do.

What's the problem?

It's about Karen and Lance.

My favorite characters. Their love story set U Hospital on its ear! What's the problem?

Lance is still there. He retires next year.

Ah! I see. Your "story-not-history" can't get juicy about real people?

I got juicy about me and Rusty.

You know you'll get no trouble from there.

So what do I do about Karen and Lance?

Punt.

What?

Skip the juice. You have another story to tell. Go tell it.

Thanks, Russell.

Rudd

Good Friday

April 5, 1985

10:30 a.m.

For two blessed weeks, Lance Rudd's heart belonged to Karen. He felt young and full, with new richness at every turn.

He tended to his diabetic management with special precision, in dedication to her. He poured himself with new energy and fresh insight into caring for his patients. He even asked a gall bladder patient how she felt about getting up to walk to the bathroom the same night as her surgery.

But the best part of those two weeks came when their two schedules found a common break, and he sprang to her side. In their intimacy he discovered sunshine even in himself.

Much of the time, they argued. She vented on doctors: over-reaching, uncaring, blind to the side-effects that their orders create, and the after-effects that their attitudes engender. He countered about inattentive nurses who see no bigger picture than the next injection. Or they debated larger questions. Professional ethics built from their lives of personal discipline. Religious ethics learned in the atmosphere of her hard-bitten pastor father. Or they wondered where their concerns will lead them, in their joined vision of a better world for hospitals, both patients and professionals.

But not all the time. They both knew the choice that Dana made with Rusty, and wanted none of it. They had times of opportunity, they had private quarters, his and hers, and they used them. Often. They rode the crest.

On this special surgical morning he plucks a gall bladder, fishes a scoopful of stones from the common bile duct, makes certain there are no stones left behind, and sews things up. He heads for Karen's new office.   Through the open door he watches her typing at her IBM Actionwriter. Her golden hair fills him with light—even in its modest bun he knows its untethered richness.

With her fingers extended, a pen wedged between them, she sits back from the machine and presses her palms against her temples.

He frowns.

"Headache?" She has had some lately.

Her smile brightens his day. "Not bad. Maybe I need new glasses."

"You look good in these. But you'd look good even in spectacles. Want a coffee break?"

"You know my weakness. I'd love it."

He watches her rise, the supple strength of her body, her spotless white uniform, the red rose, fresh each day; she has adopted it as her badge of office. She doesn't pin it on; she likes to tuck the stem behind the badge she wears:

Karen Sondergaard, RN, MSN
Patient Representative

Together they walk along the dim hallway of Old U. Before they walk on into the bright light and bustling traffic of New U, she turns to Lance, takes his hand, holds it in both of hers. Her eyes search his face.

"What is it, Karen?" Her skin feels silky against his fingers.

"You make me happy, that's all. Thank you, Lance." She squeezes his hand, drops it, and steps into the bright hall of New U.

Lance thrills to her richness, her love, her glory.

They move in leisure; nothing is urgent about coffee. Being together is what he treasures. They reach the bright, trafficked hallway near ICU, and Karen stops. She bends a bit, presses her hands again to her temples. "I do have a headache."

He touches her shoulder. "Let's go in here to ICU–I'll bum some ibuprofen."

"Lance..." She stumbles a short step. Her word blurs. "Lanthe..."

What? What is...? He seizes her arm, searches her face, sees a blank, no expression, the light in her eyes gone dark. Like an empty sack she sags, crumples, and sinks to the floor.

Lance panics. Can't be! They're in love! No way!

But on a different level his training kicks in. Heart racing, but cool and professional, he drops to his knees beside Karen. A-B-C, the protocol he practices regularly. Check the airway. Check the breathing. Check the circulation. He straightens her body.

Her jaw is limp; he lifts it forward, opening her airway. He bends close, his cheek feeling for her breath, his eyes watching her chest for movement. Nothing. He presses his fingers to her neck, feels the carotid pulse, strong, steady. No cardiac arrest for his Viking queen.

But she needs artificial ventilation. He raises his voice in a long howl for help. He tilts her head back and lifts her jaw. He places his left hand over her beautiful eyes and closes her nostrils between his thumb and forefinger. He bends down to her lovely mouth—oh mockery!—places his mouth on hers. In a kiss of life? Or—? He pushes out a strong breath, sees her chest rise then fall with his release. He counts off the seconds in the prescribed routine: twelve breaths per minute. He hears the loudspeaker blaring, "Doctor Blue, Intensive Care." Someone has seen; feet pound; he is not alone. A white uniform relieves him, as practiced as he in rescue breathing.

Action restores his self-control. As the crash cart arrives, he takes charge. He seizes a laryngoscope, tears away the wrapper, kneels at Karen's head. He slides the long blade over the back of her tongue, lifts its lighted tip, looks down it to see the open larynx. Someone thrusts an airway tube into his hand, and he passes it between her vocal cords and on into her trachea. Now her airway is assured. He inflates the tube's balloon so air can be pushed into her lungs. At the near end he connects an Ambu bag and a flow of oxygen from the tank that has appeared from nowhere, as the urgent routines of Doctor Blue bring a small army of rescuers and rescue supplies to the scene.

From experience, and from frequent drills and rehearsals, the crowd devolves into an impromptu team that works in solid coordination. Gently they lift Karen to a litter and move her on into ICU, where her life will be sustained while doctors seek a diagnosis to allow someone, somehow, to bring Karen back.

In the corridor Lance Rudd stands alone. He knots his quivering fingers together; he struggles for control. In this long, bright corridor that he knows so well, he is lost, adrift in cold, black silence. Against the wall, the emergency cart stands canted and abandoned. Old torn wrappers lie scattered on the tiles, and even a spare laryngoscope. From a square of black vinyl he sees a single blaze of color. It's Karen's red rose, and someone's foot has crushed it.

The hot, sweet memory of their passion wells up in his heart and smashes against reality. For Lance Rudd knows that Karen Sondergaard is dead.

Rudd

11:45 a.m.

Karen is not Lance's patient. Nor Dana's. But grieving at Karen's bedside, they stand together in the ICU. They know, without words between them, what has happened to her.

Silently Lance envisions the interconnecting arterial network that nourishes the brain. Somewhere among those inaccessible vessels Karen carried a malformation, an aneurysm. Silent and undetectable — until it burst. Then blood at full arterial pressure pounded into the closed space of her skull and snuffed her out.

Can she recover? Lance's heart says Maybe. His surgical mind thinks No. Either way, alive or dead, she must receive full-bore, aggressive life support. Until her doctors declare her legally and truly dead, brain dead, Karen is alive. And then, after the declaration, her body must be given the same critical support. For her heart still beats, and while it beats, gives life to her precious donor organs that can now be salvaged.

Automatically, he checks out the equipment. A new endotracheal tube has been inserted through one nostril. Connecting to it, the plastic corrugated tubes from the respirator, pumping its oxygen in its own steady rhythm. Two IVs drip fluids and meds that support the heart. A catheter drains clear yellow urine into a bedside bag. From under the sheet a tangle of little wires passes to a heart monitor that elicits a small beep, and flashes a red light, with each pulse; it scribes on a tiny screen the sequence of regular QRS complexes, the ironic electrocardiograph of her good, young heart.

Obscuring what humanity is left, the great tangle of respiratory tubing covers her chest and distorts her face. Only her eyes, closed in her coma, and a few wisps of golden hair lie exposed to his view.

He blinks, clears his throat of…of what? emotion? "They have her under control, I guess."

"Hard to believe."

"Hard to accept."

"But we have to look ahead, Lance. If she…if…well, if there is a…you know — we'll be part of it."

"We're not there yet. Maybe she'll wake up."

"Yes. Let's hope so."

They stand close, like strangers in this place they both know so well.

He draws a long breath. "We can't come again, Dana. We're both involved if…if—"

"Right, Lance." Dana puts a firm hand on his arm. "It's a mean twist for us. But we know—hard as it is—what we have to do. So let's say goodbye now and disappear."

"Right. They've called her mother to come."

They turn from Karen's bed, quit the ICU. The corridor—cleaned up now; no discarded wrappers, no crushed rose—is no happier a place. They keep walking.

"Her team can't ask about transplants yet. Maybe she'll wake up."

"Think so?" He has no hope of that.

"Not really. If it's a ruptured aneurysm, we're looking at brain death."

"That's what I think."

In his mind he replays his lecture to the students in Keaton, a changed lifetime ago. Recalls the two dogmatic absolutes that he preached about brain death: the loss of brain function must be *total* and *permanent*.

His devastation, his grief, feels exactly like that.

PART FOUR

May 27, 2014

You insist, Dana, that you are writing a story, not a history. In fiction I doubt you would allow the loss of a person like Karen. But here you're stuck in what really happened, and the hard truth had to prevail. She was a truly tragic character.

She had just begun to find richness in her life. She fluttered her wings like a bright new butterfly in a garden of blooms. I still grieve for her.

And poor Lance, my friend and surgeon. He was stricken beyond grief; he was changed. We both loved her.

But you went on, open throttle, to pursue your career. He was never the same again. It was as if he – well – as if he lost his –

Easy on him, Russell. You need to know the rest of his story. He was changed, yes; but a major and productive compendium of research papers has come from his lab and pen. He did not waste his life.

And your story goes on? To talk about organ salvage, with Karen so newly dead, gets very close and personal.

It's always close and personal – for somebody. And sometimes unsuccessful. We are grateful when the critical person, the next of kin, knows about transplants, sees the benefits, has even signed a donor card — as we have done, you and I. Even then, the donor interview is a deeply sensitive encounter. That's why we have special people to do the asking. Usually someone from the regional allocation organization, someone without local ties.

Aha! I see an escape valve for Brovek! Send Karen's liver off to some other center. She's an ideal heart donor, too.

You're getting ahead of my story, Russell. The big steps, like harvest and implant, can't happen without supporting players. Do you remember my thesis? That a transplant is like a woven web? The warp and the woof are the lives of people. Some are only brief players, like short threads in the web; but without them there's no transplant!

We've already seen one transplant in your story. Where were the — the what? — the short threads? Whose lives wove in for that heart transplant?

Dr. Bockman. Jack Herold. Danny Hovelund. And his family, huddled together in their misery. You yourself were a short thread in that case.

I didn't want to be weft out.

Now you're crying 'woof.'

But I suppose you, Dana, were a big shot, a long thread.

Yes, because I was part of the surgical team that goes on from one transplant to the next.

Isn't this web idea a little artificial?

Of course it is. Metaphors are always artificial. Take it lightly, as a unifying idea: that people weave their lives, individually, into a coordinated effort with others, to give one dying person a new life.

And?

Without those people — the short threads — all of them — the transplant won't happen.

More characters then? Bring them on.

Karen's mother

Good Friday

April 5, 1985

1:00 p.m.

When the phone call came to her in Prairie Falls, the widow Sondergaard was eating her lunch. She picked some eggshell out of her chicken salad and a few other inedibles to toss to the chickens. From her worn old boots, melting snow trickled toward a narrow crack under her wooden door. In her airtight stove she kept the draft pinched down: better to be a little cold than to burn up too much firewood. Last fall, when she split the logs, the extra cord of stove-length firewood seemed like an excess. They are nearly gone now, with another month of ice still to endure.

As a new bride to Pastor Sondergaard, then as wife, mother, and widow, she had endured here for thirty long years — years of hardship she would not question, and joys she rarely recognized. Her emotions, like the hardy gray lichen that clings to her north-country granite, were not for display.

"Hullo."

"Is this Mrs. Sondergaard?"

"It is."

"I'm a nurse at University Hospital, where Karen works."

"Yah?" Fear and foreboding churned inside.

"I'm sorry to tell you that Karen is sick. She collapsed, and we have her here in the Intensive Care Unit."

"I see." So. In life, more trouble comes.

"Do you understand? Will you want to come to the hospital?"

Impassively she would move to do whatever she must do. She folded her feelings like wings, with no flutter left outside.

"Are you there, Mrs. Sondergaard?"

Of course she would go. There was nothing to keep her here in the old manse. She could catch the two o'clock bus to Minneapolis. Connections would be what they would be. If she had to, she could sleep in the bus station.

"Mrs. Sondergaard?"

"Yah. I will come."

Brovek

10:00 p.m.

Sandor Brovek swirls his Courvoisier and churns inside.

His department is just too small. On his credit side he has one exquisite, flawless heart transplant. One. And the next one? Who knows? He hasn't seen even the shadow of another. Meanwhile his competitors, in the bigger schools, are surely getting transplants to do and building success. Next year they'll report their cases at the national meetings and publish their research in the leading surgical journals. All the necessary stuff to build their reputations. And they'll say: *Who, Brovek? Good man, but how many transplants has he done?*

He gazes at Lotte, knitting away in the other recliner. Once upon a time he would ponder his cares out loud, and she might even set down her busy needles to listen. Then often, in her soft Viennese accent, give him her quiet support. Yes, Sandor. You know always what to do.

One transplant he's done. A bare beginning.

It's imperative to expand this hospital. Essential. Buy that church, build our center, become a national presence.

Or not: stay as we are and go dead in the water.

Suppose we get a liver — it could happen. Like, soon, while Stern is still alive. What the hell would I do? Give it to Stern? Make it work? Horace got it right: if Stern lives, *I* die. Unless, instead, somehow, I let Stern die. Then the world would open. I'll compete, grow, build a program. Be somebody.

With a program built on betrayal? On a failure? That's a bad foundation. Who the hell is Martin Stern anyway? A dying man. Let him die. Send his liver somewhere else. Why not? He is in my way.

Why not? Because he is my patient, that's why. Rudd's and mine. We took him on, with the implied promise that we'll do everything we can to help him. And we still have that old oath: Do no harm. If I harm Martin Stern, and blaspheme the goddesses of healing, how can I ever again expect their blessing?

What I should do is so damn simple: keep faith with Stern. Find a liver. Give it to him. Get him well. That's what Horace wants me to do: honor my commitment to Stern. Commit, yes. Like, suicide.

How can I commit to that?

He retrieves Lotte's ball of yarn and restores it to her lap. He decants another brandy. His third.

That's absolutely the last one — for tonight.

Dana

Holy Saturday

April 6, 1985

7:30 a.m.

For Dana it is a quiet morning. No operative cases scheduled. Easy rounds. No problem—until she comes to the ICU, where one bed holds the body of her friend, Karen Sondergaard.

Dana has no role in caring for her, but she cares a lot about what happens. Has there been even a flicker of life?

From a couple of beds away, she looks over the same situation she studied last night: Karen inert, her body attached to monitors, IV drips, oxygen mask and tubes, her face smothered, her chest heaving with the repeated, triggered shove of the ventilator.

Dana could go to Karen's bed. As resident staff, she wouldn't carry the deep organ-harvest shadow that Rudd or Brovek would project. Should she go for a moment? Stand by her friend? Say goodbye? What harm could lie in that?

She takes a small step but stops. Draws back. Standing at Karen's bedside is a small, still figure in gray, who must be Karen's mother, come in the night from Prairie Falls.

With a sigh, her footsteps dragging, Dana leaves the ICU. With her unaccustomed leisure, she finds herself in the doctors' staff room. Coffee, Dana? Go for it. How about a chunk of this frosted almond roll?

She breaks off a piece and tucks it into her mouth, as Lance Rudd stalks in. Neatly dressed, as always. But with a face of grief echoed by a shadow of beard. She sets the roll and coffee back on the table.

"Any news, Dana?"

"She looks the same, Lance. Still unconscious. Still on the respirator."

"They'll probably declare today."

"Final tests. She hasn't stirred." Her almond roll tastes like dust.

"We were in love, Karen and I. We never talked about dying! Damn it! It shouldn't be like this." He turns away, hiding his face. "I need to see her, Dana."

"You can't. You know why. You even lectured about it."

He edges to a leather chair, rests a hand on its back. But he doesn't sit down. "I won't go near. Just close enough to see her. While she is still...still Karen."

"Her mother is there. Next of kin. If we hope for organs today, we'll need her permission. Don't screw it up."

He paces, shuttling between chairs, on to the coffee bar and back again. "I need to say goodbye."

"No, dear man. Her mother still hopes Karen will wake up. She sees that noisy awkward respirator as treatment. As life support. As hope."

"Well, it is. But even if she doesn't wake up, we still have to keep her organs alive."

"She doesn't have to know that, Lance. Not yet. First, Karen must be declared dead. That's the critical point. Then her doctors try for permission to save her organs. Yes or no. After that you can see her."

"After that I may have to see her. But then she's not Karen anymore."

"You're right. Good point. Cling to that, dear friend, for what may come next."

"I don't care about <u>next</u>. I'll go see her <u>now</u>..." In a sudden stride he breaks his circling and arrows toward the door. "I'm going, Dana. I've got to —"

But Dana jumps ahead of him. She plants her slight body squarely in his way and shoves the flat of her hand against the middle of his chest. She stops him as if he has run into a tree. "You can't go, Lance. Give it up. Grieve. Hurt. Cry. But don't go!"

He wilts against her hand, his fight all gone. "It's hard, Dana."

"Sure, it's hard. Let's say how hard it is. Karen is probably dead; we're waiting for the declaration. Then it's over for her."

Lance drifts back, slumps against his leather chair.

She lets her body unwind and breathes again. "But it's just beginning for Martin Stern. For a heart patient somewhere. For people who need kidneys, or corneas, or skin — whatever our science has learned to use." She captures his eyes in her steady gaze. "And for you, Lance, the job is just beginning. You are the liver guy, the only one."

She gauges him. His eyes. His hands. Can he handle more truth?   Well, he has to. "Let's say it all, even the hardest stuff. You'll be the one to harvest her organs."

Lance nods, beaten. He sinks into his chair. And she wonders — for him today, and some day for herself — what sacrifice could there be that their profession may not demand of them? She watches, troubled, as he accepts his duty and makes his gift.

And his light goes out, as if part of him has died.

Wilma

9:05 a.m.

Wilma Gale, light of heart and hopeful, revs up her 1982 white Chevette and sets out for University Hospital. At twenty-eight years she has earned her RN and a new bachelor's degree (say *bachelorette*, you're dead!). And she is turned on by her new job, to be the very first director of the Regional Organ Procurement Organization.

It's all so new. Transplants. Teaching people about taking living organs from dead people to save the lives of dying people. Winning consent for transplant from grieving families. Wearing her own clothes — her fresh size tens in her own colors. Being a trailblazer — so far there aren't many rules. She thrills at her job. Last year it didn't exist.

But now it does, and here she goes this eve day of Easter, on this warm and sunny morning, off to U Hospital for organ salvage. Always a new challenge.

She's good at this new skill, counseling the mourners. At least she hopes to be. First, she works to gain their trust. She likes to explain the machinery — the tangle of equipment that distorts and obscures the person they mourn. So she explains the importance of life-support even after death. That a brain-dead person does not breathe. That the respirator makes artificial breathing and enables a well-oxygenated heart to keep beating and drive the circulation so that other organs stay alive and can be rescued for transplant. If the family can hear more, she may even describe the good feeling that families feel when organs of their loved ones go to save the lives of other people.

To gain consent from the next of kin is always a win, but she wants more. She wants agreement in the family, and hopes for visible signs of the consolation that follows. A new firmness in their step, a lift to the voices. Seeing those signs becomes her own reward, her sought-for double win. She considers herself a very lucky young woman.

She sails along on a two-lane county black-top. The fields are still winter-bound, but a cock pheasant poses on the roadside ahead, and scores of little black birds perch on the power lines alongside. She rolls her windows down—next time she'll buy a convertible.

She's glad to be out of the office, to spend a few hours away from her fast-changing lists of names at ROPO. Rosters of dying people waiting for organs, each record showing which transplant center is involved, what organ is wanted, how urgent the need. The names come at her in a constant stream—like those power poles alongside—then drop away into her files. She'll know them a few weeks later when they crop up again. A lucky few will have won the draw. Most simply run out of time.

She checks her watch. The sun's up, but it's still early. She crosses the freeway on the overpass and slows to city speed, alert for kids and cycles. She knows where brain deaths come from.

She'd like to get more chances to ask for donations. Not for more people to die! Not that! But for more organs to be salvaged from those who do die. People haven't learned yet—and she'd like to teach them—how organs and tissues from one single cadaver donor can bring life or help to lots of patients down the line. Not only organs, but skin, bone, corneas—whatever science comes up with next. She still burns that a couple of months ago one of her hospitals suffered a brain death and rescued no organs. No lives saved. And why?

Because nobody thought of it! Nobody asked!

There's always somebody who doesn't get the word.

For the last block she drops to slow, because she likes the contrast between the two sides. That little red-brick church on her left, and its empty playground. The gleaming chrome and marble bulk of University Hospital on the other. She turns the corner, keys the gate to the doctors' parking lot, and slides into an empty slot.

Today is a new day. Another case. Somebody thought of transplants. And here she comes, Wilma Gale, full of hope, riding in to win the life-giving donation of somebody's vital organs.

Exciting.

But asking for donors is also scary. Meet the mourners. Get legal permission from the next of kin. Hope for approval by everybody else. But all she gets is one chance. She has to do it right. Her waiting names need a whole lot of Yeses.

And if she fails? Does her best, and gets a No? If she brings nothing home to those waiting names? There is the stuff of her nightmares.

But that's for nighttime and this is now.

She crosses to the staff entrance and moves inside. Into the arena.

She wants to reflect confidence—even if it's shaky. She chooses simple clothes in light colors. Nothing sexy. Never black nor any shade of red—and never a uniform. This morning, in celebration of the spring season, she wears a white carnation pinned to her favorite green sweater.

Well, what will she find today? What attitudes in the grieving kin? How many mourners to deal with? For starters, she likes low pressure, slow pace, and lots of sympathy. But she has to be ready for resistance. Ready to move quick and adjust fast, to find what works.

She marches directly to the ICU. The charge nurse confirms her target: Yes, the near bed, its still figure hidden under the ministrations of life support. The patient: Karen Sondergaard, her chest rising with the thrusts of artificial ventilation. The motionless figure by the bedside: Astry Sondergaard, the patient's mother and next of kin.

From there at the nursing station Wilma observes the woman. She stands drawn in to herself, a pinched figure in unfashionable clothes, unmoving, her hands resting on the bed's white sheet. Not at all the picture of anxious tension that Wilma usually sees in hovering families near the time of death.

Or, in this case, after death. Wilma knows Karen's attending physicians made the declaration early this morning — the loss of brain function having proved total and permanent.

She moves silently to the bedside, opposite the still figure of the mother. A round-shouldered person in the dull colors of winter clothing. She does not look up but stands motionless, expressionless, her hands resting on her daughter's knee. So severely withdrawn into herself, she must surely be a larger person than she looks.

"Hello, Mrs. Sondergaard." Wilma is careful not to say Good Morning. "My name is Wilma Gale. I believe the doctors told you about me. May I talk to you?"

Gray eyes shift to Wilma's face. Hooded, dull, they reveal no emotion. Nor any interest. There is no other movement, and no word is said.

Wilma tries again. "I'm sure you are tired. Would you like some hot coffee? I have a pot in my office."

"I will stay here." The voice is uninflected, the words final.

A difficult challenge, this north-country woman. Can she get her to respond? Again, she tries. "Do you understand why I am here? Did Karen's doctors tell you I would come to see you?"

Nothing. She waits.

Then: "Yah."

A beginning! Wilma feels a lift of hope. "I am so sorry about all this. The people who knew your daughter were very fond of her. She was a good nurse."

She uses the past tense purposely. Can she draw a response? She sees none.

"Do you expect Karen's brother to come? Come here to the hospital?"

"Erik. No." Simple words. No inflection.

"Have you talked to him?"

"Yah."

"But he's not coming?"

"His baby is sick, little Otto."

Wilma makes a sympathetic sound. She looks at the long body under the sheet. Could it truly have been brought into life from this cold little woman on the other side of the bed? And nursed at the breasts of that hollow chest?

She tries to proceed. "Do you understand what is happening to Karen?"

"Yah." Flat voice. No emotion. "She is dead."

A tough old bird. Does she feel nothing? Wilma has not seen such stoic realism. But her opening is plain, and she pursues it. "You are right. The doctors had to be absolutely sure there was no chance at all for her to recover. This morning they were able to declare that she is dead."

"Yah. I know."

Yah. Sure you do.

Wilma labors on. "Medicine today can do wonderful things for people. We can't restore our brain, of course. That's why Karen is dead. But we can restore other organs for people by transplanting good ones from people who die. Have you heard about organ transplants?"

"Yah."

Nothing. Then: "Karen was going to teach about it."

"I know she was. Did she ever talk to you about transplants? How did she feel about giving organs after death?"

"She didn't know she was going to die."

Silence.

Has she blown her chance?

Don't quit, Wilma. Try again.

"Mrs. Sondergaard, how do you feel about organ donation? You, yourself. Karen's organs could mean new life for other people."

The first motion Wilma has seen: a slight shake of head.

"Mrs. Sondergaard?"

The same flat voice. Quiet. Unmoved. "No. I can't."

Wilma feels sucker-punched. Knocked dead. *No, I can't.* Nothing could be plainer than that.

If she had to describe an ideal organ donor, this Karen Sondergaard would be the pattern. But donation must follow consent—true consent, freely given. And Karen's mother has just said No.

Bad try, Wilma. Somewhere you missed.

But it's only round one. Try again. Get yourself back in the game!

"If that is your choice, we will surely honor it. But I would like to have you think about it for a while. I'll go back to my office and bring you some of that hot coffee. Aren't you tired, after your journey here?"

"I slept some. On the bus."

"Would you like a biscuit or a sweet roll with it?"

No response. Has the old lady even heard?

Nothing changes.

Wilma sighs and turns away. She needs that coffee herself.

Fr. O'Leary

9:45 a.m.

"You're early today, Father O'Leary. Mass let out ahead of time?"

He chuckles, loving the good will of nurses like this young woman, friends he sees on his daily rounds. But even here in ICU he can't resist a chance to tease. "Someone's a little shaky on her liturgy, I see. We celebrate no mass today. None at all anywhere. It's Holy Saturday, you know, with our Jesus lying dead in the tomb. Remember?"

"Of course. Tomorrow is Easter, isn't it."

"And all will be restored and bright in the risen Lord."

"Not like today!" She nods to the nearest bed. "We've just had a death."

"Yes, I came early today." He nods toward Karen. "And she is the reason. I hoped I'd find her waking up."

"Not a flicker. It doesn't change anything in our care level, but we got the declaration a few minutes ago. That's her mother over there."

"Karen was Lutheran, wasn't she? A caring, gentle nurse — I've watched her at work."

"Wait 'til you see her mother!"

As quietly as he can, the old priest hobbles to Karen's bed, fingers his rosary but leaves it in his pocket. Silently he recites a prayer of blessing. He wishes he could offer the richness of the sacraments at the time of death. But he has never felt they are necessary.

At last he raises his eyes to Karen's mother, and finds her silent gaze fixed on him.

"I am sorry for your loss, Mrs. Sondergaard."

He sees no response.

"If I can help you in any way, I would like to...to help you."

She looks at her hands, folded together on Karen's knee. She does not speak. She offers no response. No guide, no clue.

What can he offer? "Would you like me to call Pastor Johnsrud? He comes in sometimes for...for people."

She mutters one dismissive word. "Missouri."

"I beg your pardon? I don't understand."

"No, thank you."

Missouri? He's heard of separate Lutheran synods in America, disputing something. Doesn't know what it's about. But her No is clear enough.

She offers nothing more, and he wants to walk away. God knows he is uncomfortable enough, standing before her granite face.

But hold it, O'Leary. She's supposed to make *you* comfortable? In your own hospital? She's the stranger here. And that bitter word, *Missouri*? That's a clue. She is a woman of faith. Away from her church. Standing by her dead daughter. And alone.

His heart opens to her. A few more quiet moments won't hurt. He returns to his silent prayer.

Then: "M-m-mister...ah...Father?"

Aha! "What may I do, Mrs. Sondergaard?"

"You don't like cremation." A flat statement of fact.

Why would she say that? He replays her words, and yes: at the very end her voice ticks higher. It's a question!

"My church does not prefer cremation, because the body was the dwelling place of the soul. It merits respect, after death."

"Yah." Silence. Then, "If it shouldn't be burned, a person maybe shouldn't cut it up, either."

Again that final little question mark.

Surely no one has been after her about an autopsy. It's too soon. "That would depend on why someone wants to…as you say…cut it up. For a proper reason it might be acceptable to…to separate certain parts."

He sees now what troubles her: are organ transplants okay? "Does that worry you, Mrs. Sondergaard. About changing the body?"

"Yah." She takes a long breath, rests her eyes on his collar, lifts them to his face. "If something goes missing in the body, how can it rise again in heaven?"

Father O'Leary takes a matching deep breath. How little we prideful folk credit the majesty and omnipotence of God! "He made us, remember. Created us out of His own desire, right there in the Garden of Eden. God can do anything. And if He wants to restore our bodies in heaven, then restored they will be. No problem."

"Yah…. Maybe…."

He edges closer to the foot of the bed. "Still unsure, are you?" He settles his hands on the white sheet, a comfortable few inches below the mother's hands.

Her eyes have followed him, his Roman collar, his Irish face. "What if a person gives away a heart and another person has it, and dies? Who gets the heart, do you suppose, in heaven?"

His own heart aches for her. From such a literal idea, such a deep question. "God promises life in heaven. If he needs hearts, he'll create them." He wants to tell her not to sweat the small stuff. But she needs more than his own pat answers. She needs something to count on.

He straightens, stands — pontifically, he hopes — at the foot of the bed. "One more thing I want you to know. It's about transplants. About taking good organs from dead people to help living people. Every religious authority approves of it.

Every church supports it. Not one single responsible voice has said No. Even the Jehovah's Witnesses do not object. Donating organs is a good and moral thing to do. Don't you agree?"

Her head moves in the tiniest motion of a nod. And her voice comes as he has heard it before: "Yah. I suppose."

Well, he has done what he can.

He steps to the head of Karen's bed, passes his hand through the curls of tubing to touch her brow. He whispers a prayer, makes a sign of the cross, and steps back. He nods to her mother, crosses himself, and limps away out of ICU, back again into the living world.

Wilma

10:05 a.m.

The coffee helps. Wilma fills a second cup to take back to her — what? — her candidate? Her supplicatee? Her...prey? Maybe. That ice-cold woman is a tough target, but Wilma Gale does not give up.

From her office she strides steadily along the corridor, hoping for insight. For inspiration. At ICU she presses the wall switch for the double doors, and — rats! She has forgotten the coffee for...for her target. Yes. That's the right word.

"I meant to bring you coffee, Mrs. Sondergaard. But... well, I forgot it."

Nothing has changed. The same still figure stands by the body, her hands folded on its knee. The same stoic face reveals nothing. But watches, sees everything.

Wilma fusses with her carnation, tugs at the hem of her green sweater. Where to begin.

"I wish we could save Karen's organs. And tissues. They would go to people who need them. A failing heart. Failed kidneys. Blind eyes. It is a whole new world for those folks, when suddenly they can live again."

"Yah. I know."

Does she? Does she really know? Wilma decides to push harder. "Today could be their best chance, too. They can't wait too long. They run out of time."

No response.

"In other words, they die."

Nothing.

"We can't save any of their organs, either. Because all their organs die when their hearts stop."

She waits, but the old lady remains inert. Her eyes are fixed on Wilma's face, and Wilma wonders: What bomb must she throw to move this mountain? She decides to go where she has never gone before.

"You know about transplants. Karen approved of transplants. Karen's heart is beating. Her organs are alive. Only her brain is dead. I do not want to be cruel, Mrs. Sondergaard. But what possible reason can you have for saying No to the people who need Karen's organs to live?"

At last she has struck a chord. Something new flickers in that impassive face. "Yah," she says. "I can't afford it."

Can't afford it...!

Wilma's heart leaps in hope. In a heartbeat, she sees into this woman's Spartan reserve, where she volunteers nothing but responds when she must to words that matter. Whatever is trivial she ignores. Is it a lifetime of hardship that makes her this way? So that Wilma, from her own impatience and blinded insight, has very nearly fallen short? Her own generosity wells up in her heart; she fills with new respect for this granite-like survivor. She speaks tenderly, as she would to a bewildered child.

"But you don't have to afford it, Mrs. Sondergaard. Your expenses stop the moment Karen dies. Oh, there is great expense in reclaiming her organs, and transplanting them somewhere. But you don't have to pay for any of it."

The old woman looks now, as if for the first time, at her daughter's body, those long limbs lying so still, the hidden face hardly recognizable under plastic tubes. One golden tress has escaped the tangle and lies in a curl by the shoulder.

She turns now to Wilma Gale. Two lonely tears glisten in the corners of her eyes. She nods her head. "I didn't know that."

"Does it make a difference?"

"Yah. All the difference."

"Would you like to give us permission to save Karen's organs for other people?"

"Yah, if I can. She would like that."

The tears are gone; they never reached her cheek.

"What about her brother?"

"Does he have to know?"

"Yes."

Silence.

"Let me call him for you. We can go to my office. You want to be sure he agrees, don't you think?"

"Yah, I suppose."

Wilma waits patiently now. She wonders at this remarkable old woman. How deep can repression run? Is there a torrent seething beneath that ice? She sees no trace of it. Astry Sondergaard stands silent, her elbows pinched against her side, her gnarled fingers a hard contrast to the smooth white sheet.

Wilma waits. No pressure now. Her heart is full; her prize is won.

At last, the old woman steps back and folds her hands against her waist. She looks directly into Wilma Gale's eyes, and delivers her words without inflection. "Yah. Maybe a person could still find coffee in your office?"

Brovek

April 7, 1985

11:15 a.m.

Sandor Brovek eases up on his heavy foot, lets his black Lincoln fall back from the lumbering tanker truck ahead.

Collect yourself, Sandor. You haven't even buckled your seat belt!

He snaps it on. Still making freeway speed, but he is safer now. He's worked enough emergency rooms to see how seat belts save lives — heads that didn't smash windshields; fixable bodies that stayed in the car.

He champs with impatience. If he wants to build a big transplant center here, he has to develop patterns. Routine procedures. How can he plan ahead if nobody tells him he has a donor? A head injury on life support? Hell, everybody knows it's a candidate. They should have let him know yesterday.

He slows again. Don't push your luck, Sandy.

What is it about luck? You can't count on it, and you can't make it happen. But you can sure as hell flaunt it, and maybe turn it off.

He drops down his exit ramp, and cruises—talk about needing luck!—past St. Luke's Church. So critical to his hope and desire. He can't bear to look at the place. At the doctors' parking lot he keys the gate and steers into his reserved slot.

He hasn't built his career on luck; he's built it on hard work. But luck is a leaven in the dough. And he wants good luck today. The big challenge: a heart, two kidneys, a liver.

Oh yes, a liver. And that's his own problem.

But not yet.

He cuts into the surgeons' dressing room, whips into scrubs and his OR shoes, and bombs on into the operating suite.

How will he assign the rescued organs? Where will they go? Here on his own turf, he'll decide that. With ROPO of course. Maybe do his second heart? Great opportunity. And Rudd has his liver! He's waited for weeks for his chance. And Stern is here. Martin Stern. With St. Luke's in his pocket. He should have died—but he didn't. And he's here in the hospital. Ready to go. Part of my problem.

Let that bit cook awhile.... Maybe I —. No...I don't have to decide anything yet.

In Mizzoh's glass-walled office—strategically placed at the crossroads of the OR suite—he sees a few scrub suits gathered to wait. He'll review his troops there. Plan the campaign for today. One donor, multiple organs. Do the harvest, assign the organs and the crews that will sew them in. A nice string of transplants, chalked up and reported. Like trophies.

Neat? Not.

Can he handle everything? Is he too small here even to think of that? May have to release some of those precious organs. Farm them out. What he can't handle here will have to go somewhere else. ROPO. Some ambitious center close enough to serve. That farming out won't happen when he gets St. Luke's. A one-donor day like this? No challenge. His dreamed-of center will handle multiple transplants as a routine. No problem. Skilled teams of clinicians, surgeons, research folks. Bigger hospital. More people.... If he gets St. Luke's.

And it all comes down to Martin Stern. Which way to go? Heads or tails? Live or die? Call the shot.

No. Not yet. This is what Horace Potts was pushing me about, back at the University Club. Decide about Stern. Hell, Horace, I'm still on the fence.

Through the office window he looks his people over. Mizzoh behind her desk. Rudd leans in a corner looking wasted. Garrison saying something earnest to him. Pete is there, and some juniors have crowded in.

The harvest, of course, comes first. I'll put Rudd and Garrison in Room Two to collect the heart, the liver, the kidneys; maybe more. I'll take on the heart transplant in Room One. With a couple of junior residents. Rudd should get the liver — it's his big chance. But that means Martin Stern. And Mizzoh's going to strain about capacity. I'll push her. We've got a lot of rooms to operate in.

Sure we do. For little stuff. A gall bladder, no sweat. But for major cases all at once? No way; we're too damn small.

Okay. So we're small. Get to it.

The harvest comes first. Room One. Then the heart and the liver in — well — where? Mizzoh has a lot of rooms, but many aren't big enough. And I have no more people. We're too thin.

We learned how important size is when heart surgery exploded — all the cardiovascular stuff, the valves and the stents. The pattern was plain: big centers thrived. Little guys lost funding and faded away. So we got big. We made it. But transplants are coming — hell, they're here — and we're not big enough. Not yet.

I've built my career — and good rep, if I have one — on growing the department. On hard work and solid ethics. And my full share of good luck. But not enough to take Stern out of it today. He's here. Is that bad luck?... No. I couldn't count any man's death as good luck.... But if I give Stern his new liver and he survives? That isn't exactly good luck either. Not for me.

Okay. It's decision time. Stern is here. I need to get St. Luke's and build my center, or I'll be stuck in nowhere. Can I let Stern block me from that? He's a fine case for us today. A foundation stone for a reputation in transplants. A career builder for Rudd. And he's a patient we've taken on; he's entrusted himself to us, to our care.

I'm thinking, Horace.

My duty is clear. Treat him right; get him well.

And prepare to die.

Mizzoh, ensconced behind her desk, nods a good morning as I walk in. Mrs. Maureen O'Hanahan. Mizzoh. Her round face is a fixture here. Always the same: her head encased in a green hood; her sturdy body in a matching scrub suit. I've never seen her in anything else. She has run her operating rooms out of this little fishbowl since I was an assistant professor.

Rudd stands propped in the corner, looking haggard. Unusual appearance for him. His career should take off today — if I give him a liver to transplant. Garrison is next to him, in those damn silent shoes of hers.

The team is here. It's game time. They should be keyed up and ready to go. I move in, snare the one chair before the desk, and sit on it.

"Okay, people. Today we have a fine opportunity. We have the best cadaver donor we can hope for, and we can retrieve a whole hatful of organs."

They stare at me like I'm an enemy alien. Rudd is a ramrod. Mizzoh fiddles with a yellow pencil. Garrison shakes her head.

A bad start. I forgot the cadaver was staff; maybe they knew her. Can't stop now! "Rudd, I want you to take charge of the harvest. Garrison can help you. Okay?"

"Okay, Chief." Subdued. Flat.

"Then, Mizzoh, we'll overlap in a second major room. I'll start the heart for the top name on our list. Okay so far?"

Mizzoh looks at her desk, spins the yellow pencil on her desktop. "So far we're okay, Dr. B."

What is wrong with these guys? Where is their spit?

"The kidneys can wait a day or two, with the perfusion machine. But not the liver. That's another room, a major room, Mizzoh. To start during the harvest. Okay?"

"We're getting thin, Dr. B. Holiday weekend, holiday crew. Room Three is getting the new light you ordered. Can't operate in there."

Problems. I forgot the damn light. I snare Mizzoh's pencil. When we build the new OR suite, we'll take on challenge days like this without a ripple.

I twist the pencil in my fingers. Why all this reluctance? I don't understand their pussyfoot attitudes.

"Dr. Brovek?"

Garrison. Is she going to weasel around too?"

"Your plan sounds good to me, sir. But I haven't heard you mention ROPO. They have some interest in these organs, too, don't they?"

"We have the organs, Dr. Garrison. We have the control. We'll use ROPO if we can't handle all the organs right here."Rudd leans forward from his corner, eyes intense. "No, Chief. Our first priority today has to be for these organs to survive. Call ROPO. That way you find the best candidates for her organs."

Easy, Sandor. Stay cool. Rudd sounds like a preacher, not a surgeon. "But those 'best candidates' you dream up may be miles from here. Anywhere in five states. Hours away. That's important."

Here comes Mizzoh, attacking from my other flank. "ROPO is a good thought, Dr. B. If the heart or liver could be shipped, we'd be in better shape. If we try to do both of those we'll be stretched tight. I need some leeway in case another emergency comes along."

Damn. I'm calling on my engines for full speed, and all I hear is backfire. Consider ROPO. Holler for help. Settle for less. By God, we need more rooms, more people, okay. But we need more spine in my doctors.

Like a stem of glass the pencil snaps between my fingers.

Damn. Am I the only one here with the guts to go the limit?

Hold it, Sandor. Your head is dreaming expansion; Mizzoh has to deal with what she's got today. We're not a big place. Not yet.

I tilt back in the chair, balance on its two skinny legs. Precarious. I watch them focus on my balance. These are good people. My good crew. I need to listen.

"Okay. Call Wilma Gale and see if she knows anything."

Garrison speaks up. Too soon, as if she's waiting for a cue. "She is waiting outside, Dr. Brovek. I asked her to stay a minute, just in case."

"Ain't that dandy, Dr. Garrison. Why don't you go and ask her in here then?... Just in case."

I bang my chair down on its four legs, pace the tiny office — two steps and a turn. I feel like a bear in a cage. I rumble something at Wilma Gale, as she comes in and —. By God! She takes my chair. She had to put on a gown to come in here, and look at her. It's open at the top, and she's wearing a green sweater and — what the hell — a flower?

"Ms. Gale, I want you to check possible recipients at other institutions within range, for use of today's cadaver organs." I shoot a glance at Dr. Garrison. "Just in case."

"I checked things out, Dr. Brovek, as soon as we had the permission for donation. Mercy has a heart patient; they could be here by 3:30 to harvest the heart for themselves — I believe that's the usual procedure. They are waiting for a call. More: North County has a patient for the liver, and they'll be here at 5:00 unless I call them off. Both candidates are type O blood like your donor."

"Yes. Martin Stern, too."

"And he is urgent." I surprise myself. After all my stalling, have I placed my chips?

"Chief?"

What is Rudd going to say? He's looking at his big chance to step into surgical history.

"Martin Stern is pretty far gone. His proteins are down. He's just out of coma. He's a high-risk candidate. Our liver might have a better chance at North County."

Our liver? Why isn't he fighting for his own patient? For Stern? He knows nothing about St. Luke's. About expansion. It's no matter to him.

But it's a big deal to me. And there's my escape! My chance to let somebody else do it wrong. An innocent, unassailable way to take me off the hook. And if the North County people screw up, Stern goes out of the game. I get St. Luke's. Build my transplant center.

It's my way out.

"Dr. Rudd, do you have Martin Stern under care?"

"Yes, sir. By the medical department."

"Still under active treatment, not terminal care?"

"Correct."

"Then he is still a candidate for liver transplant, correct?"

"Yes, sir. But it doesn't have to be here."

Get off my shoulder, Lance. You know only half the story. "Garrison? You have an idea, I suspect."

"Our heart patient is ideal, Dr. Brovek. She lives in town. She's ready. Another young woman with kids, like Millicent Herold."

"I want our organs to go where they'll survive, Chief." Rudd. "That's first."

They all have opinions; I must suffer them.

Rudd gives the screw another turn. "Best chances are for the heart to stay here. Send the liver to North County."

North County. How many times must I turn away from sin?

"Mizzoh, can we harvest and do both heart and liver here today?"

"One or the other, Dr. B." Straight and tough. "Try both and we'll bust the barrel."

"Lance?"

"Do the heart, Chief. It's getting too late for Martin Stern."

"Dr. Garrison?"

"Send out the liver, Dr. Brovek. The heart should be a shining success for you."

They do not know the thorns I must swallow.

"Ms. Gale?"

"Whatever you say, Dr. Brovek. I know Mr. Stern has been on your list for a very long time. But what about the doctors coming from North County? I'm not sure I can catch them."

I lean across Mizzoh's desk and pick up her broken pencil. "Okay. Enough talk." The broken ends fit together pretty good. I pull them apart, fit them together again. "Here is how it's going to go." I spit my words at each one in turn. "Lance: you harvest. Start with the liver. Mercy can come and take their own heart. I'll start Stern. You bring the liver and put it in. Dr. Garrison: you shadow Lance today. You'll be good help and you'll learn a lot. Pete, you come with me. Mizzoh: call in your team; we have a game to play. Wilma, you do have the final consent, don't you?"

"Sure do, Dr. Brovek. But what about the people from North County? What can I tell them?"

I seize her elbow and talk down to her damn carnation as if it was a microphone. "Tell them we're going to do a liver transplant. Right here. A transplant that's going to work. Tell them they can come and watch."

I let her go and she flees. Rudd squeezes past me, with a harder shove than he needed. "'Scuse me, Chief. Now I can go and see her."

Whatever that means. He disappears.

Garrison lingers in the doorway. Something on her mind.

"Dr. Brovek, this is a tough deal for Dr. Rudd. More than you know. He may need some back-up. I hope you'll stay in range." And she too is gone.

"What's all that about, Mizzoh? Is our crew a bit screwy today?"

"Young folks, Dr. B. Who knows anything about young folks?" She scurries out to marshal her nurses.

I sit down on her chair, rest my arms on her desk. The broken ends of her pencil fit together. I can match them precisely. But they'll never heal. Like the decisions I've made today. They may be right or they may be wrong, but they can never be undone.

Are you satisfied, Horace? The time finally came. I had to place my chips, and I did. The hard way. Denied my staff. Subverted their counsel. Turned away an ideal heart. Took on a moribund Stern, who odds on will die — and will serve me best if he does die. But I will drive my crew to get him well.

Why did I do it, Horace? For my integrity? Really: why did I throw away my own interest? For Hippocrates? Because I'm honor-bound to Martin Stern? Did I do it for ethics?

I'll let you think so.

I drop the pencil to the desk. The two pieces bounce, roll a bit, go still.

But it wasn't ethics. Or not only ethics. It was superstition. Not to offend whatever spirits there may be that bring good healing.

But no matter the reason, Horace, I stepped up for Martin Stern. He will have his liver. I'll get him well and send him off to buy his church. And he will block me from my dream.

Have I destroyed myself? Like this broken pencil? A sharpened lead that isn't what it says it is, but only carbon.

I flip the yellow fragment into the wastebasket.

Or have I saved myself, my integrity intact?

And what about that good young heart? An ideal organ, and I send it away? Gamble that it will find a life out there with the Mercy team? Because of Stern again?

Who wins today? Who has lost? How many lives depend on these arbitrary decisions I made today?

And can't change.

I snap the eraser end into the basket.

And I ask you further, Horace—you got me thinking this way: can a man try so hard to get things right that he ends up wrong?

Rudd

12:30 p.m.

Only an hour ago, bitter and frustrated, Lance, the transplant surgeon, was barred from his beloved Karen. Now he is sent to her, not as a mourner but as a dissectionist.

Tight with anger, a professional on autopilot, he stalks to her bed in ICU. He sees little that is Karen—only a single blond tress lying a-curl by her shoulder. A white sheet stretches over her body. Urine drains. IVs drip. Respirator blows its disturbance every eight seconds. He checks the chart: stable blood pressure, urine output okay, normal body temp, IV fluids and glucose given as scheduled. Exactly as it is supposed to be. Exactly as she was when he saw her last.

Except, she's dead. No longer Karen. What was it Dana said? Cling to that idea against what comes next.

Well, *next* has come.

An orderly appears with a litter. Nurses make the smooth transition, switching the gear to portable life support that continues unruffled during her move to the OR. For a second time, Lance watches an expert team of gentle hands lift Karen's body to a cart and roll her away.

Dana

Through the windows of her scrub room, Dana watches Myrna's five-nurse team transform a bare, cold Room Two into an operating theater. All are hooded and masked. Some wear only the universal handout uniform of the hospital's work areas: floppy, bare-arm tops and shapeless, drawstring bottoms in faded blue cotton. Those who have scrubbed are further shrouded in long gowns and latex gloves that present only sterile surfaces to the operative area.

With dispatch, the team drape their work stands, open packs of sterile instruments and array them in orderly rows on surgical trays. Gleaming instruments in a range of sizes, forceps and clamps, scissors, needle holders. From training and discipline, they all protect the integrity of sterile work areas.

In a few minutes Dana will enter the same discipline. Now she scrubs, watches the action. With life support fully maintained, Karen's body is brought in and transferred to the operating table. The anesthesia people continue her ventilation and fluids. An assistant resident folds back the sheet, exposing the full length of chest and abdomen. He paints all exposed skin in deep brown antiseptic. Then nurses apply the sterile surgical drapes, covering all but a long midline strip of chest and abdomen. Karen has disappeared.

Dana's scrub is dull routine, and she thinks about these last two terrible days…. It could have been herself. Just as likely as Karen…. Nobody knows who might have a flawed artery like that—until one breaks…. She spreads the rich brown soap in heavy lather over her hands and arms…. It could have been me…. She begins the same-old-same-old with file to her nails and the bristly brush to her fingers and hands…. And if it happened to me, I would want my organs to be recycled…. Given to people whose organs have failed…. She holds her arms, elbows down, under the running water, rinses away the suds…. What would Rusty think of that? We should talk, he and I, about what-if….

She turns off the water with the knee lever, enters the operating room…. Maybe his pilot's license lets him say what he'd want…. She dries her hands on a sterile towel, careful that it touch nothing but her own skin.... I'll have to check the new donor thing on my driver's license. I haven't even looked at it since way last year!

She shoves her arms into the gown held out for her by a surgical nurse already garbed. And then her hands into her small stretchy Latex gloves.... I hope Lance doesn't show up here yet. I ordered him to stay away 'til I called.... But of course, he's his own guy....

The students make room for her at the surgeon's place. She steps up to the long field of bright light and rests her hands on the white drape for her usual moment of reflection. This time — over this cadaver — her thought is of Karen, and — in a special turn — includes herself.... How close we all live to the edge... And how little we believe it!... Goodbye, dear Karen.

She checks the familiar geography — the sternum, the xyphoid, the pubis — and draws a straight red line the full length of chest and abdomen. She controls the bleeders, applies skin towels, folds them back. A textbook picture remains: a clean, dry surgical incision. Anonymous.

"Myrna, you may notify Dr. Rudd that we are ready for him in Room Two."

Rudd

After his own full scrub, Lance elbows his way to the center ring to take over the procedure that Garrison started. The open incision is home territory for him; the tissues are anonymous. They move through standard maneuvers they have done many times: split the sternum, open the abdominal wall, incise the pericardium — my God! The reality of her beloved heart, Karen's heart, beating there beneath his hand, knocks him back.

"You okay, Lance?"

"No, Dana, not really. Let's get it done."

Back to routine. They cannulate the aortic arch.

He checks the clock. The harvest team from Mercy should have come by now, to remove the heart they expect to transplant. He hopes they're good. He shouldn't have to wait for them. Timing is critical.

Smoothly, he and Dana divide attachments that support and suspend the abdominal organs. The spleen comes out for further tissue match to candidates for the kidneys. Working together, the two surgeons slide other cannulas into the lower aorta and its vein, the inferior vena cava. They place a third cannula into the unique vein that carries blood from the gut not to the heart but to the liver: the portal vein. Short, but of large caliber, it is critical to the liver's economy.

Lance looks again at the clock. Those guys should be here now. Carefully, he passes blood vessel clamps around the arteries and veins of the heart and another clamp across the aorta at the diaphragm. Closing that clamp will stop the blood that now still flows to the abdominal organs.

It's time to proceed with the harvest, heart first. Where are those people? It's so easy to do harm. To lose even small amounts of blood. To shut down blood flow to an organ before it can be removed and cooled. And these are Karen's organs: they must survive.

The anesthesiologist raises her head above the drape. "Her blood pressure is sagging a bit, Lance. I'm pushing her volume but she's getting weaker."

Lance reviews the protocol. Heart first. But the Mercy guys haven't come. They should be here now, gowned and gloved, moving in to take the heart. Reality check: they are not.

Time is the last thing to waste. He proceeds with key dissections for the abdominal organs. Without a beating heart, the vessels will be bloodless. But now they pulsate. While he waits, he passes vascular clamps across the aorta, vena cava, portal vein. He could close the clamps now, cut loose the liver and the kidneys and deliver them to ice. But also lose blood. Lose time. Damage the heart. Those guys ought to be here.

"Myrna, slip over into Dr. Brovek's room. See how he's coming with Mr. Stern. And tell him the Mercy guys aren't here yet."

He senses the students getting nervous, wondering what's wrong. Teaching time. "Do you see the problem? The heart should be taken first, by its transplant people. They aren't here. If we proceed with our organs, the liver and kidneys, we delay the heart procedure. If we wait further, for the heart, we damage the abdominal organs. We try to do the most good and the least harm, but real-world decisions are not always easy."

Myrna returns, her eyes wide above her face mask. "Dr. Brovek says he's nearly ready for your liver, Dr. Rudd. And he said to put it first! That's what he said: save that liver."

Rudd nods, glad to have the decision made for him. "Thanks, Myrna. Let's have the cold Collins solution."

He and Dana move smoothly forward, closing clamps, flooding the isolated organs with ice-cold salt solution. They stop the heart, flood it with cold saline, divide its vessels, and lift it, in an icy bag, out of Karen's rib cage.

"Just like Danny, in Hangarville." Dana passes the packaged heart off for Myrna's series of icy bags.

"Except you didn't have to wait for the Mercy guys. As it's turning out today, they're not harvest surgeons after all; they're just delivery guys."

"Or girls, Lance." She chuckles. "Girls like me."

"No way, Dana. There are no girls like you."

They turn to the liver, already flushed and cooled. Gall bladder comes out. The bile duct emerges from the liver to drain into the nearby duodenum. Dissected and snipped. Access to the liver's single artery and the portal vein is easy; they divide those vessels. But behind the mass of liver lie its multiple short and inaccessible veins, essential structures that return liver blood into the inferior vena cava and on to the heart. Those short hepatic veins are confounding. The answer? Leave them alone. Smoothly, and at this stage easily, Lance includes with the liver the short length of vena cava that receives those pesky hepatic veins.

The liver dissection is done. Lance slides his two hands behind it, one on each side, and eases the solid, three-pound organ from its great cavity under the dome of diaphragm. With a gentle sucking sound it comes loose. He lifts it out, lets it drip red stain onto the towels Dana holds beneath it. Careful of the heavy prize, Lance slides it into an ice-filled sterile basin for its short trip to Brovek's Room One, where Martin Stern's yawning abdomen, emptied of its dying liver, lies ready to receive it.

Dana

Newly gowned and gloved, Dana approaches the table in Room One. Dr. Brovek withdraws. Under the array of drapes lies Martin Stern, bereft not only of his liver's function, but also now of the dying organ itself. Leaving the restructuring of Karen's body to Pete and students, Lance comes now to join her. In new gowns and gloves they take positions on opposite sides of the table.

From a large sterile basin, Dana, as assistant, takes the icy donor organ, the great mass of liver, into her two hands, and turns to the open cavity where it will go. And suddenly she gasps aloud, struck like a body blow by a long-ago vision come alive. It's what she saw on a high school field trip, fifteen years ago, in an auto assembly line in Kenosha: an auto engine, dangling from a conveyor chain, settling gently and precisely into its nest below.

The image seized her then—whatever it meant—with a power she has never forgotten. And never before understood. Through her years since— giving up her social life, committing to surgery, wondering was she good enough—she has clung to that image as her symbol of good karma. It was her nidus of faith that she was on the right track. Now, suddenly, she is confirmed.

"You all right, Dana?"

Her bones feel electrified. She bounces on her toes. "Never better, Doctor, never better. Let's sew this sucker in where it belongs."

With a silent nod, they appraise their precise and difficult work. Her first job as assistant is always to "expose"—to let him see—the exact field for uniting the matching structures. Also, she sustains the proper tension on the long thread of his running stitches, the tiny bites that unite the matching ends— artery to artery, duct to duct, vein to vein, or cava to cava. She likes assisting Lance, watching his deftness with the long instruments, forceps like tweezers in his left hand, needle holder in his right. With its precise jaws he takes up the tiny needle with its fine blue thread, places a stitch, releases the needle and takes it again, pulls the fine blue thread snug and, while she holds the proper tension, runs the sequence again. Steady repetition and admirable precision.

And her excitement bubbles over. "In its own way, Lance, this is beautiful. Healthy tissues. Everything in its place. Like predestined. Everything fits."

He chuckles. "Right now it's just hard work." He ties a skillful knot, his slender fingers quick and sure. He has grace in his technique, a simplicity that she admires.

Pete slips in to the table beside Dana. While he holds the wound open to their vision, Dana exposes the exact spot of their attention, now the vena cava. It is a demanding task, elbow deep, farther down even than Martin Stern's backbone. When released, the new liver will fall back, to lie in front of the big vein. With one hand she tilts the liver forward so he can see his target; her other hand holds tension on the advancing suture line.

"Not too loose, and not too tight." The old refrain sounds fresh and sweet to her awakened ears.

Lance is smooth and fast. The two junctions of the cava are soon complete, and its clamps come off. Blood begins to flow. She releases the heavy liver from fingers growing numb, and watches it settle into its new bed. She stretches her fingers, works a cramp out of her forearm. Her thoughts tumble.

Was I destined for this? Before anyone even dreamed of liver transplants? Will livers be my home turf, my forte? Livers? They're worlds harder than the transplant of kidneys. Or even of hearts. But yes! Yes! It's what that old vision has been promising all these years. I belong right here. Building the liver program. University Hospital. I'll be the liver queen!...

If, of course, they ever ask me.

The portal vein comes next. She exposes it far under the hanging edge of the big right lobe. The thumb-size ends come together nicely, and Lance starts his suture line to join them. His long tissue forceps picks up the first edge, the lower one, and steadies it as he pops the tiny curved needle through.

He unlocks the needle holder, takes the needle again, arcs it through the edge of the vein on the liver side, takes it again to pull it through, with its fine blue thread following. She takes the thread in her fingertips and follows his advancing stitch... proper tension...not too tight...not too...

What will Rusty think of his liver queen? He didn't think "surgeon" that first night. He just moved in. His first clench. How Bozo banged at her belt, and shocked him—she loves the memory—in a very...touchy—

Something is different.

Deep down under her retracted liver, in tweezing the thin edge of portal vein, the fine tips of Lance's forceps tremble. And stall. His tiny needle, already passed through the vessel wall, sits there for its regular smooth pick-up by his needle holder. But the instrument comes late, pokes at the needle, misses, trembles. Tries again.

Something wrong? We all make a meaningless slip once in a while—and make it up at once. But he's not making the correction.

What's off line here?

"Lance?"

I am louder than I meant to be.

"You okay?"

The other assistants snap to new attention.

He makes no answer. Under the edge of his hood his forehead glistens with perspiration. His eyes are blank.

Whatever is wrong is serious. Demands action.

When the time comes, girl, step up and take charge.

Enough.

Gently, I take Rudd's hands and lift them from the field. He lets me take his instruments, and I pass them to the scrub nurse. Now to care for Lance. I shoot my words to the young med student beside Rudd. "You, sir." He jolts awake. "I want you to step back, break scrub, and help Dr. Rudd."

For a moment the lad does not move. He's not ready to be a doctor, to act alone. But I give him that moment, and he obeys.

"Myrna!" My command voice strikes again. "We need Dr. Brovek. Get him in here to check Dr. Rudd."

Then back to Priority One. My patient. Nothing is more urgent—my father's dictum echoes in my head—than the operation you are doing right now...

"Come on, Pete. I'll switch sides here and we'll carry on." I cross to the surgeon's side and take up Lance's instruments. Pete slides his hand down under the liver, exposes the vessels. The half-placed suture is there, waiting. With that same long needle holder I take up the stitch, pull it through and go to work. We complete the suture all around, irrigate the reunited portal vein against air and clots, and gently release the clamps. Blood begins to flow—Martin Stern's blood into Martin Stern's new liver. It begins to breathe again, to live and not die. It still needs an artery.

Behind me, the double doors blow open in a great gust of air, and Sandor Brovek sails in. I turn to see—how could I not! He drops to his knees beside Rudd, now propped on a chair. Checks pulse. Checks pupils. Sees the sweaty brow.

"Myrna!" There is no doubt in his voice. "Orange juice. Candy. Whatever you have out there with sugar in it, get it in here."

I turn back to my own business with the liver.

"And you!" Brovek arrows his voice to the anesthetist. "Get an IV going and ram some glucose into this guy."

I stare at the two ends of hepatic artery pointing at each other.

An IV is basic. No info there. But sugar? Aha!

Now I can move. I set the first stitch.

Diabetic! Who knew? But an insulin reaction is a medical event. A whole lot better than my spooky thought, the symmetrical death of lovers.

I'm passing the last stitch in the hepatic artery union when Brovek arrives in new gown and gloves. "Stay where you are, Dr. Garrison. I'll slip in next to Pete, and you show me what you've done."

I can't show him much. The liver looks like a liver, but for its dark, no-oxygen color. The vena cava is invisible now, tucked down deep under it. I show him the suture line in the portal vein. He grunts, satisfied.

Now I open the vascular clamp on the hepatic artery. Fresh, bright, oxygen-rich arterial blood flows into the transplant, and we watch its dull purple come to a blush, then blossom into a true and healthy red.

Brovek grunts. "Let's hook up the gut somewhere. Show me."

His big hands are like spades. A world of difference from the delicacy of Lance's thin hands and long fingers. But his touch is soft, and no motion is wasted. Together we isolate a segment of small intestine to receive the bile duct. Another critical small suture line. A leak here would be not a quick bleed, but a slow and likely fatal complication. Brovek provides expert and careful assistance, and we get it done. Ready to close the incision.

Brovek steps back, pulls off his gown. "Dr. Garrison, I want you to come to my office when you're through." He strips off his gloves and shoots them into a bucket. "I'm going to check on Dr. Rudd."

"I'm okay now, Chief." Lance has come in, watching his case from somewhere behind me. "Except for being humiliated. I hadn't had an insulin reaction like this since high school."

Brovek nods his sympathy. "Let's go to my office, Lance." I have never seen Brovek's brown eyes so deep, nor heard his voice so gentle. "We'll find out what's happened to the heart."

Pete and I work well together. The incision is long but otherwise ordinary, and we work at it.

Brovek's disposal trick with his gloves is fun. I do it myself, sometimes. With my left hand I pull the right glove off, inside out, and ball it up in my left palm; then with right fingers and thumb I pull the left glove off, inside out, containing the right. Then I hang on to the fingers and stretch the cuff out like a sling shot, let-'er-go, and fire the whole package into a bucket. It makes a snappy ending to a good operation—if Brovek isn't around.

But I'm not there yet. Still closing.

Behind me my two favorite surgeons go shuffling out of the OR, and I hear Brovek's comfortable rumble. "I'll order in some coffee, Lance. We can wait there for Dana."

In mid-stitch my hand freezes. Did I hear him right?

For nine long years I have slaved under the man's critical eye. This is the first time he has ever called me Dana.

Dana

5:15 p.m.

We put in the last skin stitches, Pete and I. He applies the wound dressing and I write the orders.

Usually, at that point, I am finished. Free. But this case of Stern's is different. It's first-time, big-sky, spectacular stuff. His survival is both chancy and all-important—certainly for him. But it is equally vital for us in starting our transplant program here at the University.

So I follow the fragile body of Martin Stern as he is transferred to the recovery room. We make a small procession around the gurney: the M.D. anesthesiologist, a nurse anesthetist (at Stern's head, so she can squeeze the airbag), two attendants in scrubs to haul the oxygen tank and to keep its hoses connected to the airbag and to his endotracheal tube), another to push a couple of IV poles on wheels, their bottles clinking together as we roll along. And bringing up the rear: me.

In the recovery room I ensure that his connections get properly set up–IV, respirator, catheter, monitors, and the full attention of his own recovery nurse. I review my orders for his post-op support: hourly urine output, make-up and rate of his IVs, frequent blood pressure checks, monitoring of blood oxygen and continuous cardiogram—plus the constant, noisy, ungraceful respirator. The medical people will see to his medications for immunosuppression—a program essential for him now for as long as he lives. I feel sad that this pioneering man, so desperately ill and failing, has no family outside. No one out there waiting for word. No one to care about his groundbreaking chance for a new life.

Well, that's enough for now.

Uh-oh! I remember Brovek's summons to his office. Now?

No. Not this time.

Me first.

Not often in my servitude have I ever claimed priority. But now I do. I am spent. Eleven heavy and emotional hours in harness—and still counting. My feet are leaden; my eyes glazed. I've had it with my droopy scrub suit and my brown-blotched OR shoes. I can't abide my smelly, unfresh self, and I'm desperate for a john break.

Let Brovek wait. It's only twenty minutes.

But after a hot shower, hair scrubbed, toweled and combed, in fresh scrubs, and back in my own faithful, silent, low-heeled flats, I'm renewed. Brovek? Bring him on.

That's a euphemism, of course. What I really have to do is find him and log in. Here I am, master. What is your command?

But maybe, today—is there a new twist? Go to his office? Where he is waiting for "Dana"? I'm piqued.

I quick-step up to his sanctum. Fourth floor of New U. No sick beds here. It's academia. Along the hall I pass medical offices and exam rooms—I remember how squeezed Rudd's little office was—and move on to the end suite. Dr. Brovek's office. The Chief.

His anteroom stands empty, on Saturday eve. Low light. Lonely chairs. A bare secretarial desk, an IBM Quietwriter garaged under a black cover—I've heard her brag about it.

The door to Dr. Brovek's office, to the great man's inner sanctum, is ajar. Through the crack comes nothing I can hear, and only dim light.

He told me to come, didn't he?

I tiptoe to the door and peek in at a darkened mess. Like yesterday's birthday party. Rudd, in a wilted, blood-spotted scrub suit, has himself draped over the professor's worst chair. At his foot a cardboard cup lies crushed on the carpet, in company with a couple of twisted straws and a great smear of—what? Malted milk? Brovek looks no better. His splayed elbows roost on his unlit desktop, his chin cupped in his hands. He stares at Lance through a deep frown. Around him on the desk, more mess: a couple of paper plates blotched with ketchup and mustard, several crumpled napkins, the bun end from a hero sandwich.

The scene is not a celebration.
Brovek sees me, shrugs, says "Come in..."
I step into sadness.

Brovek

"...Join the celebration, Dana. I'm watching poor Rudd over there — he thinks he's destroyed himself."

"I'm glad I was with him when he...well, when it happened."

"I am too. Would have been disaster without you."

How does the girl do it? Rudd and I are drooping here like we were whipped and wrapped. She looks like she's fresh out of a shower. "I'm glad you were there. You did just right."

And she's smart enough not to say anything.

But Rudd needs something, I don't know what. And there she goes to stand beside him.

"Wilma called." I hate to say it again; it broke Rudd the first time. But Dana is just as deep in this as anybody is.

"The heart got put in at North County, but it was nearly six hours and it looks pretty shaky. Started a rhythm all right, but it's weak. May not be strong enough."

The report doesn't shake her. Like she expected it.

I can barely hear her. "We'll pray for it."

She puts her hand on Rudd's shoulder, and I remember what Horace Potts said after his aneurysm. Healing power in her touch — something like that.

"The heart is more symbolic, Lance. But we can hope for her liver. And tomorrow two people get kidneys."

There's more between them than I understand. Not my business, I guess.

"Her eyes, too, Dana. But it's not the same, is it?"

They're beyond my reach, those two. And it's getting dark in here. And too damn depressing. And I don't know what—

I shouldn't worry. Garrison comes firing up, and look at her go.

"Enough already! Brighten up, you guys!"

Taking charge, bless her heart. Right here in my office. One sweep of her arm—I gotta jump out of her way—and here goes the crap off my desk—all over the floor! And she flicks on the lights—I've gotta squint. Rudd sits up—I guess he's alive after all.

"Wake up, you guys. We have a grade-A jim-dandy patient down in ICU, and he's sporting a new liver. By Monday night our two kidneys will have people off dialysis so they can pee to their heart's content. Life goes on, and we have to grab the pieces we can reach."

Listen to her! Around me, she's always been such a mouse.

"Now, you two guys, quit drooping and start grabbing."

I'd like to grab a fistful of her, by God. This is the spirit I need.

From a woman? No. Potts is right: forget she's a woman; she's a surgeon!

Forget she's a woman? No, Horace. Not Dana. She's all woman. Yes. A woman *and* a surgeon. That works.

And she's got my blood running again.

But not Rudd. Poor bastard. He's hardly stirred. Hunched up on that terrible chair, staring at nothing.

"Lance, it's not the end of the world."

He moves a bit, speaks to me. I can hardly hear him. "I've got to resign, Chief. You can't have a surgeon you can't count on." Garrison's hand jumps to her mouth.

He's in shock. I won't hold him to anything he says. Insulin reactions need sugar, not suicide. I'll have to jolly him up a bit. "We've always known this could happen. All right. It happened. Your secret is out. But nothing else has changed."

"It could happen again tomorrow."

"Not with reasonable care. For nine years we kept it secret. It didn't happen."

"Nine and a half, Chief. And now it did."

He's sinking, like into quicksand. I check Garrison, but she's frozen. How can I get to him?

"You are the best research mind in the medical school, Lance."

No response.

"After me, of course."

Not a flicker.

"You can't throw that away."

He shakes his head. "My mind disappeared today. It just walked out. I can't be any good to you now."

No good? Who says? He's one hell of a good doctor, and he's got a job to do here. For me. Now.

He's getting me mad. I rise up on my feet, lean across the desk, spit fire at poor Lancelot. "Dr. Rudd, you operated on Martin Stern today. In my department that means you bust your ass to get Martin Stern well again. Now, hoist yourself out of that chair and go see your patient."

Aha. Color in his face. He has enough spark left to get mad. I'll blow on it. "The day that Stern walks out of here a well man, that day you come back in here to me. Get him well or get him dead; then we'll talk about what happens to you."

Furious, Rudd jumps up, kicks the chair over and storms out the door. Maybe we have a chance. "Dana! You better go along and make sure that Lancelot doesn't get lost."

I slouch over after them, turn off the ceiling light and slam the door. I need the gloom.

The loneliness of command comes down hard on a day like this. Someone gets an organ; another doesn't. One transplant works; maybe one doesn't. Who gets organs. Who gets hurt. Who survives. Who gets lost.

I drop into my chair.

And who decides? Me.

And who keeps score? Me.

It's part of the job—to add up what we want to happen, and learn what did happen, and see how sadly those results diverge.

Oh, Lotte... You were part of me once, and I need you still.

I fold my arms on the desk, cradle my head. These are heavy loads for me. Are they too much? How can I do better? Can I ever make things right?

I close my eyes. Breathe in, breathe out.

I can not sleep. I do not cry. I will not pray.

I let my mind run free.

PART FIVE

July 15, 2014

Easter Sunday

Dr. Brovek's free-lining was about Dr. Rudd, of course. After his collapse, did Rudd ever operate again?

You are ahead of the story. I'll get to him pretty soon.

What about you and your own surgery? Not just transplants, but vascular surgery itself. In later years you got into microvascular stuff.

Don't bring that up!

Oops. Sorry. That's when your trouble showed up.

Who knew? Those were the first signs.

Sorry, Dana. I shouldn't have mentioned it.

No harm. Yes, microvascular surgery is another huge advance in the last two decades. With the help of magnifying lenses, my fellow surgeons nowadays unite vessels as small as the lead in your pencil. Tiny needles, sutures like spiderweb. We can – well, they can – lift free grafts of skin and muscle that carry their own vessels, and replant them to reconstruct major defects from cancer surgery or trauma or burns.

Newspaper stuff. We hear about people who have lost arms or legs and had them sewed back on. Terrific. Why not use cadaver limbs to graft onto amputees?

Technically, that is doable. But transplants are more complex than their surgical mechanics. We find that immune suppression carries long-term risk. So the patient's problem must be worth that risk before it earns a transplant. Absent one hand? No. Two hands? Maybe.

When Rudd took my appendix out, there were all sorts of people who did things for me. Or to me. Nurses and aides mostly. But hospital doctors, lab people, respiratory technicians — even dietitians. I wonder why you never talk about them.

I've left the ancillary people out for good story-telling. Although they are anonymous in my story, there's no argument they're essential. In transplants, and in every other web of surgical care, they contribute mightily to good surgical results — as measured by survival, complication rate, infections, readmissions. I could never leave them out of real-life care.

Back to your story. All Brovek's down-and-dead business with Karen's organs, all his heavy decisions, happened on the day before Easter!

Almost poetic, wasn't it? Because next came a resurrection: Brovek needed a new surgeon.

And you got tapped.

Right place, right time. I could never replace Lance Rudd as a leader, as a model, but I caught the laurel on liver transplants. They became mine to do. Brovek kept the hearts.

Did you have any idea then that you'd ever be Chief of Surgery?

Hey, in those days I felt lucky to have a job. I had patients to worry about. And a lover I didn't have to worry about.

Rusty. We haven't seen him in the story lately.

The story, lately, has been in places Rusty couldn't go. But in odd moments he turned up and kept me dazzled.

A hell of a guy.

You ought to know.

You had it all.

Yes. For a few years I did. I was a happy surgeon.

At the dawn of a new era. What made transplants explode like they did?

One drug. Cyclosporine. That discovery lets us control the patient's immune response so it doesn't kill the transplant.

It's a bad thing, the immune response?

Not against measles and mumps! But in the same way that our T-cells attack infection, they recognize donor tissue as alien and attack it.

"Cyclosporine" — I Googled it — was found in the 1970s by Sandoz, a commercial pharmaceutical company. Good use of their research money!

By 1985, when my own story began, transplants offered a new world of opportunity. They became the core of ambition for major surgical centers everywhere. Dr. Brovek had to play, if not catch-up, then keep-up.

I suppose it was natural that hearts came first.

Well, kidneys first. But for immediately vital organs, and for public notice, hearts led the parade. Livers, too. But now, in 2014, look at what's happening. Transplants in children? Yes. No tiny donor liver? We can dissect an adult liver to make a donor organ small enough even for a baby. And it grows as the child grows. We — that is, surgeons somewhere — are doing lung transplants, either total or only a lobe. Intestines. Combos. Pancreas, intact or as islet cell replacement for diabetes. If there is a way to help a life-threatening condition by transplant, somebody will try it.

Brovek was right. He saw it coming.

He did. My boss. My mentor. He saw it and he wanted to be there. And he was. He made it happen.

He and Horace Potts. That's the next part of my story.

Potts

April 7, 1985

For Horace Potts, in his suburban Church of the Holy Sepulcher, the early Mass of Easter was a family tradition. The joyful celebration. Triumphant hymns, sung on this festive morning to the music of his church's great organ and three clarion trumpets.

Exiting in a crush of other worshippers, he inched his way up the long center aisle and through the narthex, and stood outdoors in the glorious warmth of the spring morning. He watched the families sorting themselves out, the women in bright colorful hats, the children skipping ahead for Easter baskets and festive breakfasts. After five minutes, he was alone.

As always, nowadays. Nearly forgotten, his scrape with death on New Year's Day. But this first Easter without his Catherine lay heavy on his heart.

He settled his black Chesterfield around his shoulders, squared his gray fedora, and drew a deep breath of the sweet air. No downers today.

With no plan in mind, he strolled down the street to his '84 Oldsmobile. Find breakfast somewhere. Maybe even in the hospital; he might see someone he'd know. And he could consider again the problem that nags at him every day: St. Luke's Church. Truly a failing parish. Only a single mass there today, on the highest feast of the year! A fine old church about to be displaced by—a hotel!

No! He feels strongly about that! Strongly troubled! The new hospital must go there, to make a single campus with the present institution. An impossible quest? Let it not be! For he himself must make it happen—Potts, the businessman. Or perhaps, Potts, the magician! Whatever it takes.

He turned his car into the small parking lot reserved for medical staff — he felt grateful to Brovek for a courtesy card. And there, by the entry door, stood Brovek's black Lincoln.

Why wasn't he home with Lotte?

Potts parked alongside and entered the hospital. He decided he'd skip breakfast in the cafeteria and go instead to check Brovek's office. Would the professor be there on a Sunday morning? On Easter morning?

Up a level he went, then down the hall to the Chief's end suite. No lights showing, but the door stood open. No one around. The inner door to The Man's sanctum was ajar. No light came through.

Potts tiptoed to that inner door and peered inside.

Chaos! The room smelled of old onions. On the carpeted floor a wastebasket showed a tangle of squashed cups and broken styrofoam. A cushion from the Professor's couch lay under a window, along with a shoe and a scrunched-up pillow from somewhere. Folded neatly over a chair back lay Brovek's coat and pants. And now in the far corner stood the great man himself, in wrinkled boxer shorts, gazing out the window, pissing in the sink.

Potts felt as if his feet were nailed to the floor.

Brovek turned, unperturbed, and grinned. "Good morning, Ho. I'm glad you're not the cleaning lady."

"I don't know about that, Sandy. You need her pretty bad in here."

Brovek washed his hands under the tap.

"It's been a hell of a night, Ho, and I've made plans. You are just the guy I want to test them on.... Oh!... Happy Easter."

Potts shook his head. Could he ever keep up with this mountain of energy?

He couldn't. Behind the professor's desk an imposing leather chair invited him to shelter, and he dropped into it.

What? It turned under him, spun toward the window. He grabbed the arms and swiveled back to face Brovek. "What happened in here anyway?"

"Oh, all this mess? It's quite a story." Brovek rummaged in a desk drawer under Potts's elbow and came up with a razor. At the sink again, he plastered suds over his face and scraped at his scrubby whiskers. "We had a day, Ho. We got ourselves a donor—heart, liver, lung, the works. We had a day!"

Good news for the program. Opportunity. Growth. But what about—? Potts's brow furrowed; his nagging question erupted from wherever he had buried it. What had the man decided to do with Martin Stern?

He held his breath.

Brovek splashed his face and wiped it clean. "Not a perfect day. Rudd had a little trouble."

"Come on, Sandy. Give me the story."

"I'm not sure about some of it, but by God it was a good day. We got our first liver done. We laid another cornerstone."

"Wonderful. But before I celebrate your milestone, I want to know about your millstone. Martin Stern. What did you do?"

Brovek marched to the chair where he had draped his trousers. "You knew damn well what I'd do. I gave him his liver."

Potts swiveled along, to follow Brovek. "If you'd said that weeks ago I'd have slept better. What was Rudd's trouble?"

"Shit happens. Too much work, not enough food. An insulin reaction knocked him out." Brovek sat down to pull on his pants. He jammed his foot into a shoe.

Potts swung the chair back and forth. He wondered if it could go all the way around and around, like his teacher's piano stool. Too bad about Rudd. Secrets are tough to keep, and now Rudd's diabetes is public knowledge. But he focuses on Brovek. "It could happen again, Sandy. What can you do to protect him? And his patients?"

Brovek abandoned his shoestring, looked up at Potts, all banter gone from his voice. "The first thing I have to do is get him to stay here. He wanted to resign yesterday. Pack up and get out."

"Oh, no! That's too much!"

"It is. I had to chew on him pretty hard before he got madder at me than he was at himself." He bent down again and tied his shoe. "But I made it. He's agreed to see Stern recover before we talk about his future. He'll be okay, I think." He looked about for his other shoe. Couldn't find it. Shrugged. "But you're right, Ho. We can't let him work for hours at a time without a break. He has to tend to himself. And that's part of my plan."

Potts nodded. What now, from the chief's expansive mind? He watched him pull a clean shirt from another desk drawer, pull it on and start on the buttons. "So what is your plan?"

"Expand, Horace. Expand." Brovek drew in a monstrous breath that threatened those buttons. Then his breath slid out in words about Rudd's future. "He's a first-rate investigator. Transplants of pancreas or islet cells for diabetes are a matter of time — time and research. Why not here? Why not Rudd? It's perfect."

"'Here,' meaning in our massive new facility."

"You know it."

Potts nodded. "St. Luke's again. Everything hinges on that. How did it go with Stern?"

"When Rudd smashed up, he was deep inside Stern. He might have ended my ethics problem right there. But Garrison stepped in like she was born for it. She took up Rudd's tools and never missed a stitch. All I had to do was watch."

Potts retrieved the other shoe from beneath the desk. "I'm glad of that, Dr. Brovek. I would hate to have things depend on a man who can't keep track of two shoes!"

He pitched the shoe at Brovek, and waved what else he had found beneath the desk: a bent soda straw. "You had a party here last night. Things like this can start rumors."

Brovek laughed, stepped into the shoe, jammed his heel inside. "That's why you're not a surgeon, Horace. We come to Garrison—I know she's the one you're itching to know about—and you fuss at a soda straw. A surgeon," he said, throwing a quick, hard bowknot into his shoelaces, "would go for the throat."

Potts let himself smile at his surgeon friend. His taut energy seemed to activate the air around him. Yes, Sandy. Go for the throat and maybe right in over your head. "But I do want to know about her. She was all I want her to be?"

"And more. You were right about her all along. She's got the balls, and she's smooth as cream. And with Rudd out of the OR, we'll need her here. She belongs with us."

Potts clapped his hands and dropped again into the professorial chair. "So we still have to get the church. How are we going to do that?"

Brovek faced the mirror with a smug smile, threw a smooth Windsor knot into his tie. "*WE*, Horace? *WE* don't get the church." He patted the tie and turned to Potts. "*YOU* do. I've given Stern his liver. Now it's your turn."

Potts shook his head.

Potts

Haven't I always known that Brovek's Quixotic mandate would drop on me? And why not? He could have no one better! Horace-Potts-the-businessman, moving in to break up Stern's contract and buy the church for the good guys.

But how to do it? Stern's dream for a hotel is as grand and dear to him as the new hospital is for us. Dollars won't move him. I'll have to find something else—another force, a new motivation—to make Stern move. The hospital gives me enough backing that I can make something happen. Real-world influence. But am I smart enough? To make him deal, will I find a key? Or need a crowbar?

Okay, Horace. Let the game begin.

"What's his chance now, Sandy?"

"Who the hell knows? He's our first one. Four-to-one, maybe. Give him a month and then he's yours to deal with."

"A month? No. Too long. He's in my ballpark now, Sandy. I'll give him two weeks at most—'til he's out of the hospital. Then I'll hit him while he's green—before he can write new contracts and commit more money."

"Sure, Horace. Hit him with what? Right now you haven't a clue. Or a key. Or a crowbar."

I retrieve my hat, stride to the door. "Happy Easter, Sandor. I think I'll take another drive around the neighborhood."

I forget breakfast. I go straight to my blue Olds, throw my hat and coat in the back seat, roll the windows down and move out into the deserted streets.

So.... I'm in a duel. Potts the civic leader against Stern the developer. And Stern holds the high cards.

They're always the same, these blocks near the hospital.

I've idled around, scouting the area many times before. Standing strong and alone: University Hospital. Across the street, our prize: St. Luke's. Everywhere else, all around, it's small commercial buildings, shabby apartment houses of two or three stories, side by side, alley to eave. Another block or two farther off, the freeway. The only possible space for us, to build our one united campus, is the church — the doomed church, with its spacious playground.

Okay, Horace. Make it happen. Find a way. Key or crowbar.

And when I pull it off, what's my prize? I'll sit Brovek down in his office chair and spin him dizzy.

Rudd

April 20, 1985

9:30 a.m.

"Excuse me, Dr. Rudd."

Standing inert by Stern's bed, I watch the young nurse check Stern's blood pressure. Then his temperature. And his urine output. His monitor. His respirator, and hoses. The routine observations that will become dots and numbers on his considerable chart. They have marginal interest to me. For nearly two damn weeks I've stood here looking at him, still unconscious. Still he wears a tracheal tube jammed through his nose, connecting his life to the huff and puff of his respirator.

But two weeks is too long; it's time he should wake up.

And past time I should be out of here. Leave the medical guys to monitor his liver tests and run his immune suppression. Team medicine. They don't need me. Except for Brovek the dictator, I'd be long gone.

Don't know where, just gone.

And here comes Dana. I should be invisible.

"You look dreadful, Lance. Can't you get some rest?"

I glare at her. She's floated into ICU in those silent shoes and found me—where else?—at my duty station. In her usual casual elegance she's posed across from me, Stern's chart clutched against her breast.

"Why shouldn't I look dreadful? All I've done for two damn weeks is stand beside this bed."

Not because I care about Stern. Nor about me. Neither of us is worth our cost. But Brovek writes the rules: "Get him well or get him dead; then we'll talk."

Talk, hell. When I'm done, I'm out of here.

But I can't say that to Dana.

I cock my head toward the nurses' station, and we move away from the bedside. I pull at my white coat, smooth the collar, and try on a smile. I'm surprised at the tension that releases around my eyes.

"Dreadful?" I put it to her. "Is that how you say hello? So how should I look?"

Maybe dreadful is right. I stand here because there's nowhere else to go. I check my only patient more often than my own blood sugar, and neither one is doing a damn thing.

But hey: I'm not the only one under stress. She looks like always—scrubbed cheeks, that elusive fragrance she wears. But she's too thin, and has shadows under her eyes. "Come to think of it, you look pretty scrawny yourself. How are you holding up?"

"You know how it is for a Chief Resident. You've been here."

"You ought to put that boyfriend on hold. He's hanging around here a lot."

By God, she can blush!

"I'll consider your advice, Doctor. Did you say I should hold on to him?"

Yes. Hang on to him, before.... Yes.... Before your world caves in.

I take the chart from her hands. "Go on with your rounds, Dana. I'll wait for lab results and then write some orders."

"Thanks, Lance."

I watch her small figure move off to her considerable responsibilities.

Wait for lab results? Nothing else to do. My assignment is Stern. Nothing else.

Ironic, because I don't care what happens to him. Who is he? A loner, like me. One step above nothing. No family. Nobody cares.

Except me. I do care. He's alive on Karen's liver, and I want her to survive. To become Martin Stern's liver. And today I think something's not right with him. Don't know what. I only feel it. You're two weeks out, Martin, and you've been okay so far. Except... Except what? Your lungs? Your precious liver? Rejection?

Something. You're pushing me. What do you need?

Against the white sheet Stern's arm moves. I adjust the IV tubing so it won't snag and have to smile at myself. It's a reflex response, built during those endless frustrating nighttime hours when I struggled, as an intern, to make IVs drip through steel needles stuck into clotted, used-up arm veins. Today? Stern has a central IV, a flexible little tubing that carries his fluids and meds right into his subclavian vein; it's a lot less fragile.

But everything carries risk.

What's going on with him? Rejection? Infection?

I need to shape up. Stern needs something. He needs his physician to think straight and nail this complication — whatever it is. ID it. Fix it.

If it even exists.

He is my patient. The question is: am I the right physician? Can I treat him properly, or should I holler for help? Am I his good doctor, right now, or do I get the hell out of the way?

It's close....

We're in this together, Martin. You as a builder. Me as a doctor. In our own ways, we each damn near died in the OR. And ever since, for two weeks here in ICU, I've been as useless as you are.

But if I can get you well again, make you be a builder again—maybe I can be a doctor again.

Dana

From ICU, I step out in quicktime for my first morning-hours tryst with Rusty. I asked him to meet me at the hospital's entrance. Symbolic. Will he remember our short foray outside and our first serious clinch? My heart pounds and my step is light, because I'm not in Hangarville any more. I've arranged for Pete to cover for me over the Memorial Day weekend. Yes! And Rusty doesn't know it yet.

And, as if we need more spice: if I'm late, he may not wait. He's gotten pretty aggressive about his writing. Every day that he doesn't fly "our" Cessna for the University, he's pounding out manuscripts on his "single-engine IBM." And now he's had an article accepted for publication by a magazine. We celebrated that last week in good old Keaton Amphitheater. Dear place. Love has intervened. My life became more than Brovek's six months.

It's all a stark contrast to my friend Lance. I'm about to strike fire; he lost the only hot love of his sequestered life.

Poor guy. Duty ruled, and he crashed. How could he not? If Dr. Brovek hadn't put him on a chain, he'd be out of here.

But not me! I'm in the lobby by the information desk; where is Rusty?

Of course, Lance's problem was only an insulin reaction: perfectly ordinary. I remember the sweet roll I offered him, not knowing then that he has diabetes. I wish he had eaten it! He wouldn't have crashed. But we were both in emotional turmoil. I tried one bite; it was like sand in my mouth.

If he'd had a little time for himself, he might have been okay.

I walk over to the entrance doors, looking for "that boyfriend." Where is he?

But on that fateful day I was the lucky one. Right place, right time to *step up, girl; take charge!* And I feel good about that. I did what I knew to do. And Dr. Brovek finally saw me—I think he did—for who I am.

And now, at last, for who I *know* I am.

Well, Rudd and Stern are a pair. I hope they survive. Both of them.

I look about the great atrium; no Rusty. I push through the entry doors, out on the great landing, into the fragrance of the April morning. Don't see him. I told him I could take a quick break. But…where is he?

I grab a couple of sweet, deep breaths and turn to go back inside. And here he is, with his mischievous grin, right in my face! He seizes my shoulders in his strong hands and pulls me in—no resistance—for a quick kiss.

"You rascal! Where were you? Did you follow me?"

His green eyes dance. "All the way from ICU. I'm researching a detective story: how hard is it to tail somebody?"

"How hard was it?"

"Look where we are, Dove. The second time in four months. Outdoors together. Fresh air. Sunlight. Take a deep breath."

Yes. He remembers. I'm busting to tell him about our break. But not too fast to savor the day. "Ten more weeks, Rusty. Then I'm out of here."

"With me?"

"Do you want me to be?"

"Like sun and air. For always."

"Don't play games, Rusty. When July comes I'm a free person."

"Not if I have a say about it."

"Meaning?"

"I'm serious, girl. You know how I feel about you."

"Do I?" Two people can play games, and I'm in the mood! "You haven't told me lately."

"You're too damn busy lately." He takes my hands, glances at people coming up the steps, looks into my eyes. "But now you're here."

"Yes. I'm here. Outdoors with you. In the spring sun and fresh air." Wait up, girl. What is he up to?

"Bond to me here, Dana... Outside your hospital... Seriously, Dove... Will you do me the honor — "

He stops. Lets the people go by. Shakes his wiry red-top head. Then: "Damn it, Dana, don't make me kneel here on the concrete."

My heart is pounding. "Go on, Rusty. What is the 'honor, seriously, Dove,' that I can do for you?" I want to grab him, hold him, twine my fingers in his hair, and say Yes-yes-yes. But I'm still a bit old-fashioned. I want to hear him say what he's stumbling around to say.

"Dana?"

"What, Rusty?"

"Right here on these hospital steps — "

"Yes?"

"I want — "

I've never before seen him hesitant about anything.

"Let's…. Dana—"

"I'm listening, Rusty. What—"

"Dr. Garrison. ICU, stat. Dr. Blue." I jump out of my skin, avulsed out of dreamland, a million miles from Bozo.

It's only April. It's not July. Rusty's got to understand. I whirl and hit the hallway double time.

What is there in life that my profession may not demand of me?

Dana

I had no choice. Jumping fast to a Code Blue is a prime obligation for house physicians like Pete and me. And I know my quick response was important to our successful resuscitation. I was the first doc there.

But I sure didn't like being torn away from Rusty at that lifetime moment—and it must have been bitter gall for him.

But now I'm free—could it be an hour already? I grab a phone, punch in his numbers. It dings once, he picks it up, and I give him no chance. "Hello, my dearest Bricktop. Will you still talk to me?"

He doesn't miss a beat. "Did you save a life? Anything less, I may be inconsolable."

"I'm already inconsolable. But yes. Dr. Blue saved the day."

"But he did a job on us…on me."

"I want a rematch. Come over for lunch."

"You might bug out and leave me with the check."

"Don't let's talk about bugging out. I feel destroyed already."

"Don't be. Bozo has no heart."

"Right. But it's only ten weeks 'til I rip his batteries out."

"Ten weeks is too long a damn time for me to put my life on hold."

Oh, ouch. Didn't he accept being on hold? I rein in my heart. We settled that way back in winter! Didn't we?

Surely my fear reflects in my words. "Yes, Rusty, it is too long. And if there was anything I could do about it" — I can't tell him now! — "I'd have done it long ago."

"I'm thinking there's not much you can do about it in the future, either. I want a wife, a full-time partner. You'll always have to put me second."

"I'll have obligations, Rusty. That's normal. You'd tire of me quick-time if I sat home and did laundry."

"I'd also tire of a wife who splits when the phone rings. And I'm tired right now of a wife who can't come to bed at all. I was about to ask you to — well — I didn't. I caught on in time, Dana."

Dana. That's my name with friends. Rusty calls me — has always called me — Dove.

Cool it, girl. Give him room. "Okay, my friend. Take a break."

For sure, don't beg. What is, is; say goodbye. But don't lock the door. And I will not cry…. Not while he can hear me…. "I'd have said yes, you know."

The phone carries only a faint electric sound that it's alive. Like me, perhaps. "But I hope, if either of us has news, we're still friends enough to share."

He says nothing. Maybe he's not there. I cradle the phone.

It's one more sacrifice — of my own person, of me — that I have made to my career. And it's the bitterest one of all.

But I can't go back. Not now.

April 23, 1985

The longest, bluest days of my servitude. I feel no pleasure in my work. I resent the ineptitude of Duane, my new junior resident. I even snapped at a nurse who brought me the wrong instrument package. Apology can't make it up to her, and I feel worse. I'd feel better if I could sleep at night. Even without calls, I toss on my cot, wakeful, crabby.

And right this minute I am challenged to be gentle. Duane's young patient has a pneumothorax — an uncommon result with a broken rib. But there it is. Duane put in a chest tube, connected it to a jug of water on the floor. But he can't get it to bubble. The x-ray shows the tube in place all right, inside the chest cavity, but the left lung is still hanging there like a busted balloon.

Well, it's minor trouble, easy to fix. We cut the skin stitch, wiggle the tube, and bubbles begin a nice unsteady disturbance in the water bottle.

I wish Rusty was that easy.

Stern

May 10, 1985

I must be getting better. Out of the stalag at last, that they call ICU. No more oxygen hoses, no IV, no monitor. Martin Stern in a normal hospital bed. And this morning — wonder of wonders — I came awake with an erection. For the first time since the other side of darkness! By God, I'm getting well after all!

Morning sun floods my room. Baruch Hashem.

I climb out of bed and poke a foot around for my slippers but come up bare. I grab a more urgent need, the plastic handle of my urinal. Another new blessing! Gone the long tether that drained my bladder for the last five weeks. Master of the Universe! A man should not take simple things for granted.

I splash cold water over my face, dry it with a scratchy white towel that I toss under the sink. I settle carefully into my one sittable chair and feel something else new and wonderful: an appetite.

No more trays in bed. I'll wait for the soft thud of a nurse's foot against my door, and it'll swing open, reveal her smiling face with a tray of — what will it be — oatmeal?

I drum my fingers on the chair's wooden arm. My stomach growls. If it's oatmeal, it might even be hot; it should be here already.

How long did they have me trussed up there in ICU? It's nothing I can know or count: my brains and the days are all blurred together, in a miserable slurry. Like a day of atonement it was, nonstop, with no nightfall.

Now, they tell me, we are into May. And I'm alive again. As weak as wet straw! But I can start to plan, study specs, make contracts. Time is running. I've lost a lot of fair weather to get started on Stern Towers.

A bump on the door; it swings open into the room. But I see no smiling Nightingale face. Only Ben's scrub-suited green tuchas, as the silent orderly moons his backside through the doorway. He's trailing a wheelchair.

Dreck. Again? Too many times already the tiny Hmong has wheeled me away, on too many litters, for X-rays, scans, biopsies. Jerky elevators. Torture. All in Asian silence.

But now: a wheelchair. Progress maybe?

Ben pivots it around, locks the wheels, points to me and then the chair. Never a word. But two messages, and I understand both: *climb in,* for him, and *no breakfast* for me.

At the nursing station Ben stows a metal-jacketed chart on my lap. I check the double label: "Stern M," and "Dr. Rudd."

Correct.

But this morning, Stern-M is me, and I'm alive again. "Young lady!"

No response.

"Miss!"

At the desk a startled young woman in white looks up.

"May a person ask what is happening to him this morning?"

"Oh, good morning, Mr. Stern. You are to go to Keaton Amphitheater. It's Grand Rounds today."

"What about breakfast?"

"We'll hold it for you, okay?"

I've heard it a zillion times. "Okay?" they say. But it's not a question; it's a sign-off. Let it go, Martin. You'll know soon enough where it is you're going. "Keaton Amphitheater?" Outdoors, maybe?

Down we go, three or four floors in the jerky elevator. But it doesn't hurt this time. Along a dim hallway we roll and stop at a narrow doorway. Ben reaches past me, pulls the door open, and shoves me — what? where? — into a blinding, bright light.

I squint and have to shade my eyes. I'm on a stage, for God's sake? Rows of faces peering down at me — like a theater. No. It's what they called it — an amphitheater. An arena, already. Who the hell are the people up there? Young folks. Some white coats. A nurse or two up near the top. I should have worn my glasses.... Shit.... I haven't even shaved yet.

I squirm around in the wheelchair. Up a few rows I spot my savior, Dr. Rudd. But who's down here, with me, in the pit? Lions?

No. Here comes that lady doctor — Garrison. Walking right up to me.

"Good morning, Mr. Stern."

Her message is clear: "Do not answer." I bite my tongue.

"This is a teaching conference of the surgery department. We are all physicians, nurses, students, here to learn about your kind of problem. Okay?"

Okay again. It's code is what it is. "Shut up" is what it means. Go along with the program. But I could have worn my slippers, for God's sake.

Dr. Garrison turns to the crowd, taps a fingernail on the metal chart. Her short, white coat fits good across her shoulders. Very neat backside.   She's talking to the balconies. Not to me.

Why should such a short person wear flat shoes? Her feet hurt, maybe?

"About five years ago this patient developed sclerosing cholangitis..."

Hey! That's me! My story here?... all these people?

" ...Despite steroid therapy his liver tissue degenerated, squeezed out by increasing scar tissue. In January he was placed on the waiting list for a liver transplant."

That day I remember! In Rudd's office. My chance for a new liver that had to be a gift. And the same day I bought up the bishop—with my crazy offer he couldn't refuse. Maybe I found a new way to do business!

" ...And we never have enough donor organs...."

Problems. Everybody's got problems. They've wheeled me out here, a big shot, already, with my bare feet sticking out. Tied in. Can't fix my own blanket. Where the hell is Ben?

"...Missed chances... Need better protocol—"

But Rudd got me a liver, like he said he would. If he'd done it back then, I'd have the church torn out by now. Even foundations dug, maybe.

"Lost opportunities, while his liver function got worse and worse—"

The young lady doctor talks like she knows it all. Nice voice. Low and husky. I think I heard it before, back there in the fog.

" ...almost died...hepatic failure...coma. We had to decide if he was too far gone for a transplant."

What's she saying...? Too far gone? That's what they'd have said if they'd found out I own the church. Sorry, Martin. Too bad, Mr. Stern.

But they never found out, and here I am.

Where is Dr. Rudd? There, on the left. In the fifth row. Blessings on his house.

But hell, I missed the operation! What's she saying?

"...five weeks ago. He's had a tough recovery."

Look who says it was tough! Let me tell her about tough!

"He stayed on the ventilator for fourteen days before we could wean him off."

Mostly, I was out of it. The end I remember — the hose in my nose, the machine pumping air into me, how I gasped for air when they turned it off. I damn near died — and wished I could. Except that old priest, sitting there sometimes. I owe him something.

She's still telling. It's too much attention. My stomach's growling. Master of the Universe, when's the last time I was hungry?

"...he developed fever. Was it rejection of the graft?"

She's still talking about me? Enough, already.

"Or some hidden infection? Three times we studied needle biopsies of his new liver. No rejection."

Three times? Like, five times with the big needles. Five times if you count the times you jabbed into me and didn't get anything.

She's still talking. "... sputum.... Pneumocystis... trimethoprim..."

Don't they know any real words? Sounds like code. Who knows...

"...immune suppression...the new disease called AIDS."

AIDS I didn't have! Pneumonia I had. Bad enough without AIDS, God forbid.

"...discontinued the ventilator...began to eat...stitches out...up and around..."

What good does it do I sit here while she talks? They should bring a dummy in. Dress a dummy up like Martin Stern; let a dummy sit here in a wheelchair. Who's to know? I could have had breakfast already.

"We expect he'll leave the hospital within a few days. Are there any comments?"

I look down at my bare feet, uncovered, sticking out there in plain sight. With a bunion, for God's sake. I feel naked and diminished.

A voice from up in the seats asks something, and Garrison talks more big words, and then a new voice booms out. A deep rumble. Everybody sits up to listen.

Deference. I know it well. I get it from architects and subcontractors. That big voice has to be the top boss. The Dr. Brovek I've heard about. Easy to find him, third row on the right. I didn't know Brovek was so big.

"Well, thank you for coming in, Mr. Stern." Garrison again. Behind her the silent Ben, like a magic genie.

Not so fast. It's not a dummy in this wheelchair. You're through with my body? You'll trundle me back to my cold oatmeal. If you need me again, you just send old Ben along to haul me, hell, anywhere you want?

Nuts.

You're forgetting somebody. Me. Martin Stern. And I've got my macho back. "Does a person get to say something here?"

Garrison jumps like I pinched her behind, and I wish I had. I look up at all those faces peering down. What the hell should I say?

"Surely, Mr. Stern." Garrison. "If you need to, you may say something."

I don't need to, Doctor, girl. I just want to. Complain? Kvetch? They'd never even hear me. Give Dr. Rudd a plug, maybe? "Many of you had a hand in my care—you should pardon the expression. So I should thank you for my new life. But specifically I give thanks to Dr. Rudd, who never stopped fighting to get my new liver."

I squint up at all those faces staring down at my bunion. No reaction. Did they even listen?

But look at Rudd! Red face. Scowling. Angry? My compliment is a bad thing?

What about Brovek? He's picked up too; he's paying attention. But he's not upset. More like he's been dealt a new hand.

Okay, Martin. You've plucked a string. Pluck it again, quick, before they shut you down. "Maybe a person..." What'll it be? Not another compliment. Sting them a little?... Yes: " ...Maybe a person should be so grateful he forgets what was bad, and swallows it."

I stop, wait. It might be a cue for somebody; who will pick it up?

Garrison is stalled. Rudd looks whacked. Nothing.

Then, Brovek: "We would like to hear what you mean, Mr. Stern, if you want to get something off your chest."

Oh, good! I like a measured response like that. Smart. If there's a problem, it's not Brovek's.

I enjoy this kind of debate. Like *pilpul*. Start nowhere, end up—somewhere. But it takes care. Sharp words win no friends. I let the words come out.

"It is hard for a person to be a patient in your hospital. He gives up control of his body, while you do your tests and procedures. He has no choice. But *you* have a choice. It is a bad thing if you work on his body and forget that a person is living inside it."

I like the sound of that. If they don't respond, I'll still be glad I said it.

I watch Brovek. Nothing.

I rub the scratchy stubble on my jaw. I look to Rudd. Eyes narrowed. Aha! He's into this somehow.

"Do you feel we have failed you in some way, Mr. Stern?"

Hang tight, Martin. You have a rare chance here. Don't mess it up.

"Your miracle, Dr. Rudd, can't be a failure. But all those long weeks, wasting away, waiting for my liver, who gave me hope? Nobody in your program. Who kept at me, made me fight and not give up? A stranger, that's who. You made my miracle happen; but an outsider made it possible."

Rudd's face looks all screwed together. "Are you saying that without that personal support" — his eyes are on me like black lasers — "you would have died?"

I forget the staring faces. "Dr. Rudd, as God is my witness, I would have quit. Yes, I would have died."

There. I decided to say something, and look what came out! I sit back; I'm ready for Ben and for breakfast.

But no. From down in my insides, new words tumble into my mouth and I say them: "There is a hole in your program, Dr. Rudd, and you ought to fill it."

Dynamite! Rudd's flushed face turns to fire. He rocks back in his seat as if stunned.

What did I say that would rock him like that? And what about Brovek?

No. The bomb has missed the boss. "Thanks, Mr. Stern. Every patient has challenges to meet; he has little choice but to go along with the program."

Okay. I've said my piece. I sit back. Time for breakfast.

Oh? Not yet! Dr. Rudd jumps to his feet. Look at him. He's talking too loud.

"No, Dr. Brovek. We can't let it go like that. This is testimony of a real deficiency. I have heard the same opinion from — from someone else."

There's a catch in his voice. Sit down, Dr. Rudd. You'll get fired. Nobody talks to his boss like that.

"If our transplant program is deficient, it's our job as physicians to fix it."

I look to Brovek. Fireworks?

No!

Brovek's face is a sharp-eyed mask, like he's playing a new hand. "Very recently we started a support program of that sort, under the direction of the late Miss Sondergaard. Perhaps we should renew it. This time under a physician." He swivels his great shoulders around square on to Dr. Rudd. "Lancelot, you feel strongly about this program; may I count on you?"

There's a surge-current of energy between these men, something extra, deeper than their words. There is more on the table than some program or other. Brovek looks like a cat with cream, and Rudd's slump is gone. He's looking at Brovek with a serious face and a trace of a smile. A curious expression, like — affection? or gratitude? There's more message here than the words can carry. "Yes, Dr. Brovek. You may count on me."

Let's go, Ben. We're out of here.

Ben wheels me to the elevator, but I beat him to the button.

Something big happened here this morning, because I rocked their boat. I, the builder. They don't know me yet, but I own their church.

I'm back.

No oatmeal for me. It's gotta be bacon and eggs on a day like this.

Dana

May 14, 1985

"Okay, Dr. Garrison?"

Yes. I suppose something must be "okay." I nod to the anesthesiologist, and our patient slips into lethe. I go back to work.

No matter the reason, cracking the chest is a big deal. Turning the anesthetized patient to his side. Supporting both arms safely out of the way. Padding and protecting pressure points. Securing sterile drapes over a curved surface.

But we learn procedure by being part of it, and Duane is doing it for his first time. I bite my tongue and hold tight; I'd have it done by now.

I'm not happy about this case anyway. We make the big incision, cut a lot of muscle, maybe strip a rib and take it out, then put in the metal spreader with its gears that crank the ribs apart and open up a major body cavity. And all for what? To identify a lung nodule seen on the chest x-ray, most likely benign and of no significance.

Not like the days of pain that follow.

I'd like to find a better way. Some day maybe, with x-ray guidance, we'll be able to biopsy a lesion like that by needle.

"Come on, Duane. Get the drapes on and let's go."

Careful, girl. Be unhappy if you must. But don't take it out on the people you work with.

At last I move in with Duane, do the cutting, spread the ribs, and admire again the beauty of the chest cavity. Glistening pleural surfaces. The firm, speckled lung losing its inflation and turning marshmallow-soft. The nodule is easy to feel. I gather it in my fingers, apply a stapling clamp across the lung tissue at my fingertips, fire the staples and cut away the specimen. While the pathologist identifies the nodule—some harmless old inflammation called a *granuloma* — I make sure the cut lung is air tight, punch in a chest tube through a stab wound, and begin to close.

It's a good, neat, successful surgical operation. Once upon a time it would have given me joy.

Rudd

Lance Rudd, BS, MD, Alpha Omega Alpha, Diplomate, Fellow—my office wall proclaims my credentials as a doctor of medicine, and a surgeon. Six weeks ago I was all of that. Also a prideful, go-to guy who retrieved live organs from nameless cadavers, and the anchorman for liver transplants.

Then suddenly my cadaver was Karen; the precious beating heart was Karen's beating heart; the liver bore her DNA. I should have shut out the world.

But duty allowed no delay. She is my own true love? Suck it up. I'm in grief? Cry some other day. Diabetic? Bluff it out. In her transplanted heart she can live on; her liver and her kidneys will give new life.

So, like a tin soldier, I marched to work.

I smothered my grief and harvested—oh God, how could I?—her heart! Implanted her liver! And crashed, in that shameful, preventable insulin reaction, my skills wiped out, my secrets exposed, my integrity thrown into doubt.

I resigned. I meant to walk away. But Brovek seized me. "Get Stern well" — that was his order: "Get him well, or get him dead; then we'll talk about you."

So now he is here, waiting in my examining room for a post-op check. I expect to find him well and discharge him from surgical care.

Then I'll go to work on me.

Physician, heal thyself?

All the shards of my shattered life are linked to Martin Stern. My collapse in the OR. My desolation at his bedside. His sneaky atypical pneumonia, a tricky challenge that I ferreted out. And his recovery, that I had a hand in. And then my shake-up in Grand Rounds when Stern nailed us with Karen's own words, and Brovek offered her program to me, and my insides caught fire.

Yes, I can heal myself.

And to begin, I must be straight with Martin Stern.

In my adjacent exam room, he gives me his usual grouch about his paper sheet. I make a weak joke.

He looks good. No jaundice. His face is rounding out from his cortisone. But his belly is flat. No more ascites. His new surgical scar is thick and red, and healing well. It's at least triple his old cholecystectomy scar. But incisions heal from side to side. How long they are counts only in stories.

"You're good, Mr. Stern. Your wound is healed. You've made a total turn-around from last January. Today I can dismiss you from my surgical care."

He grins, adjusts the sheet over his lap. "So I just take my pills and live forever, right?"

It's a joke, and I grin back. "You know it is absolutely essential that you follow up with our medical people. They'll monitor your liver function and your immune status, and watch for rejection."

"But not you?"

"Only if you need more surgery."

"God forbid! I have a hotel to build. And for that I thank you always, Dr. Rudd."

Thank me? Hear the whole story. Then we'll see. "When you have dressed, Mr. Stern, please come in to my office. There is something I must tell you."

When he comes, I won't want the desk between us, so I roost my behind on its front edge. At my knee is the chair where Karen sat and shared her dream. Where she stood to let me pass—but I didn't pass—and we came together like magnets in our blazing affair that lasted two beautiful weeks, and crashed.

Now, today, this chair will hold her again, in the person of Martin Stern.

His brown gabardine drapes loosely on his frame. He looks about and settles himself on Karen's chair.

How should I begin?

"Thank you for coming to the Grand Rounds conference. It may have seemed needless to you, but it helps students to see a real person. They get their fill of books."

"Probably I talked too much."

"No. I'm glad you spoke your piece. No one else could have said what you said."

"One thing was too much, maybe. I bragged you up for fighting to get my liver, and you turned all red."

There is my opening. To start a fresh slate, I have to wipe the old one clean.

"Mr. Stern, these last weeks have been difficult, not only for you, but also for me. I need to tell you two things that happened. Both concern you, and what I did for you. Okay?"

"'Okay' is a word I've heard enough. Talk already."

"I had a bad spell during your surgery. I could not finish your operation. Only the skill and dedication of Dr. Garrison and Dr. Brovek brought you safely through."

I watch his face. His eyes are like steel. One cheek twitches. His lips move, as if he is calculating. Then: "So you were not the only one to fight for me? Thank God for them, then."

"In fact, Mr. Stern, the person you have to thank the most for your new liver is Dr. Brovek himself."

Stern shrugs, shifts on the chair. "Dr. Brovek? I haven't had the pleasure. He was the big voice in the conference?"

Big voice? For sure. "Yes. He is our chief. And he wants to meet you. I am to bring you to his office when we're through here today."

Stern frowns, shakes his head. "Maybe a person has plans? I could have appointments to go to."

"He was insistent. I hope you will come." I squeeze past him and pause by the door.

Stern nods, as if he holds all wisdom. "If I do not show, it would be bad for you. So it is for you I accept the kind invitation of Dr. Brovek." He stays in his chair.

"I have no idea what he wants."

"A big donation is what he wants." He does not turn to me, now behind him. "Maybe to buy a big-enough gown to cover my tuchas. For that I might listen."

"His office is down the hall from here."

"Not to go so fast, Dr. Rudd. Two events, you said. Your bad spell is one. Number two is Dr. Brovek in some way?"

I want to duck. To turn away. I swallow cotton.

But before I can rebuild, before I can heal, I must erase every blot, every lie, every stain of my unhappy memory. My clammy hands tremble, and I lean back against them on the doorframe. It would have been easy to slide past this part.

"The second is Dr. Brovek, yes. Some of us, myself included, thought your liver was too far gone for you to survive a transplant. We wanted to send the donor liver... away. Dr. Brovek stood alone. He insisted that it should go to you, and he made it happen. He was right. I was not your champion, Mr. Stern. Dr. Brovek was."

Neither of us moves. His expression is impenetrable. Grave. Then: "Dr. Rudd." He draws a long breath. "The truth is always good to tell...even if it is too much." He gets to his feet, checks the knot of his tie, looks at me. "You are a good man. May your troubles lose their sting." He adjusts his coat. "Now," he motions to the door, palms up, "introduce me to this big voice Brovek."

Potts

The arrangement of furniture in Brovek's office is not my usual business. I don't even belong here. But our meeting with Stern is critical, and I'm the guy, businessman Horace Potts, who has to make it work.

"Why put a chair over there, Horace? In front of my window?"

"That's where I'll sit, Sandy. When Stern checks me out, he'll have the sun in his eyes."

"Are you planning a battle? I thought this was a business meeting."

Different folks. Brovek is a professor. A scientist. In business he'd be eaten alive. "It is a business meeting. And a critical one. Your first chance, your best chance—and maybe your last chance—to get your church."

"You scare me."

"Good. You gave Stern his liver, all by yourself. And you stuck me with the job of bagging the real estate. All by myself. Okay. I have made preparations."

"You moved a chair."

"More than that, Sandy. I'm ready. You'll see."

"You damn well better be ready. But I'd have waited a couple more weeks. He's not well yet."

"Catch him when the tear is in the eye. Don't let it get out on the cheek."

"Hell, Horace, we don't know if he's grateful at all."

"What we know is, he's a shrewd and honest negotiator with legitimate goals for profit. He intends a huge development for our property. I doubt he'll be a willing seller."

"If he's grateful enough, he ought to give it to us."

"Don't hold your breath for that! No. We have to move big to make this deal happen. In the last several days I've taken on a major gamble."

"Then you'd better do the talking."

"You're the authority figure. He doesn't know me at all."

The professor grunts, fusses with a sheaf of architectural drawings rolled up under his desktop lamp. "Okay. I'll put our problem to him. But he's a businessman like you. You'll have to step in if there's a fight."

Oh, no! "No fight, Sandy. That's a definitive no-no. Must not happen. We would lose for sure."

"We've given him his life."

"You were supposed to do that. Forget it. He has our property. We want it. If you make him mad, the chase is o—"

At a quick rap on the doorframe, I clamp my mouth shut. Lance is there with Stern. Through the doorway I glimpse the man who controls St. Luke's Church and Brovek's future.

Rudd ushers him to the front of the desk, makes the intro. "Dr. Brovek, this is Martin Stern. Mr. Stern, you met Dr. Brovek at the conference."

Brovek rises to greet him. "Thank you for coming in, Mr. Stern. Here in my office we can have a more personal meeting."

Stiff response. "The other one was personal enough."

"Different perspectives, sir."

Ritual handshakes across the desk. I place a chair for Stern at the desk and retreat to my window. He squints in my direction and sits. Rudd retreats.

Brovek settles into his desk chair. "You have been through a dramatic few months. I am pleased for your fine recovery."

Stern nods. "It is a miracle. After five years of being sick that didn't do my business any good. My thanks to Dr. Rudd."

"Dr. Rudd is a fine surgeon. He did superb work for you. We are proud of him—and of you."

Stern says nothing. He's barely polite.

Brovek is sailing without a chart. "Dr. Rudd would be the first to tell you that a fine outcome like yours requires the cooperation of a whole host of people besides himself."

"He told me that already."

Maybe Stern is a poker player. But a poker face is not what we want from him.

Sandy tries again to get him engaged. "Part of my job, Mr. Stern, is to develop all those special people into a coordinated program, so that we can help patients like you. Kidney transplants. Hearts and lungs. We are starting a research program for diabetes. Your Dr. Rudd will direct it. If we can find the funds."

Rudd jerks in surprise but is wise enough to be still.

Not Brovek. He goes on about money. "We need to grow here, Mr. Stern. We can become a major national center for transplants and for research. But development takes very much money."

Stern doesn't twitch. "Everybody wants money." As if he is bored. "Join the race."

Stay cool, Sandy!

"We have an expansion project in mind. This gentleman on your left is Mr. Horace Potts, a member of our board. He is the leader of our development efforts. I want you to meet him."

I stand and stick my hand out to Stern. I have to hold it there. He searches my eyes, looks over my Brooks Brothers jacket, white shirt, bow tie. His dark eyes return to my face. And I size him up, too. He has played his share of commercial poker, this man; he knows to count cards.

He touches my hand, a light flick, then turns away and sits.

He's going to be a tough mark, Martin Stern. He's seen us coming, and he doesn't want to play. And I see that telltale red tinge begin its creep over Sandy's collar. I mustn't wait too long to get in the game.

But Brovek picks it up. "We hope, after your 'miracle' here with us, that you may feel some interest in our…institution. That you may want us to grow, so we may help more people as we helped you."

Stop talking, Sandy. We'll go nowhere unless we get him to open up.

I give that a shot. "A few months ago, Mr. Stern, I went through emergency surgery here. I personally feel very grateful to this institution for saving my life. I suppose you may feel somewhat the same way."

Aha. Stern swings around, squinting, to stare at me. His lip curls. "Ain't that nice, Mr. Potts. So you know how I feel?"

Bingo!

"But no, you don't know how I feel."

Open up, Mr. Stern. Blow your cool.

"Yes, my liver is a miracle. I'm glad to get well. Not quite Auschwitz was it, but for my worst enemy I wouldn't wish it to go through again."

"No, sir. Of course not." Talk some more, Mr. Stern.

"So the Riviera it wasn't either. Now I want to get out of here and forget about it. Thanks for the memories."

I don't care what he says! He's off dead center!

And here goes Sandy, giving another try. "You certainly are due a change of scenery. The Riviera might be just right. But before you go, I hope for some help from you."

We've cracked his dam, and now the waters pour through.

"Dr. Brovek, in my wallet is my driver license. My birth date doesn't say yesterday. For your pitch I was ready the minute Dr. Rudd said to come over here. You are talking maybe to the wrong guy."

I almost laugh at that. No, Mr. Stern. It's the other way around: the wrong guy is talking to you! Sandy is huffing up, fingering his plans. He'll go for the throat, and maybe over his head.

But I'm too slow. Sandy barges on.

"No, Mr. Stern. You are the right guy. We are at a crossroads here at the University. We want to grow and lead this nation to a glorious future in transplant surgery. We must grow now, expand now, or we will wither on the vine. We need your help."

Now he's got Stern's back up. He's too smart to be angry, but he could close his mind and shut us out.

"You are pushing me, Dr. Brovek. Pushing I don't like. For my miracle I don't even have a bill yet. Probably I'll need another miracle to pay for the first one." He lurches to his feet, kicks his chair back. He leans over Brovek's sacred desk, his hands only inches from those scrolls. He hisses his words like projectiles. "I don't want to be ungrateful. Also, I will not be pushed. So don't ask me for your big donation. Let me go to get acquainted with my last dollar, if I still have it."

He rears up from the desk and wheels toward the door, pointing a bony finger at his surgeon. "Dr. Rudd, maybe you'd be so kind to show me out of here."

Rudd stands up, helpless. Brovek is lost. Stern is moving. We are a millisecond from failure.

And my moment has come. After a thousand imaginary rehearsals, I step in to center stage. "Mr. Stern!" — my words like a javelin at his retreating spine—"we don't want one dime from you."

I watch that loose sack of dull tweed moving to the exit. Will it stop?

He balances over braking feet, slowly, slowly turns back to face me.

Our dynamic has reversed. I lift Stern's chair back into position and offer it to him.

"I'll stand."

As I am standing, my hands folded together at my waist. If there's a saint for new hospitals, I'm praying to him. "Hear me, sir. It is absolutely vital to our institution that we expand. Dr. Brovek would be pleased to show you conceptual drawings of our proposal—a beautiful modern hospital integrated into our existing campus. Our difficulty is—location. We must build it exactly on the site of old St. Luke's Church."

"So buy it."

"We hope to, sir. It belongs to you."

I expected him to be surprised. I did not expect shock! His eyes go wide, his mouth hangs open. He spreads what look like guardian fingers across his belly. He sinks slowly onto the chair.

"You know?" His voice is a whisper.

"Yes. We know that."

"The old priest said he wouldn't tell."

"Father O'Leary? He didn't tell."

"Then how...?"

"The bishop told me. Weeks and weeks ago. He and I are old college friends."

When the waters move, let them find their way.

Stern turns to Brovek. "You knew?"

Brovek nods. "Since February."

"Rudd says he didn't fight for me—you did."

"I'm afraid that's true, too. Yes."

Stern retreats into a tight frown then brightens a bit. "But you figured if you let me die, you'd get somebody else owning the property, somebody tougher than me."

I step in here. "We know the terms, Mr. Stern. Dr. Brovek always knew the terms. One million dollars cash. The option is to you alone, as an individual, and is non-transferrable. If you died, the bishop would keep the money and sell the land to us. You see, we do know the terms."

His brow dips once—he's heard me. But his eyes stay fixed on Brovek. "You knew? Always you knew? And still you fought for me?"

"That is our mission here, Mr. Stern. That is what we do for our patients."

"You knew? And still you found me a liver?"

Brovek nods. "I never considered anything else, Mr. Stern."

Oh, Sandor. You are a pillar of virtue!

Stern nods. "So now I build my project."

I reclaim my alpha position. "Yes. We think your project is impressive, Mr. Stern. We would like to see it prosper. Perhaps another site nearby would be even better for you."

He squints again at me. Briefly. Reverts to Brovek: "You knew? You had your site in your hand if I died, but instead you gave me a liver. And now you ask me, please Mr. Stern, to walk away from a million dollars? Meshugge. I don't understand you, Dr. Brovek."

Catch the moment, Horace. Don't let it fall! "Look, Mr. Stern. You don't have to walk away. Exercise your option, buy the property, and then resell it to us. You come out a wash."

Aha! There's glitter again in his eyes. Straight in his chair, feet tucked beneath, he's not walking out on us now. He's joined the game. More, he likes it.

"A wash, Mr. Potts? Washes are for losers. A winner like me takes a project to completion and makes money. If for some good reason I back out, I don't wash. A little value rubs off already, just for the experience."

He's dealing. I can breathe again.

And if he's dealing, it's time at last for me to take center stage. No drifting now. I have crafted a scenario, the biggest gamble of my life. To draw Stern in. Keep Brovek out. And win that little red church for the good guys.

My lines start with a chimera. Be still, Sandy!

Scene one:

"One way or the other, Mr. Stern, we are going to add our new hospital directly to the present one. One campus. We want the church site. But if you insist on building your project there, we will have to face our grand entrance the other way. Your site would face our loading docks. Your guests could watch our dumpsters."

Score! Stern's face goes dark.

Please, Lord. Don't let Sandy say anything. We looked at that plan a thousand times; it would never work. I keep talking, so Brovek can't sink our boat.

Scene two:

"On the other hand, Mr. Stern, if we build on the church site, we would have every desire to cooperate in whatever you do nearby."

Stern is listening, but he sees the obvious problem. "No, Potts. It doesn't jell. I looked over all those blocks, same as you did. Dogs. All dogs. I have my site, and that's it."

Brovek looks like it's over. All lost.

But I'm not done yet. Keep still, Sandy, and listen up!

Scene three:

"Mr. Stern, think for a minute of a checkerboard. St. Luke's is one square, and we build our expansion there. Suppose then you build your project in the next square toward the freeway. That would be an advantage to you. And then our projects can face each other. Magnify each other. We can have our architects plan together, perhaps put a small park between us. A connecting tunnel for wintertime. Wouldn't that appeal to you?"

He's too smart to say anything. I watch his wheels turn as he paces off dimensions in the spaces of his mind. I glance at Brovek, to share the brink.

Stern clears his throat, and I snap back to him. He shrugs, spreads his hands. "It could be worth considering, your suggestion. That block is not a dog if it has a new hospital across the street. I would have to see who owns it."

I give him one second to think about records and deeds and easements and impairments, and then: "As a matter of fact, Mr. Stern, we own it. Would you care to swap?"

I hear Brovek suck in his breath, but my eyes are fixed on Stern, staring back at me. His mouth is open but no sound comes out.

And then he laughs! "Look what happens! A touch gratitude, and right away a person goes soft in the head." He presses his hands together, fingers spread. "You have maneuvered a sick man into a trap." He aims his right hand at my chest. "But it is a good-looking trap." He comes to his feet, narrows that open hand to the stiletto of his index finger. "The whole block? All the properties?"

I nod yes. "Options, not titles. But it's all in order."

"Extra time it will take. But extra time you have given me, thanks be to God. If my lawyers agree, I need one condition, then we shake hands."

I stand up, face him, my hand at my side. "Tell me what it is."

"A little rub-off, Mr. Potts. Something better than a wash."

"I think our lawyers can work that out, Mr. Stern. I surely do."

Our eyes lock. I offer my hand, and Stern takes it in the age-old sign of agreement. He can't quite contain his grin of delight—to be on stage, to be back in the chase. He takes Rudd by the elbow, nods at Brovek and exits, laughing.

Brovek sits in his chair, open-mouthed, stunned.

But I'm on a high. The meeting played to my script and we won. For a plain vanilla businessman like me, such a touch of show business is an escapade. So it's only fair, isn't it, that I take a curtain call?

Go, Horace!

I step around Brovek's desk, into the great man's private space. I plant my feet and put both hands—yes!—on the back of his chair! And spin it around! Hard! And there he goes, hanging on for dear life, whirling all the way around and starting around again, before he comes alive and hollers his outrage.

I don't think he even knows I bought his church.

PART SIX

September 5, 2014

I love it. Potts finagled the church site from Stern with sheer wit, financial smarts, and flat-out daring. And then he twirled Brovek's chair? How did the big guy react?

He was furious. But he cooled quick enough when he saw the prize. And he still needed Potts to fund the whole thing. Government grants, commercial support, private money. Potts quit his business and led a three-year fundraising campaign. He matched his timeline to the construction schedule, and it all came out right.

He was a hero, wasn't he?

To me he was. One of my favorite men.

What happened to him?

After he cut the ribbon to open the new building, he went home and had a stroke.

Oh, no! I didn't know that.

You didn't hear about it because they un-stroked him, right in his own brand-new emergency room.

"Un-stroked him?"

Yep. They have IV meds now that dissolve arterial clots, like in the heart or the brain, so the blood can run again.

And the stroke goes away?

If you treat it soon enough. Time is the key. Heart attack and stroke are red-hot medical emergencies. Call 911. Don't mess around.

People should know that!

Tell your friends! First symptom, the clock is running.

Like it does for your donor organs. That's why you risked your life and your airplane to bring your first heart home.

Danny Hovelund's heart for Millicent Herold. Our first transplant web. She is still alive, by the way.

You've been part of that scene a lot of times now. You can't remember all the names!

You never forget the first time. Nor the first liver. It was Karen's, and she lives on in Martin Stern —

— who built Stern Towers, the great hotel across the street.

Father O'Leary lived out his years there. Did you know? Courtesy of Stern! He could look out his window right at the new hospital. He still went over there sometimes. Worked with Wilma Gale and Lance in Karen's ombudsman program. The good priest died a while ago. He was ninety-two.

No one dreamed when you saved Horace Potts in 1985 that he would become the hero for your present-day temple of transplant. In a way, you made the new hospital possible.

I'm glad I didn't know that at the time. Responsibility for his life was all the gravity I could handle.

He became a rooter for you.

The champion I needed with Brovek.

And now you are Professor and Department Chair, Emeritus.

Emerita. Perforce.

Yes. Retired too soon.

Fifty-nine years old. But look on the bright side. I get to write a book.

About the transplant web. Do you still carry that image?

Oh, yes, I do. But in telling about Stern and St. Luke's, do I obscure it?

Yes, a bit.

Well, I have to anyway. If I want to weave a web, I need a loom. We couldn't have done our dozens and dozens of transplants without that modern hospital, nor weave those scores of transplant webs without that loom.

And the webs are...? Remind me.

The people. We professional staff are the warp, the long fibers; we run from case to case. A new web begins when a patient is registered to receive a donor organ. Then the short fibers weave in, the relatives and friends who show up in support. The donor families are in the weave too. All those lives become part of the web.

Like, for example...?

Well, Millicent Herold carries the heart of Danny Hovelund.

Brovek's first heart transplant.

Her web involved her husband Jack, and her kids Francie and Eddy; Danny's family, all eight of them; Dr. Bockman in Hangarville; a certain heroic airplane pilot. And Father O'Leary, who stepped into the web in the Herolds' waiting room. All these lives contributed to the web of Millicent's transplant.

You still know the names, after all these years.

They were my first transplants.

Let's get back to your personal story. I know how it turns out, but you still have to write the book!

Dana

May 25, 1985

Saturday morning. My rounds are done and I'm glad. I head for my quarters, two things on my mind. Not Rusty; he doesn't count.

I should be exploring the market for my future. Where to go. What sort of surgical offer I can draw. I haven't put nine years into post-grad education so I can draw unemployment! But I have given almost no thought about where I want to live or what kind of surgeon I want to be. I need to breathe free for a while.

The second thing is more urgent and much less interesting: to bury myself in study. I have a stack of journals piled by my cot, publications of current thoughts and new discoveries at the top surgical centers around the country. For my surgical Board exams this summer, I need to study them all — two days of lab practicals and written tests and personal interviews. Certification by one or more of the American Boards of Surgery will be my essential badge. But reading and study do not draw me.

But then, nothing does. Every day calls come to me, and I always hope one might be Rusty. But the voice that claims me now is not Rusty but Bozo. Duane needs help starting a central IV. Can't hit the subclavian vein.

It happens. It's happened to me. Lance was always patient, and I learned from him.

I join Duane in ICU. Check his set-up: the small sterile field by the patient's shoulder, painted brown and draped with towels. Several discarded tools scattered on a tray nearby — the debris of his unsuccessful stabs at the big vein. A senior nurse standing by, looking doubtful. Duane's brow beaded with sweat.

The patient is cooperative, resigned, waiting. Anesthetized skin makes a good difference.

"Give it another try, Duane." He feels the landmarks, angles the syringe, presses the needle through the skin, advances it in the prescribed direction, hoping for a free flow of blood back into the syringe. And there it is. He threads the long plastic IV tubing through the needle, down into the central circulation, probably the superior vena cava. He slides the needle back out. Applies pressure. Hooks up the connections, applies the bandage. Easy.

"Sorry, Dana. Thanks."

I cut him short. "Don't be sorry. Be right."

I walk away.

Five weeks before I walk out of here.

Into what?

Rudd

Memorial Day

May 27, 1985

Ignoring the holiday, Lance Rudd looks into his new medical home, the research labs of Old U. In exile? Well, no. Just feels that way. Here he will bury himself in the silent subterranean level of the hospital, behind Keaton Amphitheater. His neighboring facilities are the morgue and the autopsy rooms, deserted today. Little traffic here any day.

He stands without moving, listening to nothing. A faint knock in an overhead steam pipe accents the silence.

Here will be his domain. In the company of white rats and inbred mice, he will spend his days in experiments, speculation, study of patient records, and the generation, if not of progress, at least of articles for scientific journals. The advancement of knowledge about diabetes.

In his creased slacks and tasseled loafers he feels out of place. Today, under his long white lab coat, he wears an open shirt, no tie. How long, he wonders, in his isolation, before he will fall back to wearing his old favorite scuffed boat shoes and worn Levis, with a length of rope for a belt.

Dana

June 4, 1985

Home stretch. And still no Rusty. Not a whisper.

Nor have I called him. We can both be stubborn. But he should call me; he's the one who broke us off.

For six whole damn weeks I've done my work in mourning, waiting, waiting for his call that never comes. But I keep hoping. Doing my job. Counting the days. And trying to be civil. I've quit snarling at Duane. We have just finished a thoracotomy, and he's putting in the skin clips. He'll write the orders. I'm out of here.

I strip off my gown and drop it, inside out, into the hamper. Next, my gloves. For the same six weeks I have never felt jazzy enough to strip-'em-and-shoot-'em. That's Brovek's maneuver. But the waste bucket to receive them is sitting there, and it's round like a target, and it could be Rusty's face frowning up at me. Hah! I stretch them out and nail him good.

The move feels right after an easy case like this... Actually, it feels good anyway.

I dictate the op report and head for the nurses' dressing room.

If I were queen around here instead of slave, I'd change a lot of things. But my first big change would be the locker room signs. *Surgeons* or *Nurses?* Out! *Women* or *Men?* Yes. Better. I wonder whether our male nurses use the *Surgeons* dressing room.

I mosey on down the hall, past Mizzoh's office. My mind is far from Dr. Brovek but jerks back in a hurry at the sound of his voice.

"Dana. Can you step in here a minute?"

He's sitting on Mizzoh's desk, his heels bumping a faint rhythm against it. He's in green scrubs and cap, a mask dangling from his neck. I duck into the room and stand before him. "Good morning, Dr. Brovek. How can I help?"

His broad hands lie flat on his thighs, their veins traced by lines of residual white glove powder. The v-neck of his scrub top sags, and I choke back a giggle. I never thought before of a man's whiskers growing all the way down, so he has to decide where to stop shaving. I'm glad Rusty doesn't have all that hair on his chest. Not that it matters.

"In another four weeks you'll be finished here."

"Yes, sir." My giggle dies. *Finished?* Like, gone? I force a smile. "Yes, sir. The first of July."

My first day of release. Will Rusty be here? Will I have a job? Do I have a chance to stay right here? Be a liver surgeon? I still feel in my muscle and bone the rightness of that moment when I held Karen's liver in my hands and settled it into its new home.

But my future is up to Dr. Brovek. He can invite me in — or send me packing.

"You have done well here, Dana. I have learned to depend on you."

"Yes, sir. I hope so."

"My chief residents usually take a weekend once in a while."

"Yes, sir."

"But you never did. That was your own decision, wasn't it? I've been curious about that."

"Everyone assumes the men you appoint are competent. A woman has to prove herself."

'To be as good as the men?"

"No, sir. Better."

"I hope you never felt you had to prove yourself to me. I have always — "

"Frankly, sir, you were my principal challenge."

He nods. Rash of me to say it, but he makes no denial.

In fact, he breaks into a broad grin. "If you repeat this to anyone, I'll deny it. But five years ago when I accepted you into my program, I thought Dana was a man's name."

I smiled cautiously. Concave or convex, it fits either sex. "Yes, sir. Sometimes it is."

He goes back to business. "I've had inquiries about you. Dr. Bockman at Hangarville, for example. Are you making plans for your future?"

My hands tremble. I lace my fingers. "I've given all my attention to you here, Dr. Brovek. I've thought ahead a little, of course. But I've waited...you know...to see what might happen" — go ahead and say it — "here."

My cheeks turn to fire. Even my forehead glows hot.

He flashes an unusual quick smile. "You'll be surprised what happens here."

I step back, drop into one of Mizzoh's chairs. His hair pushes out from under his cap. Gray, like his chest. I've never thought about his having concerns beyond his own department. Research, of course. His students. And everybody knows about his wife.

"You know that I'm switching Lance to a research position. He is a good mind."

Here I find words. "I nearly died when he wanted to quit. He's too good for that!"

Brovek nods. "But he's no longer clinical. I need to replace him on the surgical staff — patients, students, clinical research."

"Yes, sir." It's a breath only. My heart races. Not an axe for me?

He nods. "It is not yet public knowledge, but the university plans a huge expansion here."

I stay silent.

He slides forward to the edge of the desk, his feet braced on the floor. "A major transplant center. We'll build a large department, and we'll do more and more transplants. I expect to do hearts — and lungs when we can. But I want someone else to do the abdominal stuff. Urologists will keep the kidneys."

Abdominal stuff? Like livers?

Brovek draws a deep breath, lets it out, looks right into my eyes. "Dana, would you consider staying on here?"

I jump to my feet. I want to hug him, but I don't dare. "That's what I want more than anything, Dr. Brovek. If you want me to stay, I would never consider anything else."

Brovek's smile melts me. Was I ever afraid of him?"I like that answer, Dana. Welcome aboard!"

His two great hands engulf mine. Caution flees. I throw my arms around his shoulders and plant a solid kiss on his cheek. "Thanks, Dr. Brovek. You'll never be sorry!"

Prudence be damned. I race to my room, throw myself onto my cot, seize the phone and punch in Rusty's number. It rings once. I think again, break the connection and set the phone down.

Should I call him at all? Ever? Think it through.

Do I want him to know? Yes, I do.

Do I want him to care? Of course I do.

Will he care? I haven't a clue.

Do I care? Yes! I care a lot.

I touch his numbers again. The line buzzes once and he's on it. "Hello?"

"It's me."

"Oh! Hello, Me." Polite.

"I've missed you."

Pause. Then, "I miss you, too."

"I wouldn't call, but—"

"I'm glad you did."

"I have news to tell."

"So tell." A harder tone. He is not my Rusty anymore.

We have always played games. I'll try one. "I've been propositioned by a gentleman."

One-second delay. Then: "I tried that once. Good luck to him." His voice flat.

Game over.

Okay. I'll spit out my news and split. "The gentleman was Dr. Brovek. He asked me to stay on here, on his surgical staff. I said Yes."

"I'm not surprised. You sacrificed everything else. Congratulations."

"Thanks—except, what you said doesn't sound like congratulations."

"What I say doesn't make any difference anyhow, does it?"

Lighten up, girl. "It might—if I really heard you say it." Make him talk. "Try me."

"As long as you're holed up in slavery over there, you'll hear nothing from me."

"Twenty-six more days. I'll be sprung."

"Yeah. Sprung on a spring. You'll be right back in the old routine."

"No, Mr. Waters. Not so. I will work on my own schedule, and most days I will eat breakfast at home."

I don't wait for a reply. Maybe he doesn't make one. I drop the phone onto its cradle, lie back on my cot, spread my hands over my face and blot out the world.

Ice your heart, girl. His fire is out.

Dana

July 1, 1985

Way before dawn I awake to the big day. In the dark I lie on my cot, thinking of the good stuff from the past. I promised total commitment, and I gave it. I proved my worth—even to me. And soon I'll be Brovek's "liver queen."

But at what cost? On this signal morning, with all its promise, my heart is heavy. The last four weeks dragged by in daily routines—surgery, rounds, random urgencies, tedium. Even my eagerness to count off the days and be free felt dull. As if I were on automatic pilot, holding out for July to come at last and print my new labels: fully trained, board-eligible, a free person and available.

And Rusty? Over and over again I replay his last few words on the telephone. I search them for any hint of interest. "As long as you're holed up over there..." Was he thinking of a day when I'm <u>not</u> holed up over here? Because, today is Day One. I'm out of here. I am a free woman. Will that mean anything to him?

Briefly, because today I could lie here as long as I want, I think of Pete down there in the mix somewhere, with Bozo on his belt, ready as I was for whatever might come along. Good luck, Pete. Goodbye, Bozo. There's something to feel good about.

At seven the sun is up and the day is bright. I slip into the shower, soap up, rinse down, towel off, comb out, and throw on my civvies — the same slacks and blouse I wore in here six months ago. I look at the wedgies I wore in here on that day. Elevator shoes, open toes? No way. I've lived in my cushioned flats, and I've covered miles these last six months. My "winged heels" are like part of me now. I slip them on.

Breakfast? Yes. But not here! Somewhere outside, out there in my new world.

I jam my few things into my backpack, ready to head out. Where?

Anywhere.

Face it. I'm alone. Not far from here my old room sits empty, waiting. That's where I'll live, I guess. For my new job at the hospital I'll need new clothes. New shoes. Soft-soled flats, if I can find them. For my new life as a surgeon — a surgeon alone.

Suck it up, girl.

Through the familiar halls I go, wearing my pack, passing memories. I ramble through the hospital's huge front lobby, past an empty information desk, walk through the big entry doors and into the morning sunshine.

This is the spot. I stood right here, and he came up behind me. He'd followed me, tailed me as research for a story! Oh, Rusty, I would have said Yes. You must know that. And would again, if you ever…

I hear a voice. His voice?

My heart thumps and my breath sticks in my throat.

"I followed you again, and you didn't catch me. Maybe I should be a private eye."

I want to wheel about and throw my arms around him. But he didn't see me cry before, and I won't go giddy now. I set down my pack and turn around. "Were you speaking to me, sir?" Grinning, I look up into his beloved face.

"Yes, madam." His grin matches mine. "I want to express my congratulations on your new job. Can you hear the words?"

"Better than I dared hope."

"Do they sound like congratulations?"

I clutch my hands tight together. "They do. Is there a hug to go with them?"

He is not laughing. His green eyes bore into me. "Depends. What have you planned to do today?"

I love the games he plays. Where is he going this time? I go along. "I thought for starters I would buy new shoes. Want to come along?"

No smile. He shakes his head. "I'm too straitlaced. No, I have to go home and write a story today."

"You're as much a slave as I was."

"But only when I want to be. Now comes the big question. You ready?"

I am ready. With this man, for anything.

"Let's assume you don't go shoe shopping. Then, tell me, what do you most wish you could do today,"

For a long moment our eyes lock. My answer springs from my heart, straight to my lips, with the barest pause at my brain. "I would like to see where you write your stories."

For a moment, nothing. Then he grins a great, giant Yes, and opens his arms, and I fall into him.

Now the tears run free. "Oh, Rusty, I am not whole without you."

"If half of you is mine, my Dove, you're enough. You are all I want and the woman I need."

In the best way possible, in his arms, I kiss goodbye to my six months of indenture. Rusty one-hands my backpack onto his shoulder. I take his other hand, and follow him into the rest of my life.

July 15, 2014

After all these twenty-nine years I am still in love with you, Dove. You are still all the wife I can handle.

I flash him a teary smile. You have to handle me more than you bargained for, dear man. In and out of my bed, my bath, and my wheelchair. You are a living saint.

A living one is the best kind, I suppose. I couldn't help you if I was dead.

Dead. Yes. Like my right hand that terrible day. Suddenly my scissors wouldn't snip. I had to watch my resident finish a nice lobectomy, and I couldn't even tie my shoe.

You came home scared. I remember.

I'll never forget. Five years ago last month.

You were okay again, for a while. Back in the OR.

But I knew it was MS.

Multiple sclerosis. People were shocked when you quit operating.

They would have been more shocked if I hadn't! I ran the department until last year. But MS won. When I couldn't walk, I hung it up.

Emerita. Perforce.

Good words. My dictation software knew "perforce." No problem. I hope my readers will know it and what it says about me.

It's a fine story for a gal who can't type —

— who has a husband with the patience of Job and the smarts of an editor.

That's my privilege, Dove.

I wish... Well, you know what I wish. I wish we had made a child together.

God knows we tried! For those first years we really worked at it. And loved it.

Maybe you scrubbed up too much, gown and gloves and all that.

I see your eyes dancing. What's your point?

Trying so hard to be sterile? Maybe it rubbed off!

If I could move my arms I'd rub you off, you joker.

Sure you would, Dove. Sure you would.

I love you, Russell. You are a good man.

Who, me? I'm just Russell Waters, redhead, ex-pilot, struggling writer, trying to build a name. It's my wife who's the big shot.

You're teasing me again. You never give up.

Of course not. You're the gal people know: Chief of Surgery, Endowed Professor, transplant surgeon, educator of surgeons.... Victim.

And from everything but victim, I'm Emerita.

Yes, my dear Dove, you are. Emerita.

Yes, Rusty, I am. Perforce.

The author is grateful to the Sanibel Writers Group
for 30 years of constructive criticism,
patience and friendship.

We hope you thoroughly enjoyed S.R.Maxeiner, Jr.'s novel, *The Transplant Web*. Be sure to check the other great novels and works of non-fiction at www.bluewaterpress.com.

www.ingramcontent.com/pod-product-compliance
Lightning Source LLC
Chambersburg PA
CBHW020548020726
47494CB00006B/1975